MARVELOUS WORLD

BOOK 1.5

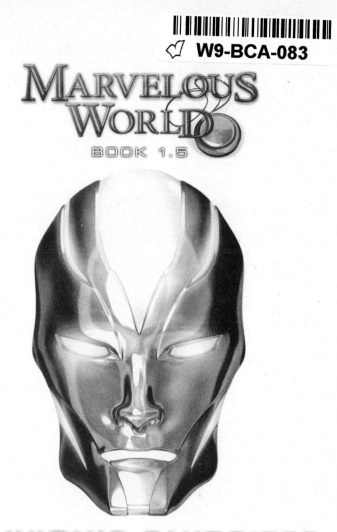

OLIVION'S FAVORITES

Also by Troy CLE

Marvelous World Book 1:
The Marvelous Effect

MARVELOUS WORLD

BOOK 1.5

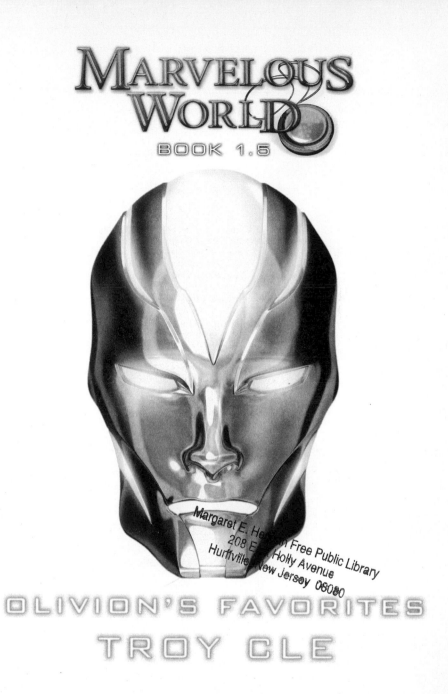

OLIVION'S FAVORITES

TROY CLE

Simon & Schuster Books for Young Readers
New York   London   Toronto   Sydney

For my friends

who have seen the best and worst of me and at every turn never abandoned

me. Instead, you all knew it was just me becoming a Favorite when I

was once only a CLE. I love you all. (Now forget I said all of

that and just carry on as if I hadn't.)

SIMON & SCHUSTER BOOKS FOR YOUNG READERS
An imprint of Simon & Schuster Children's Publishing Division
1230 Avenue of the Americas, New York, New York 10020
This book is a work of fiction. Any references to historical events,
real people, or real locales are used fictitiously. Other names,
characters, places, and incidents are products of the author's
imagination, and any resemblance to actual events or locales
or persons, living or dead, is entirely coincidental.
SIMON & SCHUSTER BOOKS FOR YOUNG READERS is a
trademark of Simon & Schuster, Inc.
For information about special discounts for bulk purchases,
please contact Simon & Schuster Special Sales at
1-866-506-1949 or business@simonandschuster.com
The Simon & Schuster Speakers Bureau can bring authors to your
live event. For more information or to book an event,
contact the Simon & Schuster Speakers Bureau at
1-866-248-3049 or visit our website at
www.simonspeakers.com
Book design by Tom Daly
The text for this book is set in Weiss.
Manufactured in the United States of America
2 4 6 8 10 9 7 5 3 1
Library of Congress Cataloging-in-Publication Data
Cle, Troy.
Marvelous world. bk. 1.5 : Olivion's favorites / Troy Cle.—1st ed.
p. cm.
Summary: Transported to the fantasy world of Midlandia, Louis
Proof, an inner-city boy from New Jersey, tries to return
home using his newly acquired powers.
ISBN 978-1-4169-4216-0
ISBN 978-1-4169-9736-8 (eBook)
[1. Fantasy. 2. Heroes—Fiction. 3. Adventure and adventurers—
Fiction. 4. African Americans—Fiction.] I. Title.
II. Title: Olivion's favorites.
PZ7.C579185Mas 2009
[Fic]—dc22
2008053515

FIRST
EDITION

Glossary

Celestial Entities (CE):
Living, thinking energy. Both eNoli and iLone are CE.

eNoli: Desire. Passion. Self.

iLone: Compassion. Reason. Others.

Midlandia: Place of the impossible.

The Midland Isle: Passageway to all places and times.

The Olivion: Everything.

Pronunciation Guide

Alonis (ah-LON-iss)

Alorion (A-LOR-ee-un)

Arminion (ar-MIN-ee-on)

DiVarion (di-VAR-ee-on)

Elynori (EL-in-or-eye)

eNoli (ee-no-LIE)

iLone (eye-low-NAY)

Kiyonrae (Kee-YON-ray)

Olivion (OH-liv-ee-on)

Orenci (o-RHEN-cee)

Perilynn (PEH-ril-in)

Timioosiyon (ti-mee-YOU-see-on)

Vivionya (viv-ee-ON-ya)

Dear Favorites,

Finally! The missing levels of *The Marvelous Effect* have been found and you are gazing upon them at this very moment. If you remember correctly they occur between levels I and V of *The Marvelous Effect*, during Louis Proof's mysterious coma and Cyndi Victoria Chase's "kidnapping." They reveal MANY secrets and promise to be more important than anything you have learned about the Marvelous World thus far. I'd like to add that I'm not one for rumors, but there is one floating around that a few highly important *Olivion's Favorites* prologues and tons of information about Midlandia can be found online at *marvelousworld.com*. Who knows? Anyway, that is all I have to say and I have said it.

Thank you,

Troy CLE

P.S. If you are indeed a Favorite and there is anything else . . . Iamafavorite@marvelousworld.net

Marvelous World

A.K.A.

The Marvelous World of the Supposedly Soon

to Be Phenomenal Young Mr. Louis Proof

Book 1.5: Olivion's Favorites

Level II

Chapter **One**

Snatched up! Taken! Kidnapped! Borrowed? Whatever you want to call it, this is what happened to Young Louis Proof, Cyndi Victoria Chase, and Devon Alexander. They didn't understand how or why, but they suddenly found themselves on Midlandia.

Midlandia can only be described as a limitless place at the center of all things known and unknown. It's like heaven's electric kiss only better. It's like hell's unrelenting scorn only worse.

They didn't know one another but Louis, Cyndi, and Devon would be bound by their quest to return home. They didn't know it, but first they'd need to find the Olivion, for they were Olivion's Favorites—children of ultimate power and importance.

The three Favorites' pathways seemed to stretch behind them into forever. In front of them was a magnificently large bluish ball of living light. Yet, oddly, within this light they could see only the pathways and one another; the children were surrounded by total darkness.

The light greeted them with all sorts of hellos that could not be heard but sure could be felt. The light was happy to welcome them. They were its hope, because it and all things known and unknown were in grave danger.

"Where are we?" Louis asked.

"I have no idea," Cyndi said.

"Me neither," Devon said.

Well . . .

Louis, you are a long way from your uncle's store in New Jersey, where you collapsed.

Cyndi, you are a long way from your brother's kitchen floor in California, where you fell silent.

Devon, you are a long way from your attic in Chicago, where you were looking for one of your old toys to give to your sister.

But still you belong here, for now . . .

The light began to wildly radiate. Blues, yellows, reds, oranges, gold, and platinum plus limitless more colors flashed. The light's power lifted them from the platforms. The three felt like they were dancing in heaven. But this would not last. Everything began to shake, and with that, the light sent the children flying in different directions, far from one another.

Louis. Cyndi. Devon.
Welcome to Midlandia.

Chapter **Two**

So there Louis was, flying through the Midlandian sky nowhere near his mom, dad, home, the JunkYard JunkLot, or his beloved radio-controlled cars. Blue and white light radiated from his body, making him look like a human comet. He felt limitless, as if he were being reborn as a god.

The night sky streaking by was like none he had ever seen. Electric shades of violet, deep blues, and rich purples wove together around him. Way off in the distance there was a massive, glistening mountain range and beyond that a large city with shiny buildings blanketed in light. Everything felt vibrant, as if it were all somehow alive.

This had to be a dream. And now he was sure he would wake up, because he was heading straight for a mountain. The collision would kill him and he had never before died in a dream.

Okay, wake up! Louis thought. But nothing changed. Panic set in. Louis screamed and crossed his forearms in front of his face as if that would ease the impact. Yeah right! *Blam!* He blasted straight into the mountain with such force that his twelve-year-old body tore a twenty-foot-wide, sixty-yard-deep hole through it. Surprisingly, slamming through rock reminded him of the cool, wet, and exhilarating sensation of traveling down the water slide that led to the Junk Yard Junk Lot, but this time it was much more intense and all over his body. He was still screaming, but it was amazing!

Then he crashed hard on his right shoulder, hitting the lush, grassy Midlandian ground and tearing a chasm six feet wide and hundreds of feet long. He lay still and silent but not unconscious. Finally, he pressed his palms to the earth and rested on his knees. He slowly stood, unharmed. There was a quiet power growing inside him.

Louis Proof's Celestial Infection Rate = 8%

Louis looked up at the sturdy mountain hundreds of feet away. It seemed like nothing would be able to shake it, but there it was: a twenty-foot hole that he had made. He could see the night sky on the other side.

The mountain . . . didn't hurt me?! This is a dream? It doesn't feel like a dream, Louis thought. He didn't have a scratch. Plus, he couldn't recall ever being more alert. Everything was so vivid.

There was no moon, yet light radiated from the odd violet, star-kissed sky. Louis began to walk. In the last five minutes, he'd collapsed in front of his uncle's store in frantic pain, stood before a bluish light with two other children, and blown through a mountain, and now here he was wandering in this strangely bright night. Where was he?

Suddenly, a voice grabbed Louis's attention. It had a vibration that he'd never heard before but he could understand it clearly.

"Perilynn, it tore through the sky; it must be one of the children. You have to hurry. Reign is on his way to destroy this child—and you, if you get in his way. Why are you so eager to reach this child alone anyway?" the voice said.

Louis looked everywhere but saw no one. He couldn't even tell what direction the voice was coming from. It was like it was being transmitted directly into his head, as if he was meant to hear it. Louis figured the city he had seen was the best place to go for help. *Destroy this child.* He had to be the child, so he began to run, but there was no place to hide from whoever was speaking.

"aZRon, when I find all three children, Olivion's Gate will reappear to welcome them. And if I cross the Gate with them, Olivion will make me a Favorite," a second voice said.

Where are they? Where am I? Louis thought as he ran, frantically looking around.

"You fool! You're going to battle all of Midlandia, fighting both eNoli and iLone to become a Favorite? Of course, I can't wait to see such an exciting show. Things have been boring even with Galonious, Trife, and Arminion escaping. But you do know there's no way you can win, right?" aZRon said before barging right on with hardly a pause. "I'm not taking any falls for you, though! And when you're caught, I want to be the one to cast you into the Infinite Abyss. I've always wanted to do that to someone."

"Fine, if I get caught, you can be the one to throw me into the Infinite Abyss, but I won't lose. Thanks for telling me about the child," Perilynn said.

"The next time we meet, we may not be on the same side, my

7

friend. Don't take it personally." aZRon laughed, and the laugh slowly faded, as if aZRon was flying away.

The sound was swift, compact, and deafening. It came right before the three spheres of red and yellow light hit the ground in front of and to the sides of Louis. He could feel heat and was blasted off his feet and onto his back. Quickly, he rose to see the spheres of light turn into imposing figures. At first they were electric outlines, then solid beings of light, and finally three people who seemed human but were unlike anyone Louis had ever seen before. They moved with an air of superiority and flawless perfection. Their blue-gray eyes seemed otherworldly. They wore slick, fitted clothing and each clutched dual glowing blades as if they intended to slice Louis in half.

"You need to be more careful. You created such a sight when you got here. It was not hard to find you at all," said the one in front of Louis. Red light briefly rose from his body like mist.

This was not one of the voices Louis had been hearing.

"Know me as the eNoli Reign, and we are here to . . . well, you'll soon find out." He nodded to the others. Their blades hummed as they moved through the air toward Louis.

Louis knew he had no answer for the oncoming attack. He was ready to run when he felt a tug at his center that pulled him back into a wave of radiant golden energy. The energy moved toward his attackers. It was now solidifying in the spot where Louis had been less than a fraction of a second ago. It became a man with a silver mask that radiated a fluorescent blue light from its eyes and carved patterns.

This masked man moved faster than Louis could follow. His hands held two glowing blades that caught the attackers off guard. He sliced through the one on the left while flipping backward, evading the attack of the one on the right. In midair, behind his enemy, he delivered a well-targeted blow. Two beings had turned into energy bursts that violently faded away before Louis could twitch. No blade had met this young masked man as he landed.

Only Reign was left, and Louis and the masked man both knew he would not be beaten as quickly as the others.

"Stay behind me. Don't run! I'm the only one who will keep you safe," the masked man said. This was one of the voices Louis had heard earlier.

Reign charged the masked man. They exchanged a few blows, but everything stopped when Reign's fist shattered the man's mask, revealing his identity. In a second, the mask had rebuilt itself as if it had never been broken.

"Perilynn, I should have known. Why do you fight for this iLone child? You and your brother are traitors," Reign said as he grabbed Perilynn by the throat. Perilynn released a shock of energy from his body that forced Reign to free him.

However, Reign was no longer the problem. Hundreds of beams of light rocketed to the ground like meteors. Hot white sparks flew wildly from each impact before the lights turned into figures like Perilynn and Reign. Perilynn grabbed Louis by the wrist and ran, guiding him through the falling lights.

"You have to trust me; I'll lead you out of here," Perilynn said.

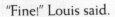

"Fine!" Louis said.

"Fine?" Perilynn was surprised he didn't have to do more persuading. "Okay, stay close!"

In front of them.

In back of them.

To the left of them.

To the right them.

The vicious lights hit everywhere.

Perilynn stopped all of a sudden in the midst of this.

"Come on, let's go!" Louis yelled, trying to pull Perilynn forward.

"We can escape here," Perilynn said as he stomped twice at the ground. The land was bending under his foot.

"Are you crazy?" Louis asked.

"All things considered, I guess I am! We're going to break through, and there's only one way we can do that." Perilynn answered. He had a plan.

"Do something!" Louis yelled as Perilynn started his plan.

Step One!

Perilynn kneeled and punched the ground. The punch created a circle; written symbols spiraled from it and a ripple of jagged red light traveled outward along the ground, forcing back everyone near them. But it wouldn't take the fallen long to regroup, and more were coming from the sky.

Step Two!

Perilynn threw Louis hundreds of feet straight up into the air. Louis looked like a perfect target. But Perilynn jumped right after him, turning to pure energy and traveling almost instantly to meet each Celestial Entity (CE) that was closing in. When he reached one, he would take on his human form with sword in hand, strike, then turn into energy again, twisting to rush to the next target. Every movement left a trail of streaking light. He struck the first in its chest, the second in its abdomen, the third in its head, the fourth in its neck. He was in human form again as he darted toward Louis, who was still flying up. Perilynn grabbed Louis by his hand and threw him even farther into the sky. He could see Reign speeding after them. It was time to go.

Step Three!

Perilynn caught up to Louis, snatched his arm, and pulled him close. He flipped backward so they were aimed headfirst toward the ground. They began to spin as they plummeted.

Louis could see the many following them, but he and Perilynn were moving too fast; there was no way they could be caught. It didn't matter, though, because the ground was about to make a quick mess of them both. Screaming was not going to help. Louis didn't think he even had the air to scream. So he closed his eyes.

There was no impact. They pushed right through the surface. A clean exit!

They were gone with no telling where they would appear next. That was the way of Midlandia; if you knew where to look and how to access it, just about anything could be an entrance or exit. It was up to Midlandia, though, where you would turn up.

Chapter **Three**

Pushing through Midlandia was a great thing if you knew how to do it. Some had to force their way through as Perilynn just had, but it was believed that some could make the ground open up and welcome them.

Although they had crashed through dirt, grass, and rock, Louis and Perilynn were now falling gracefully through air, and Louis felt this place all around him, as if it were embracing him like it cared about and needed him. A few glowing colorful lights took a moment to travel in front of Louis's face and examine him. They took off after saying unspoken hellos and good-byes.

Soon, Louis and Perilynn landed on a path, and it was like they were underground but not. They were in a huge expanse, yet Louis sensed that everything ended just beyond his range of vision. There were many other pathways around them—some interwoven, some not.

There were upways ascending and downways descending.

There were sideways winding on their sides and slantedways on a zigzag.

There were oldways coming apart and newways being built.

There were frontways in full sight and backways somewhat hidden.

There were rightways leading to good places and wrongways leading to bad places.

There were all sorts of ways but oddly there were no doorways . . .

Perilynn found a way, grabbed Louis, and they were off.

"Where are we? Where are we going?" Louis asked, staring at everything around him.

"This is Midlandia and I have to get you to Olivion's Gate, but before that can happen we must find the other children . . . ," Perilynn said from behind his silver mask, which reflected all as he led Louis with quick steps down a shiny metal pathway.

Each time their feet touched the ground, tiny glowing sparks flew up. They were moving through what could only be explained as "it all." They were actually inside of Midlandia, traveling through the fabric of existence. It was if they were walking through an invisible fog, pushing through something that was tightly woven yet contained loose patches at the same time, and it gave Louis an odd, prickly feeling. Marvelous!

"Other children . . . like me? I saw them when I first got here. There's another boy and a girl," Louis said, trying to keep up with Perilynn's pace.

"You were with them? Why did you separate? That was the worst thing you could've done."

"We didn't separate on purpose. I was with them one minute, and the next I was flying through the sky and you know what happened after that. . . . You saved me. Thanks."

"We're not safe, so there's no need to thank me yet." Perilynn was trying to figure out where they should be going among the many paths surrounding them. Louis realized now that he'd been hearing a faint background noise ever since he'd arrived on Midlandia. The sounds were becoming louder in Louis's ears as he was becoming more accustomed to this place. It seemed as if everything had a sound as identifiable as its appearance. The interwoven melodies comforted Louis.

"Always remember that the best and only way is your own way and you should never be afraid to take it." Perilynn had hardly finished speaking when he leaped, pulling Louis with him, to land on a platform that met his feet as if it were called to him. There were more, and Perilynn was leaping from one to the next with Louis in tow. Upon each landing a shock tore through Louis's body, vibrating his insides with an exciting, energizing tingle. Louis didn't know it but the effects of a celestial virus were being accelerated. He was becoming more in tune with Midlandia and it was becoming a part of him both here and in his body back home.

Louis Proof's Celestial Infection Rate = 19% and Rising

Louis didn't notice but he was also becoming thinner and more muscular. He was distracted by the realization that colors were different here. They seemed to be living entities that chose to bring color to objects as sort of a cool job. They radiated this place with patterns that were unpredictable yet complementary, as if this were a wondrous painting accented with blackness.

The platforms read each of Perilynn's moves, pivoting with his steps. Some even catapulted him forward when the next one looked too far to be reached by just jumping. Of course Perilynn could clear just about any jump, but nonetheless he always appreciated assistance.

There were no more platforms, and they came to a complete stop. There seemed to be no way to go forward in the darkness. "Hold on," Perilynn said. Louis braced himself for Perilynn to leap into the unknown but he didn't jump.

Hearing the sound of running water, Louis looked down to see a stream of illuminated water rise up in front of them. Perilynn smiled. The water took on the shape of a woman's face, which had to be over ten feet tall. It didn't speak as it looked Louis and Perilynn over. Finally it smiled and opened its mouth. Instead of a tongue a stairway rolled out and met the platform. The woman's mouth kept opening wider and wider until there was no more face left. There was only a massive liquid passageway. It beamed with light and Louis could feel its warm invitation.

"I'm pretty sure this is the way, but if not . . . well, hey, we won't worry about that!" Perilynn said as they began to climb the stairs that led to an illuminated waterway.

It seems that Louis and Perilynn did indeed find their doorway.

Chapter **Four**

Cyndi Victoria Chase found herself falling from a tree. But it was a slow and guided fall as if the branches were grabbing her and passing her down so she wouldn't hurt herself.

"Be careful. They're in the trees. You don't know if they're friends or enemies. They're in the trees." Cyndi heard whispered words as she was dropped six feet from the last branch.

She landed on her feet in a forest, all the same height and perfectly trimmed as if a groundskeeper were well paid to keep them that way. "Who's in the trees? Where am I?" Cyndi asked, looking around. She saw only the trees and a long path of clear, still water with evenly spaced square stepping stones along its length. This place was lovely but foreign. She remembered the two other kids and a magnificent light. Before that she'd been in her brother's kitchen . . .

Cyndi walked onto the stepping stones, mesmerized by the colors and by the clarity with which she was able to see. Her clear California nights could not compare to the purples and violets that streaked along this sky. It was as if the colors were alive, vibrant with playful energy.

Stopping on one of the stones, Cyndi could feel eyes. They

were in the trees, but she didn't turn around. Instead she looked into the water. Fear squeezed her heart as she saw the beings reflected there. Vile-looking snake-, crab-, spiderlike abominations were carefully peering at her from high in the branches. They had many legs and an upper body that could stretch and coil around objects like a serpent. For now only their heads and upper bodies were visible among the leaves.

She continued down the stepping-stone path, wondering if each tree had one of the beings in it. They were less hidden now; they were beginning to creep out of the foliage. She thought to run but that was not the way to go. She could see it—her running, falling into the water, and being attacked by these mysterious creatures.

She was going to have to talk to them. "Will any of you help me? I have no idea where I am, but you must know. Why don't you come out, so we can talk?" Cyndi said.

"Help you? Talk to you? You're an iLone child. Surely you jest," one spoke from deep within a tree.

"Yes, you're an iLone child and you have no business here," another said.

"But where is here and who are you? And what is an iLone child?" Cyndi asked as countless numbers of them came down from the trees. Cyndi had to use every bit of energy to stop herself from screaming.

"This is Midlandia. Don't you know anything?"

"Of course she does. This is a Favorite using iLone trickery! Arminion demands that she be captured because she'll destroy our chance to escape."

Midlandia . . . iLone . . . Favorite . . . Arminion. Cyndi had no idea what the words meant. The creatures began to circle her, and she couldn't come up with the right thing to say.

"Really, I have no idea where I am or what this is about. I don't know anything about being iLone—is that what you said? And Midlandia. Can you explain?" Cyndi said.

"Well, you're here because—" one began.

"You cannot be serious. You're being tricked into believing her lies," another said.

Cyndi had made it out of the water. Now she fled. But she didn't get far. They circled her, grabbed her, and took her away.

Chapter **Five**

The glowing waterway led Louis and Perilynn into a water-filled cave whose smooth walls were etched with images of CE that seemed to point the way out. The current forced them through a short underwater tunnel, then they swam to the surface and found themselves in outer Midlandia, floating in a river in bright daylight. Climbing out of the water, they began to wring their clothes out.

Perilynn had faith that this was where they needed to be. He'd soon find the second child, with Louis's help of course.

They sat on the ground because Louis had no desire to move. He was still taking everything in. He listened to the sounds of Midlandia; they were as brilliant as before if not more so. He looked at the Celestial-graced landscape. Gray-blue mountains with glistening snowcaps hovered in the sky miles away, and the river led to a gorgeous crystal building in the distance.

This is not a dream, Louis thought. He would have sworn it was if it had not been for the wonder of the omnidirectional elevators, rides, racetrack, and the very existence of the JunkYard JunkLot and for one of the last conversations he'd had with Uncle Albert in his store.

* * *

"Have you ever seen something that you knew couldn't be real? But you knew it was real?" Louis blurted out.

Uncle Albert thought for a minute. "Wasn't real? What does that mean? The world is a big place, where just about anything can happen, good or bad. I know that for a fact—and man oh man, I can tell you some stories . . ."

It now seemed as if his uncle had told him something much bigger than he was able to realize at the time. Yes, this was all real.

Louis Proof's Celestial Infection Rate = 25% and Rising

"Come on, we have to move. There isn't time to rest," Perilynn said, getting up. He wouldn't stray far from the river, but just in case they needed cover, he knew it was best to walk close to the trees and to the stone statues of CE and unique beasts that were evenly placed throughout the breathtaking landscape.

"Wait! Who are you? Please tell me what's going on . . . and can you take off that mask?" Louis asked, following.

"I quite like it, but sure. I decided I'd wear it during the fight. They found out who I was anyway. You first. What's your name?" Perilynn said as the mask moved three inches forward and then turned into light that traveled into him.

"Wow! My name is Louis. Louis Proof and I'm from East Orange, New Jersey," Louis said, amazed by how the mask had disappeared.

"Louis Proof. That's a strong two-part name!" Perilynn said.

"So what's yours?" Louis asked.

"It's Perilynn. One part!" Perilynn said as he ran his finger across his chest. In its wake, a name tag with striking red letters appeared and attached itself to the stylish vest that Perilynn was wearing. To Louis's surprise, Perilynn had given him a name tag too with his full name written across it: "Louis Proof."

"Nice to meet you," they both said at the same time.

Louis extended his hand for Perilynn to shake. "Hey, you did some wild stuff back there! You're not human. What are you and what is this place?"

Perilynn paused, thinking about his life and this place. Both were at the root of why he was doing this.

"Louis, I'm something called a Celestial Entity—a CE, but really I don't know what that actually means. I just am. This is Midlandia and it just endlessly is . . . ," Perilynn said.

"How can you not know what you are and what this place is?"

"It's complicated. I guess you can think of Midlandia this way: Every place you knew of before you got here, this is not there. That's the only way I can explain it."

"Well, who knows and can tell me?" Louis asked.

"Oh, that's easy. The Olivion knows everything and I'm going to take you and the other children to Olivion's Gate. We'll cross it to meet the Olivion. After that you can go home."

"Yes! That's the best thing I've heard: Then you can go home. If that's how we have to do it, let's get to it! Other kids. Gate. Olivion. Home. All right!"

"I like your attitude."

"Hey, so where's this gate?" Louis asked.

"That's the funny part. Finding the Gate is tricky, although I was right there the last time it was known to appear."

"If you found it before, you can find it again."

"No, Louis, I didn't find it. It was the greatest and strongest of us all who found it, Myth. He was like a father to me and my brother, and his ambition led us to the Gate. You see, Midlandia is not like any place you know. Many things on Midlandia, especially Olivion's Gate, won't be found unless they want to or are supposed to be found. And even then anything can be anywhere."

"That sounds like madness, but why were you looking for it? Were there other kids like me who had to find it?"

"No. There are kids like you because we *did* find the Gate. My kind, the eNoli, want to leave this place. The Olivion would not allow such a thing, so Myth sought the gate to *persuade* the Olivion. That started everything."

"You want to leave too? That's why you're taking me to the Gate?" Louis noticed the gentle, relaxing sound of the river's pure flowing water.

"No. I don't want to leave. I want to the find the Gate so that I can become a Favorite and learn the answers to the questions you just asked. The Olivion knows all. Nothing makes sense to me, and I want it to—I need it to. From my first thought I was alone and I knew nothing. Everything was a mystery. That's why I followed Myth and took part in the war to find the Gate and the Olivion." Perilynn was keeping careful watch for anyone who might be around.

"So, what happened?" Louis asked, wondering if they'd be able to explore the building that sparkled in the distance.

"I don't know exactly, but it's said that when you touch the Gate, it shows you things. When Myth placed his hand on the Gate, it showed him something that made him flee."

"He was that powerful and he just left?"

"Yes. He abandoned the Gate and no one has seen him since. What it showed him is one of the biggest mysteries of Midlandia. We've all tried to find him, especially his beloved eLynori, but, like I said, he was never seen again. They say that when and if he returns, it will mark the beginning of a new age on Midlandia."

"But you were there too. You didn't cross the Gate?"

"Someone did cross the Gate, but it wasn't me. I was robbed of my chance—" Perilynn broke off, quickly pulling Louis behind a tree as he saw three CE many yards away. Louis realized that Reign had found them but didn't know it.

"Perilynn and his brother are traitors. I should not only have thrown them from the Gate, I should have ended them when I had the chance! I won't make that mistake this time!" Louis heard Reign say as he and the other two began to walk away from Louis and Perilynn's hiding place.

That must be why Perilynn and his brother didn't cross the Gate. But who did? Who got to meet the Olivion? Louis wondered.

Perilynn waited for them to leave, but they didn't because suddenly they had four visitors.

The one in front wore a blue stone medallion encased in white shiny metal. It reminded Louis of one that his mother had, only it was a bit bigger and a rim of brilliant white light shone around the stone. It was wondrous. The person who wore it was a twenty-year-old leader with blue-gray eyes who projected confidence. He looked as if he could command the wind and calm the seas.

"Kiyonrae. To what do I owe this pleasure? You must be looking for your three iLone children. I've met one. Don't worry, he got away but the next time I meet him I'll remove his head from his shoulders," Reign said. Then he threw a sharp, spinning, glowing metal disk at Kiyonrae.

Kiyonrae dodged it, and that was enough for Reign and his followers to take off into the sky. They weren't easily scared but they had no desire to face off with a Favorite.

Does it ever stop? Perilynn thought. He was always up for a good fight but this was not the time. Like Reign, he wouldn't dare challenge Kiyonrae unless he had no choice. He just had to hope Kiyonrae would leave as Reign had.

"Who is that?" Louis asked.

"That's someone you have to stay away from: Kiyonrae. He's a Favorite just like you. Other than the Olivion, Favorites are the most powerful beings in existence. The medallion around his neck symbolizes that. But he's an iLone and the iLone are the reason why this place is not at peace—or maybe it's because of the eNoli. Who knows? I myself don't care about eNoli or iLone. All I care about is getting you to the Olivion. If I become a Favorite like you, I believe that I'll finally understand everything. So this is the plan: No matter what, we stick together, find the other two children, and get there," Perilynn said.

Louis made a fist and raised it. Perilynn curiously did the same. Louis hit their knuckles together as a promise.

"Okay, now which way do we have to go?" Louis asked, watching Kiyonrae and his companions fly off.

"You tell me. You should be able to feel the others. Which way feels right?"

Louis didn't question. Perilynn was right. A feeling guided him to the right and away from the wondrous building he'd hoped to visit.

"This way." Louis turned.

"Great!" Perilynn said as they set off into Midlandia in search of the second child.

Louis, it seems you have been dropped into the middle of something big.

Chapter Six

There would be no brilliant living blue lights here.

There would be no intelligently moving platforms here.

There would be no wondrous building in the distance here.

There would be no such adventure here.

This was the place of Louis's birth and a place where many believed Louis would die.

This was East Orange General Hospital.

Louis was hooked up to tubes, and doctors were flabbergasted. His pupils were not responsive to light. His brain activity was registering at higher levels on the monitors than had ever been seen before. His body was at a temperature beyond what would cause spontaneous human combustion, yet his skin was cool to the touch and his heart rate was perfect.

What's more, his body had burned enough calories for him to lose ten pounds in a matter of minutes. Anyone who could bottle that would be an extremely rich person.

The doctors had taken a blood sample and it was on its way

to be analyzed. Maybe it would provide the clues they fever-ishly sought.

Trife had followed Louis to the hospital, riding on top of the ambulance, though still caught in another dimension. He was quietly observing until he saw the vial of blood. Trife knew what that was and he followed it. If Louis did make it out of this state, Trife knew what the blood would be able to do; he had to get it. He followed the nurse to the lab, and as soon as she put the blood down, he made his move. He concentrated and was able to force one hand into our dimension. He did not care who saw him. Why should he? While only a portion of his body was in this dimension, the paint on the walls began to crack and peel. Some of the glass in the room resorted back to sand, and plastics began to melt. He was forced back into his own dimension, but he had it! This would make Galonious very happy.

The room continued to deteriorate and Trife didn't understand why. *If we are to cross dimensions properly . . . balance . . . I've thrown off the balance . . . have to restore it . . .* On a whim he thought of a few marbles, grabbed them, and placed them where the vial had been. Balance restored . . .

Wait. Something was calling to Trife. It was an energy that he could sense between dimensions. He followed its draw through the hospital. It led him back to Louis's room. Trife was surprised that it was not Louis. It was his brother. There was an aura about him that was magnetic. There was a subtle darkness to him. It was his Karma, creating a precise pathway between dimensions. It only had to be strengthened.

Trife would follow him everywhere . . .

". . . We were just talking and he suddenly frowned, hunched over, then stumbled out of my store and collapsed in the street. It came out of nowhere," Uncle Albert said to Louis's mother as she wiped the tears from her face.

"I got a call from the school that he left running and scream-ing out the door. Did he say anything about that?" Mrs. Proof said.

"No. I asked him why he was at my store early and he just asked me if I had ever seen something that I knew couldn't be real but also knew was real. That's it. He didn't say he was sick. He simply clenched up and walked out the door while we were talk-ing. I called 911 and here we are," Uncle Albert said.

As this conversation continued, someone important appeared out of nowhere in a nearby room. Actually, not from nowhere. Not long ago Timioosiyon had traveled from Cyndi Victoria Chase's room in California to Louis's hospital. Timioosiyon, who while here would don the name Timothy, was the reason there were three kids on Midlandia rather than two. He was the young iLone who had left Midlandia to help Louis and the oth-ers, if they were able to return from Midlandia safely.

Have to find him and get him out of here. He would be under too much scrutiny. A Midlandian freak show, Timothy thought with a laugh.

He was in a vacant room with many windows in plain view of the nurses' station. He immediately ducked down. Okay. He was a teen and there was no way a teen would have any natural authority here. He had to be a doctor. He thought about it for a moment, then aged himself about twenty years. He was quite dashing. Perfect smile and body. A bit too much. He needed to tone it down. He messed up his hair, wrinkled the lab coat, and stopped smiling so much. He grabbed a clipboard and tried to make his way to Louis. This was the awkward part. Timothy had to struggle to keep his influence under wraps. All who saw him were suddenly overcome with the need to right everything they had ever done wrong. They also wanted to work harder so that the hospital could run better for everyone. Oh boy, it was a real love fest. None of it was intentional, and soon he had his influence under control so it wouldn't happen so easily. He was proud of himself as he found Mrs. Proof.

"Mrs. Proof?" Timothy said, leading her away from everyone else.

"Are you a new doctor? Do you have any news?" Mrs. Proof asked.

Timothy paused for a moment because he had to get this right. Oh, forget the plan; just use the truth. That's the only thing that would work.

"No, Mrs. Proof. I knew of your mother so I know you will understand what I am about to say. We have to get Louis out of this hospital. If we do not, there will be trouble. Louis may be in danger here. If he is further examined, he will be taken away from you. Do you understand?"

It seemed to Mrs. Proof that just as the new doctor said this, Louis lost a bit more weight. It was scary. She had to fight her feeling of helplessness. She refused to cry and lose her head. Then, as she clutched the medallion that hung from her neck, she suddenly knew Louis would be okay.

Timothy needed Mrs. Proof to realize that she had to do exactly what he asked her to for Louis's benefit. But he would not use his CE influence as he spoke to her.

"I know this is shocking. Look at the instruments. His vital signs are perfect. He looks perfect. He is in perfect shape. I will take care of everything so that you will be able to care for him in your own house. He does not need a hospital. Louis will get better. He already is . . . better than he has ever been. He will awaken in his own bed. You know what I am saying is true. Are you ready to take your boy home?" As a CE his words were undeniable, but they weren't actually needed to convince her.

Mrs. Proof looked at Timothy and then at her son. She thought of her mother, and at that moment she knew that the time had come. This was all part of it. She clutched the medallion that hung around her neck even harder. Timothy smiled as he realized what it was.

"How are we going to do this?" Mrs. Proof said.

Timothy showed her a silver metallic device. "I have got it covered . . . I will attach this to Louis's wrist. It will tell you how close he is to home. When it reaches zero, Louis will wake up. As far as getting him out of here goes, it is quite easy. No one will

remember him being here. I just needed you to agree." Timothy
was confident he'd be able to do his job.

Your job?
Timioosiyon, what about the blood?
If you had only known about the blood . . .

Chapter **Seven**

Reign stood in the center of Lefton Rack. Lefton Rack was where most great eNoli meetings have taken place. If there was notice that someone would be speaking about a matter of importance, all you had to do was walk and if you were meant to be there, you would be.

Lefton Rack also bent itself to what was needed. It was modest now, but as more and more eNoli filled it to hear the tale of Reign's encounter with the child and with the lone masked being who had also eluded some of their most powerful, it got bigger and grander. A circular platform met Reign's feet, raising him so that all parties could see him. Countless numbers of eNoli had come to witness his tale. They stood humbly on the ground. With Arminion, Galonious, and Trife gone, there were no leaders per se, just massive interested parties.

"Myth, the greatest of us all, abandoned us so long ago, and in his place you accepted Arminion! Not out of respect, as you did Myth, but out of fear because he is a sniveling lap dog of the Olivion. Where has that gotten us?" Reign said.

"Where has that gotten us? You must be mad! He told us he'd escape and he has when none of us could. He's on Earth now with

his closest followers, Galonious and Trife! They'll usher our exodus! The arrival of the children is proof of that!" said Holliston,
one of Arminion's most loyal followers.

Everyone began to cheer. Reign wanted to rage but for the
moment was silent. In Myth's absence he, Reign, should have
been named leader, not Arminion. Arminion had been responsible for his brother Kyll's ultimate demise. Reign was the one
who'd worked and fought the hardest under Myth's guidance,
yet he'd never won Myth's support; Arminion and Perilynn had it
instantly. These wounds wouldn't heal. If he could only persuade
the eNoli that Arminion's leadership should be abandoned . . .

"Why should we trust him to help us? Have you forgotten
that with Myth we went to war to destroy the Olivion so we
could leave this place? That's the correct path and we need to
return to it!"

aZRon was getting impatient. *Blah! Blah! Blah! All of this talk!
Reign never said any of this when Arminion was around.* He knew better.
aZRon turned to his three sisters with a disgusted look on his
face. They smiled but motioned for him to pay attention.

"We agreed to uphold Arminion's plan before he left—"
Holliston began, but Reign cut him off.

"It's no secret that I don't agree with Arminion, yet even still
I was out doing my duty to destroy the children. I'm loyal to
our cause. But someone was not; someone betrayed all eNoli.
This is what makes me stand here to tell you we should abandon
Arminion, because he cannot be trusted!" Reign said, and a great
smile spread across his face.

This was what aZRon had been waiting for. He sat in quiet anticipation.

"Who is it you speak of?" one eNoli asked.

"Who is this traitor and what does he have to do with Arminion?" another demanded.

"It was the person whom we would least expect! It was Arminion's brother, Perilynn!" Reign said.

Silence came over Lefton Rack. aZRon clenched his fist and whispered, "Yes." This was going to be exciting!

"How can you be sure? It was said the savior of the child was wearing a mask! It must have been an iLone. All of the children are iLone!" said an eNoli.

"They're going to try to protect them at all costs," said another.

"No! It was Perilynn. When we fought I broke his mask and saw it was he. No one else saw his face? He challenged you all!" Reign said.

Lefton Rack went silent. No one other than Reign and aZRon had seen that it was Perilynn. Everyone knew Reign hated Perilynn, so they were hesitant to trust him.

Oh, come on, no one else saw him? It was Perilynn! aZRon thought. He wanted the drama and excitement of everyone chasing Perilynn. He had no choice but to speak. "I saw him too. Perilynn has betrayed us so that he can become a Favorite."

"Are you sure?" Holliston said.

"Oh yes. He's my friend and it pains me to say it, but he's been driven mad with his desire. He wants to cross the Gate with the children."

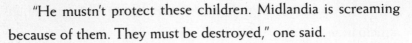

"He mustn't protect these children. Midlandia is screaming because of them. They must be destroyed," one said.

"They mustn't be allowed to reach the Olivion and return home with the power to challenge Arminion, Galonious, and Trife. Our plans to escape this place will fail!" another said.

"Perilynn must be stopped!" someone else called out.

"No, he must be destroyed!" Reign said.

"No, he deserves a worse fate. He must be sent into the Infinite Abyss, and I volunteer to kick him in when he's caught!" aZRon could not keep the sickening smile from his face. He nearly shook from side to side with anticipation of what was about to happen. Just as he'd warned Perilynn, all of Midlandia was going to be after him. Not since the war of Myth had there been the possibility of so much excitement.

Chapter Eight

Louis and Cyndi were thrown from the Midland Isle into conflict, but Midlandia would not permit that for sixteen-year-old Devon Alexander. You see, Devon had a crystal heart stained with tragedy. Midlandia would not let that tragedy find him here, at least not for now. He slept peacefully, as if he were wrapped in a marvelous dream, nestled gently high in the air among the cloudy platforms of the Ethereal Ends. Midlandia would:

Hold him.
Hug him.
Soothe him.
Love him.

But if that was the case, why was there a horde of teenagers creeping in on him? Four boys and three girls held glowing blades, double-sided axes, energy staffs, and energy bows all aimed directly at Devon. Their names were aMaya, Always, Ariel, Stance, Evidence, Carbon, and Shyft.

They were Favorites with sparkling Alonis Medallions around their necks.

They were The Young Armada.

"This is serious!" aMaya said.

"We've found one," Always said.

"Oh, really? What was your clue?" Ariel said sarcastically.

"Stop it, you two," Evidence said.

"Call Vivionya. She said if we—" Stance said.

"No need. Look . . ." Carbon said.

A figure streaked across the sky on a simple yet high-tech vehicle. It seemed to be a combination of a wingless jet and a motorbike. Compact, made of metal, and light, it was designed for ultimate speed and agility. When it got closer, the vehicle broke apart and the pieces disappeared into a light at the rider's back.

"Wonderful! You found him. What do you say we wake him? But first, put those away." Vivionya said. If the boy were to wake to the sight of this bunch with glowing blades and other weapons, he'd be terrified.

"Are you sure? One is eNoli; he could be that one," said Always.

"Always, I most certainly am. Until Olivion marks the children either iLone or eNoli we'll treat them all kindly." After everyone had put away their weapons, Vivionya gently placed her hand on the boy's chest. As she touched him, her hand

and his chest began to glow, and with that the boy peacefully awoke.

Devon was sure this was a dream. The vivid colors of the bright sky. The songs that rode in on the wind. The wondrous floating islands and mountains drifting in the distance. Actually, he too seemed to be on an island, which was drifting in the air and gently rocking under him. How could this not be a dream? He'd dreamed that he'd woken, but his dream had simply changed and gotten even better. Devon was no coward. He would never run from his life, but dreams were a way to escape his troubled world without running. What his eyes gazed upon right now was far more elaborate than any daydream or night dream he'd ever had.

"Whoa. Where are we? I'm dreaming, right?" Devon said to Vivionya while glancing at the others.

"Vivy, we need to get him back to the city. We won't be safe here for long," Always said.

"I'm Vivionya and I'll tell you everything you'd like to know. I just need you to come with me," Vivionya told Devon, extending her hand to him.

"Come with you? Where to?" Devon took deeper notice of the other seven people. They were close to his age; some seemed a bit younger, others a bit older. Then he quickly stood up and took in the sight of the Ethereal Ends. They were water-colored marvels that surpassed phenomenal.

"Come on, we have to go where it's truly safe," Vivionya said, spinning the Alonis around her neck. As soon as she did, her Alonis vehicle constructed itself and she was on her unique bike.

All Devon knew was that there was a gorgeous woman telling him to come with her. He didn't know if it was the smartest thing to do, but he was on autopilot. He would get on her bike and go wherever she wanted to take him. He couldn't explain it but he trusted her. Besides, this was probably a dream, although it felt so real, he was beginning to trust in its truth.

"Hold on," Vivionya said when Devon was seated behind her. He was happy to do so.

That gave them a head start. Hopefully they hadn't been seen by the hordes of eNoli searchers that were headed to this location.

The Young Armada stood ready to meet those eNoli. They would prevent any from following.

Sights set!
Alonises glowing!
Weapons drawn!
eNoli vs. iLone!
Battle on!

Chapter **Nine**

Perilynn and Louis stood at the top of a valley. Way off in the distance they saw a walled city with a huge dome structure in its forefront. Gunmetal gray and imposing, the dome seemed almost like an angry eye sitting on the horizon. Louis had the feeling that whoever resided there was not someone with whom Louis would want to sip hot cocoa.

"One of us is in there. I can feel it," he said.

"Just as I said, Midlandia is like that. You're all being drawn together," Perilynn said.

As he walked toward the city, Perilynn realized that there was no chance he'd be able to leave Louis on his own or let him out of his sight. He had to plan for that. A disguise? Hide him? No. Neither option would work. There was only one way—Louis would be a prisoner. There'd be no need to bind Louis because Perilynn's word would be enough for the eNoli. The reality was Louis posed no threat to the CE. Not yet, anyway. Perilynn just had to worry if word had spread that he was a traitor. He'd find that out soon enough.

They walked right up to the large door of the domed structure that led to the city. Before he did anything Perilynn turned to Louis.

"Are you sure?" Perilynn asked.

"I just feel something strong and it's bigger than the fear. I can tell . . . I remember from when I first got here. She's in there," Louis said.

Perilynn placed his hand on the door. A pattern of light pulsed from the point of contact, alerting all inside to his presence.

"It's Perilynn. He's heard of the child. He'll be so happy!" A voice said.

"Let him in . . . ," another said.

The door opened. Fin, an imposing eNoli CE, slid into view. She was similar to Trife but a bit bigger and bluish. For Louis, she was a frightening reminder of what had happened a few hours ago during his last day of school. He rubbed his arms to try to soothe his uneasiness. His stomach felt queasy. He knew he couldn't run but he sure wanted to. Making an effort, he clenched his lips and listened.

"Perilynn, you've found your own child. Such a wonderful prisoner! Your brother will be so pleased. . . . We've found a child ourselves. Do you hear its screams? It tried to talk to us but we wouldn't be fooled," Fin said, then paused. They soon heard a screech.

"We tried to keep it quiet for as long as we could, but that has come to an end. Its energy is so lovely—unlike any we've seen here before. We're collecting it. I'm sure we'll be able to find a use for it. That's how we're killing it. We're draining it dry." Now Fin turned to Louis. "We'll do the same to you. It won't hurt if you don't fight."

"This one is none of your concern. I'll deal with him on my own," Perilynn said.

How can he protect me from all these things? Louis wondered as he looked beyond the door. It led into the massive metallic domed chamber, where countless holes swarmed with beings just like Fin and Trife. They slithered from hole to hole as if they were worms crawling through a rotten apple. The sight reminded Louis of cartoons he'd seen.

"Where is this child? Take me to it," Perilynn said.

"Of course! Of course! Follow me." Fin led them through the large chamber toward a distant passageway on its opposite side.

Above, ahead, to the right, to the left. The CE were moving in an unnerving rhythm through the holes. The air vibrated with the freakish hissing sound that Louis remembered from the first time he'd seen Trife.

Terror stopped Louis from taking any more steps. One of the eNoli had fallen right in front of him. It didn't grab Louis but pointed directly in his face.

"We'll bring you no pain, but you will die. It's better if you let us do our job," the loathsome eNoli said.

"All in good time, Grynd. Go on your way and leave us," Perilynn told the eNoli. It obliged, slithering to one of the holes to the far left and disappearing.

"I'm sure Arminion will place you in the highest regard for the great work you're doing to destroy the children," Perilynn said.

"Yes, we're happy to be doing our part. And we can't wait to leave Midlandia. It's been so long, so unbearable. You know, we're proud of Trife. We didn't know what to think when he decided to serve under Galonious, but he was given a chance to leave," Fin said as they finally reached the door on the opposite side of the chamber. It opened onto a city that was cold, foreboding, and exposed to the Midlandian sky. The buildings seemed to be built on a curve as if they were all part of a circular maze. There was no maze though. A direct path led to the center of the city, and they set off down this path.

As they walked, many CE pointed and stared at Louis. He was clearly one of the children to be destroyed. Others greeted Perilynn as a hero for his single-handed capture of another child. They knew that if the children were killed, Galonious, Arminion, and Trife would have no obstacles on Earth and could usher in their exodus.

Perilynn enjoyed the praise and admiration. It was a relief that word of his actions had not reached this city, and no one suspected he was here to betray them.

But when they made it to the center of the city, Louis stopped to stare, eyes wide. Here was a wicked yet elegant metal machine with wild circles of light spinning behind it. Suspended in the center was a defenseless fifteen- or sixteen-year-old girl. Her blond hair hung in her face. She could no longer scream as her energy had been drained so low, she was a few short yards away from falling into death's grip.

Her legs and arms were bound with electric ties. The electric circles behind her were her own energy that had been siphoned off. It glowed a majestic bluish green and highlighted the beauty of all that was caught in its hue.

Perilynn had to act quickly.

"I think you should release the child," Perilynn said.

"Why do you request such a thing? It may have screamed for freedom, but it's in no pain as death slowly overtakes it. In a few tiny ticks it will be done. We're doing right by it and ourselves. You'll do well to give us your capture too. Yours may take the place of ours after it has fallen. You can enjoy watching its energy slip away," Fin said as others came in closer to touch Louis.

"Perilynn. Do something!" Louis said. Then he realized it may have been better to be subtler.

They all began to look at Perilynn with curious eyes. They couldn't believe Perilynn would allow the child to speak to him like that, neither did they understand why Perilynn would wish for their child's release.

They may have chosen a painless way to destroy Cyndi, but they were not kind. They were formidable warriors, and there was no way Perilynn could survive a battle with all of them in such close proximity.

If you alone deliver the children to me and cross my Gate with them, I will praise you as a Favorite. Perilynn remembered the words that had echoed in his mind. The Olivion had spoken to him! He *could* become a Favorite. He had to act now or lose his dream.

Perilynn had just one option. He sent up a blast of glowing light, alerting both iLone and eNoli to the location of the child.

"Traitor!" Fin yelled. It was on. No longer docile. No longer subdued. The eNoli were beasts. Louis saw them transform. Their bodies became laced with razorlike quills. Their faces became hell-bent on destruction. Ravenous eyes.

"iLone will seek the child," Grynd yelled.

The perfect distraction, Perilynn thought.

The iLone looked like massive glowing raindrops as they stormed down from above. Waves of electric mist hit the ground and materialized into soldiers.

Neither Louis nor Perilynn had time to meet any of them.

No time for handshakes.

No time for small talk.

No time at all.

Perilynn grabbed Louis under his arm; he moved freely even with Louis in tow. Louis was dumbfounded by the way he was being handled as if he were a weightless bag of potato chips. Perilynn couldn't use one arm, but it didn't matter. He was driven. He was focused. He leaped, attacking eNoli with his free hand, punching and elbowing with deadly accuracy. He also swung around so that Louis's feet knocked eNoli to the ground. This dynamic use of Louis, well-placed kicks, and the blows with his one free hand would have awed even the most adept martial arts master.

Perilynn landed on the machine. He waved his hand over the electrical ties that held Cyndi, and they disappeared. As she began to fall, he flipped backward toward the ground, trailing Louis, to catch her in midair with his free hand. He landed firmly and kicked the excess energy out of all approaching eNoli. He had yet to meet with any iLone, though they were coming to claim both children.

He had Cyndi, but she was nearly dead.

Two out of three.
More than halfway there.
That is, if she doesn't die.

Perilynn released Louis, told him to stand behind him, and called to Cyndi's stolen life force, which glowed, still captured in the machine. Just as he did, Fin called to it too. It was drawn to both of them at the same time. The energy stretched between them, sparking and fighting for its freedom. Cyndi instinctively used every bit of her remaining strength to reach for her own energy. She grasped Perilynn's arm, connecting through it to her life force. This was the advantage Perilynn needed to command the energy as he saw fit.

The iLone were charging toward the children. Perilynn began to swing the energy beam around like a whip. Fin was still attached to the other end, but she no longer had any control, so she spun around with it. The whip was powerful—something no one had ever seen. As the whip made contact, it severed iLone and eNoli alike in half. Their energy disbursed into the air, leaving the songs of Midlandia to mourn their loss. Fin finally lost her grip and was sent flying. She was lucky to be able to tell the tale of Perilynn.

As if it were a retractable tape measure, the energy sped toward Perilynn's arm. His arm was not its destination. It flew directly into the girl, knocking her from Perilynn's grip. She soared into a wall, and the impact created an energy wave that tossed all nearby iLone and eNoli away.

Cyndi awoke to chaos.

She was overwhelmed by the luminous streaks of the iLone attacking the eNoli and by the eNoli thrashing in defense of their city.

Where the heck am I now? Cyndi screamed in her own head.

Perilynn noticed that the spot where she'd hit the wall shimmered. Wish and hope! It had to be! They were coming. So many chasing and seeking. With crazy ridiculous speed Perilynn snatched up Louis and charged. He grabbed the girl an instant before he would make contact with the wall.

Did they make it?
We should all hope so.

Chapter Ten

Reign and a few of his supporters abandoned Lefton Rack for the Limited Peninsula in protest of what he considered to be a senseless allegiance to Arminion and his plans. The Limited Peninsula was a place that Reign often sought for secret meetings. It was limited in the sense that it was small and lacked the wonders that many other parts of Midlandia had. Wonders can be a distraction when you want to be the focus of attention. The Limited Peninsula had only deep golden sand and a few trees. The sky was a reddish yellow blend that suited Reign.

"You were not at Lefton Rack," Reign said.

Two eNoli came into sight as soon as he completed his sentence. One was a woman named Helenia. She was thin and pale, dressed in a white form-fitting dress with a flowing train. Five glowing red orbs floated in her hand. She was playing with them, making them dance and move in elaborate patterns.

The man was named Octavio. He had no feet, or they just couldn't be seen under his long overcoat. He hovered a yard off the ground, wearing an odd smile. Both were devout followers of Myth and commanded hordes of eNoli who were not satisfied with Arminion or his plans.

"Lefton Rack has become nothing but a fan club for Arminion. Sad. Sad. Sad," Helenia said in a wispy, lighthearted voice while playing with her orbs. She didn't seem to be paying attention to Reign.

"It's such a shame that eLynori and the Lost went mad. She'd never have stood for any of this. No one would have opposed her even in the face of Arminion. She'd have fought him, unlike others I know. She even kept the great Myth in line," Octavio said.

"Don't mock me. She did go mad, and now it's time for us to complete what Myth started. We must destroy the Olivion," answered Reign.

"You've always asked for our help to challenge Arminion and we've always refused. Why should we join you now?" Octavio questioned.

"You know that the children of legend are here. When the children are united, the Gate will appear. With your support, I'll steal the children and I . . . we will cross the Gate to destroy the Olivion. That will win us our freedom. We'll do what Myth had planned to do. But we'll be victorious this time," Reign said.

"Will you? You know what happened to you the last time you found the Gate! What makes you think you'll be successful this time?" Octavio asked.

"The children will guarantee that. The Gate *must* open for them," Reign said.

"It's one thing to attack Perilynn to get the children. It's another to go against the eNoli. We'll be starting a war," Octavio said

"We're already at war with the iLone!" Reign said.

"But this would be a *civil war*! We'd be going against the eNoli who follow Arminion," Helenia said.

"Are you scared? Are your numbers weak? Are you children? We're eNoli and this is our perfect time. Myth wouldn't have thought twice with less of an opportunity. Do you think any of your fears will exist after we destroy the Olivion? All will follow us!" Reign said.

"How dare you! You ask us for support. Without it you are nothing and blowing in the wind like Perilynn. At least he has the courage to do this on his own. You do not," Octavio said as they closed in on Reign. They radiated a warlike energy that was to be feared. They were both very powerful.

Reign stared them down and showed no fear. He began to glow and drew his blades.

"I may need your support and numbers, but do not think that I fear either of you," Reign said. Helenia and Octavio backed down. They knew Reign was a formidable adversary. They just needed to be reminded.

"Perilynn is a fool. I'm a bit more organized. I do have the courage to do this, but our numbers will guarantee success. This is our time!" Reign said.

"Fine. Do what you need to do. We'll be watching and when needed we will support you," Helenia said as her orbs began to dance wildly. She waved her hand over them, making them disappear. Then she and Octavio disappeared too, leaving Reign ecstatic. He finally had the backing he needed.

This was a very dangerous path that Reign was eager to tread upon.

Very dangerous indeed.

Chapter **Eleven**

Devon held tight to Vivionya. As he soared through the sky with her, he drank in the wonders around him. There were crystal mountains beaming with light. Rivers that seemed to sparkle with precious stones. Flying entities that were big, small, and all sizes in between were racing by. It wasn't hard to figure out that they were headed for the elaborate city in the distance.

When at last they entered its walls, he saw crowds of people.

Devon was their fighting hope or a tool for their demise. Welcome, Devon, to the iLone City of Chance.

He could hear music that was like a million ethereal violins playing in perfect twenty-part harmony accented with singing voices. It seemed tuned to his heartbeat.

Landing, he didn't feel the need for words. He felt as if he knew these people, although he'd never seen them before. But there was no time for greetings anyway, because Vivionya ushered him to a water fountain that reconfigured itself into a hidden stairway.

He thought he was entering a castle underground, but after

they'd walked inside for a bit, they stepped outside again. The sky was bright and clear above them while bushes and trees at ground level hid them from view.

Vivionya led Devon to a small room. When they were both seated in plush chairs, she said, "Devon, I bet you're wondering what's going on, right?"

"Yes! This place is amazing. The colors. The people. The sounds. Everything. Nothing compares to it." He paused and stared intently at her. "But I've got to get home. My family needs me."

"Devon, this place is Midlandia and this is the iLone City of Chance. You're here because of a war that happened long ago and that was ended by something known as the Alorion Treaty. That treaty has been broken," Vivionya explained.

"What—"

"Please let me finish. I am iLone. There are two kinds of CE, or Celestial Entities, here, iLone and eNoli, and neither is supposed leave Midlandia. We do not fit in your world. The consequences if we leave are grave not for us but for you. As you can see, Midlandia is a wondrous place without limits. We iLone love it here and are beyond content. But the eNoli see things differently. No matter what they have, they're never satisfied. Such is their nature. They're driven by their desire for more.

"The treaty says that for each of us who manages to leave Midlandia, a child, like yourself, will be transported here and will gain the power to defeat us. But you need to survive your time here. You are one of those children and must return home safely to fulfill your destiny. Three of you are here now; two of you are

54

iLone and one is eNoli. The thing is, I don't know if you're an iLone child destined to fight the eNoli or if you're an eNoli child destined to fight those like me," Vivionya said.

"How will I find out what I am?" Devon asked.

"There's only one way to find out. Once you're united with the other two children, you'll be able to find Olivion's Gate. You'll enter the Gate and meet Olivion, who'll mark each of you as either iLone or eNoli. Then you'll be able to go home. We're looking for the other children so that we can get you to the Gate," Vivionya said.

"But wait . . . you said there's an eNoli child here. So you guys broke the treaty too. I thought you had no reason to leave."

"Yes, we broke the treaty too. Timioosiyon is an iLone on Earth now. We did it to help you. Some think it was a mistake, but Timioosiyon was ready and prepared for this. He is rather unique."

"This is all a head trip. I have to get home. My family needs me," Devon said.

"Devon, cheer up. eNoli or iLone—you're a Favorite. Anyone would be happy to be that," Vivionya said.

"What's a Favorite?" Devon asked.

"I'm a Favorite too. It means that you're one of the most powerful beings in existence. Olivion smiles on you. If you speak, Olivion hears you. The things you'll be able to do after you meet Olivion will only be limited by your own imagination and will. And you'll use this power to fight Celestial Entities." Vivionya's Alonis began to glow.

"I can do anything once I meet the Olivion?" Devon began

to get choked up and his eyes got watery. He walked away from Vivionya to hide his face. It wasn't long ago that he'd begun to pray every night for such a power. That's when he started to have wild dreams of a place that had to be Midlandia. He knew exactly what he'd destroy. This lovely woman was telling him that all he had to do was get to Olivion and those powers were his. But could he believe her?

"Vivionya, if you're a Favorite and I am too . . . can you show me the power?" Devon asked.

"Devon, you've flown with me through the Midlandian sky. You're in this city unlike any you've seen. You've met the iLone people and looked into their eternal eyes. I think you've already witnessed enough to know that I'm telling you the truth. I don't needlessly flaunt my power; if you turn out to be iLone you'll understand that."

"All right, but I know exactly what I would do . . . ," Devon said.

"Do you really?" Vivionya was suspicious of his intentions.

"What if I'm eNoli? What then, since you're iLone?" Devon said.

"We won't speak on such a thing. We'll just have to hope you're iLone. You must stay here. I'll be back," Vivionya said. She knew she could kill him right now if he was eNoli. She'd already told him too much as she tried to put him at ease. She left Devon in the room alone.

Devon sat. He had no option but to wait.

Chapter **Twelve**

The Celestial Drifts looked as if they should have been cold, as they seemed to be made of ice; nonetheless, the one in which Louis, Perilynn, and Cyndi stood was not. It was clear, yet depending on how you moved, you could see colors, vivid and beautiful, playing in its smooth surface. The Celestial Drift was like a gigantic cave within a crystal mountain that was flying through the air. Light was dancing in the walls, and each passageway looked like it would lead to an adventure.

All that really mattered, though, was that they were no longer in the center of a battle.

Perilynn walked jauntily about. He couldn't keep still. He'd made it this far. He only had to rescue one more and he'd be well on his way to becoming a Favorite. He'd been doing things that he never thought he could do. He simply couldn't accept *not* being a Favorite. He couldn't accept not getting these kids to the Olivion safely.

Juggernaut Complex.

"I know this place. I've never been here but I've heard of it.

We're within the Celestial Drifts," Perilynn said. This would have been a place of legend but just about all places in Midlandia were worthy of being places of legend. It would be hard to find anything on Midlandia that was not seriously impressive in its own way.

What next? Perilynn needed to plan. Practically floating with anticipation, he walked away from Louis and Cyndi. He didn't want to let on that he was not totally sure what they should do now.

Cyndi was slumped on the ground, holding herself, in shock. "It's crazy, right? Everything that's going on?" Louis said to Cyndi. She didn't respond.

Louis didn't know what to do. All he knew was that he wanted to help. For some reason he remembered his first day of kindergarten. He'd gone up to everyone and introduced himself. He told everyone his life story, although it was short and his vocabulary was limited. By the end of the day, he had the most friends, two of whom were Brandon and Angela.

Louis, give it a try. See what happens.

"Hey, do you remember me from when we both got here? My name is Louis Proof." Louis pointed to his name tag. Just then one appeared on the girl's chest without a name. She said nothing.

"I'm twelve, about to be thirteen. Um . . . I'm from East Orange, New Jersey, about twenty-five minutes from New York

City—fifteen, if you drive like a madman. Um . . . I'm in eighth grade. I have a mom, dad, and brother. I can't forget cousin Lacey, who's like my little sister. I have two best friends named Brandon and Angela. You know, I miss them all. And Perilynn is helping us get home. Perilynn's a good guy." Cyndi still didn't respond, so Louis continued.

"I race radio-controlled cars and my last race was at this place you wouldn't believe. Oh, that's a secret; I forgot for a second. But I had such a great race; I was going to win and things got crazy, but not as crazy as . . ." Louis didn't want to call this place crazy—that just was not the thing to say. "Oh, I have a job working for my uncle. He makes specialized and personalized doorknobs, well, any kind of knob or handle. It was kind of my idea, and he can make them any way you want. He was on TV. Some are real expensive. Some are iced out . . ."

Doorknobs. Specialized doorknobs. Iced-out doorknobs. That sounded familiar. It was such an oddity. Something she never thought she'd hear here.

"I bought some. They were very . . . elegant . . . expensive. I just had to have them. They were the perfect highlight to my door . . . ," Cyndi said slowly.

"You bought some?" Louis said, surprised.

"I did. Your uncle is Albert Proof and you're Louis Proof, just like you said."

"Yeah. You got it. I work in the store."

"Hello, Louis. Thank you. I lost it for a second." For the first time she looked at the young boy. He had an honest face and a winning smile. He was sincere; she could tell that about him. He was a friend.

"I know what you mean. I was in a real bad situation—not as bad as yours—before Perilynn saved me. He's going to take us to the Olivion so that we can go home." Louis sat down beside her as if they were old friends. He thought of her as a friend. It seemed like the natural thing to do, since they were in the same predicament.

"Hey. What's your name?"

"It's Cyndi. Cyndi Victoria Chase."

"I *know* that name. I *know* your order. You're from Cali. It was going out that day . . ." Louis paused and watched her name write itself on her name tag, courtesy of Perilynn.

"The day I fell out. I was in front of my uncle's store. I felt sick, like I was going to die, and I guess I collapsed. Before that, this thing—who looked just like the ones who captured you—chased me. It had to be from here. These guys are already on Earth," Louis said, realizing that when he got home he was going to have to face beings like those he'd seen here.

"That was Trife. I know him well," Perilynn, coming up beside them, said with a laugh.

"You felt pain and fell out? I did too. The day before had been such a good day. I mean a really, really good day, one of my best—you've no idea." Cyndi was remembering how she'd exposed the corruption of her school and, after just a few phone calls and emails, brought the school year to a close with an exciting exclamation point.

"I was in the kitchen and I felt extreme pain and I fell. Then I remember the light . . . that's where I first saw you. I tried to talk to those creatures and they captured me. But before that, when I was home, some strange kid just popped into my room and told me unusual things were going to happen. I had no idea that this is what he meant." Cyndi stood.

"I guess you were lucky. I didn't get any warnings. Just weird things chasing me and distracting me during my last RC race . . . I lost the race. That was nothing; I almost lost my life a short time ago.

"Cyndi, this is Perilynn, and if it wasn't for him, neither of us would be alive. He's incredible. One of the best I've ever seen. Like Jack Bauer with superpowers," Louis said before turning to Perilynn. "Thank you, Perilynn. If I didn't say it before—thank you. I wish I could do more to help myself—to help us. But I can't fight like you. I wish I could."

"Louis—and you too, Cyndi—don't worry, it's my job and a great honor to help you. Because you're here, I'm able to seek out my own dreams. I would see my end as I am before I'd let any harm come to you. I promise to get you safely to the Olivion," Perilynn said. "There's something I want you to do for me, though. Something I want you to promise."

"What is it? Tell me. Whatever you want!" Louis said.

"Promise me we'll stay together and you won't cross Olivion's Gate without me. Promise me that. That's all I want from you."

"Of course, I promise I won't cross the Gate without you," Louis said, then looked to Cyndi. She was clueless.

"What is Olivion's Gate?" Cyndi asked.

"Well, Cyndi, I can't start with Olivion's Gate. There's much more you must know about before you can understand that." Perilynn extended his hand to her. She took it as he led her to one end of the Drift. The view was beyond anything she'd ever imagined. The Celestial Drifts were dazzling. But there were also flying cities, each more detailed than the last. And she spotted magnificent airships gliding in the sky. Even the threat that some of them might be looking for her didn't diminish their wonder.

"Where are we? How did I get here?" Cyndi said, awed.

"Cyndi, I wish I could tell you everything, but I don't know. Just as I told Louis, this place is called Midlandia. Where is it? Think of everything you know about where you're from—I mean everything, like other planets and such—and this is not there. That's all I know," Perilynn said.

"How can you not know these things? You're from here, right? This is your home, right?"

"Cyndi, I'm sorry. I just don't. No CE—or Celestial Entity—does. Most eNoli don't care; they only want to leave this place. The iLone try to keep us here, but they don't have the answers either. I suppose it *is* maddening, if you let it get to you," Perilynn said.

"How big is Midlandia? And it's got to be somewhere, every-where has got be somewhere," Cyndi said.

"Midlandia has no end, as far as I know. It goes on and on, and places don't have to be where you found them last, and you may never see anything twice."

"This sounds like hell with a pretty face. It goes on forever, you don't know where it is, and people are trying to kill us," Cyndi said, her voice wobbling a bit.

"It's crazy, but I think this can be a good place too. Maybe. There's good here too. Look at Perilynn. He's good. He's great," Louis said.

"How do we leave here? Is Olivion's Gate the exit?" Cyndi asked.

"The only way to leave here is through the Midland Isle," Perilynn said.

"Where's the Midland Isle?" Cyndi asked.

"Sometimes here, there, anywhere. Or maybe it's always in the same place and everything moves around it. I don't know. You see, this place makes no sense. Sometimes I want to explode into a million shards of energy from the frustration. I want to understand. I need answers."

"Perilynn, you told me the Olivion knows everything."

"Yes, Louis, the Olivion knows all things, and all things come from the Olivion. You're Olivion's Favorites. We'll find the Olivion at the Gate."

"Where's Olivion's Gate? Do you at least know where that is?" Cyndi asked.

"No, but that's not an issue. Just as Louis found you, the two of you will help me find the third child. When all three of you are together, the Gate will make itself known. If I deliver all three of you safely, the Olivion will reward me by making me a Favorite. She told me so herself," Perilynn explained.

"Okay, so then the Olivion will allow me, I mean us, to go home?" Cyndi asked.

"Yes, you'll return home safe and sound after all of this," Perilynn said.

"Cool. So, Perilynn, you've got it. If you get us to Olivion's Gate, we won't cross without you!" Cyndi said, putting out her hand for Perilynn to shake. He obliged and Louis did the same.

This was a pact of all pacts.

These three would become bound to one another in ways they could not imagine.

Cyndi wanted to stretch her legs. She was still wobbly from having her energy drained from her, but she was beginning to feel stronger and thought that walking might help. She invited Louis to walk with her. Perilynn followed.

They went from cavern to cavern in the Drift, finally stopping to stare through the crystal-like walls in a spot where they could see other Drifts floating by in the bright daylight. Here Louis, Cyndi, and Perilynn's images became engraved in the wall, as if they were becoming a part of this wonderful place. What they were soon to find out was that they were actually calling home and home was about to answer.

Louis and Cyndi found their lives on opposite walls of the passageway they were in. The areas where their faces had been engraved turned into mirrors that at first showed them as they were right now, and then allowed them to glimpse their lives back home.

Louis saw himself in his own bed. He looked thinner and a bit more muscular, just as he was here. What was he missing? What were his friends up to? He had the feeling that someone was upset over him. He wanted to find this person, and it was as if the mirror used the person's emotions as a homing signal. The mirror showed him Angela.

She was on the set of the movie she was filming, but she was crying in her trailer over Louis. Everything was out of whack. She was far from home, wrapped in a new life, and she wasn't adjusting without her anchor, Louis Proof.

What had happened to talking every day?

What had happened to the way they'd been doing things since they were little?

There were whispers of them replacing her if she couldn't get through this scene. Louis wondered how he was able to know all this. How was this place able to do this?

Then Louis thought, *No way!* This was Angela's dream. Louis couldn't live with himself if Angela wasn't able to do her job because she was worried about him.

"Mom, I just want to go home. Can I quit?" Angela said to her mother.

"Honey, if it's too much for you, you can. Are you sure?" said her mom.

"Angela. Don't you dare quit on your dream! I'm fine. I'm right here. I'll be back. Hugs, kisses, lollipops, and cupcakes are all great things, but not as great as you! Come on, get back out there and shut the game down!" Louis shouted into the mirror, wishing not only that Angela could hear him but that she could feel his intensity. With that desire, the mirror became a sort of two-way emotional communicator, as he pressed his hands against it. He could sense Angela's feelings and she could sense his.

That was all it took to sprinkle a little bit of a miracle on her. Angela breathed easy and deep, and all the doubt, remorse, and uneasiness of missing Louis faded away. It wasn't as if she'd forgotten him but as if she knew he was fine and right by her side whispering in her ear. She trusted this feeling because she sensed it was real. Louis was with her in a way. When she got back on the set, it was with a powerful new energy. She did indeed shut the game down. That's what's up!

Once again Louis was looking at himself lying in bed. Someone was coming. Brandon walked into his room without closing the door behind him.

"Louis, so much crazy stuff is going on here! I wish you could see it, but you know I'm here to keep you updated on everything. I brought you some new music to listen to." He turned on Louis's stereo, plugged his iPod into the auxiliary jack, and new sounds poured out.

"Oh, I know you want to see what's up with this new game you got. Since you're still not up, I'm going to have to play it for you. Can I open it? It's a federal offense to open someone's mail. Stay still if it's okay. Fine! I'll open it because you insisted." Louis had been waiting for this game right before he fell out.

"Excellent choice. I swear, I wish my mom ordered games for me," Brandon said.

Brandon, be careful what you wish for.
Someone just might be listening.

Brandon began to play the game. But watching the flashing lights and pressing the buttons was not joyful for him.

"Awww, man! Louis, come on. Angela is gone and you're in a coma. Don't you know, my life pretty much sucks right now? Seriously, it sucks. And it's summer. That's the worst time for your life to suck! I don't mean for just me. I mean for you too. You missed your birthday and stuff. Crap! I would've gotten you a gift, but I never get you a gift and I didn't want to break tradition. But I promise you this and I swear. When you wake, I will always have your back! I will always be a good friend. If the cars in the JunkYard JunkLot shake, I won't run. Never! For real, you'll always be able to count on me. I'll be your best friend for-ever . . . BFF. I get it now! That's what that stands for? That's for girls, so scratch that. I'll never let you down. Just come back!" Brandon didn't realize that Lacey was eavesdropping on the whole conversation from behind Louis's partially open door.

"You got it, Brandon. I swear I'll be back," Louis said, and the feeling of his promise washed over Brandon.

Brandon sat taller and his eyes twinkled. "Okay, back to that video game. Pay attention, because I'm about to show you how it's done!"

Louis began to walk away from the mirror, but something caught his eye, and he quickly turned to it once again. He didn't know if this was the same day, yesterday, or when. He didn't even know if time worked like that here in Midlandia. The image in the mirror had changed and Louis smiled. He was watching his cousin Lacey and three of her friends playing in the park. He thought it odd that they were there by themselves, but Lacey was known for sneaking away to go on adventures.

"Lacey, not the sandbox. People pee in the sandbox. I've seen them do it. It's not just a school myth," Louis said. As if she'd heard Louis, Lacey led her friends away from it to the jungle gym.

What the . . . Louis couldn't believe it. Ill, horrible, compact beings were closing in on Lacey and her friends.

"Lacey. Lacey. Lacey. Get out of there!" Louis yelled.

Lacey looked up and screamed. Twenty or so beings were nearly upon her and her friends Harrison and Imani. They meant to do harm. The jungle gym, swings, slides, and sandbox offered no cover or escape. The creatures were everywhere and the kids were alone.

Harrison was scared out of his mind but had enough sense

to pick up a stick to beat them back if they got closer. Imani screamed for her mother. Lacey began to tear up but remembered Louis's promise. If she were ever in trouble and called him, he would come.

"Louis! Louis! Help me! Help us!" she yelled.

Louis didn't know what to do. He called to Perilynn, who saw the sight but couldn't do anything. It wasn't his connection. A fire burned inside of Louis, and with it his Celestial Infection Rate rose even higher. He thought of all the fighting that Perilynn had done and wished Lacey could do the same. He wanted her to be able to protect herself since he was not there to do it. With that desire he touched the image. The sand began to stir and the swings began to sway.

Lacey's tears were gone. A feeling of confidence and power blew through her as images of skilled fighters tumbled in her mind. She *felt* Louis. Somehow he was with her. Lacey focused. As the creatures began their attack, she had something for them. They leaped with claws and foul-teethed mouths voracious for the taste of her and her friends, but she would feed them round-house kicks, upper cuts, and jabs. She used the jungle gym to swing and flip, delivering a creative assault. Her friend Harrison cheered her on and used his stick to hit the ones she downed. Imani tried to keep Lacey between her and the beings.

Soon it was over. Lacey and her friends left unharmed; the Crims did not.

She had kicked some serious assets.

Score one for Lacey Proof.

69

* * *

The image in the mirror changed again. Louis saw his room once more. It was a different day and Brandon was no longer there. Louis's brother had just entered and was searching for something. Cameron was always yelling at Louis for "rambling" through his stuff, but now he was doing it.

What was he looking for? Louis knew. He was looking for money.

Louis could read his brother's feelings. He was in trouble and he needed the money to leave. It was a serious situation. Not only that, there was Trife. Louis could see him shadowing Cameron, although he wasn't in Louis's room. He was someplace else. It was like another dimension.

Louis wanted to help his brother get out of there.

Behind the desk, hit that panel in the floor. Then you can reach into the wall to pull the red fireproof box out. It's there. Take what you need, Louis thought.

Cameron suddenly moved with purpose. He strode toward Louis's desk, pounded a panel in the floor, and found the secret compartment and Louis's money box. He took a sizeable amount but left some for Louis. He couldn't just take this money. He sat at Louis's desk and grabbed some paper and a pen. It took him a moment but he began to write. He welled up with emotion because this was the most truthful he'd ever been to his little brother. He had to tell the truth, for he was actually stealing from Louis; he needed to explain why and what he was doing to make it right. When he was done he tucked the remaining money into an envelope with the letter, gently placed it in the box, and returned the box to its secret location.

Until now Louis hadn't noticed that Cameron had brought a garment bag into the room with him. He took it off Louis's bed, pausing to stare at Louis's still face. Then he turned abruptly and placed it safely in the closet among their father's out-of-season clothes. It was for Louis.

Cameron started to leave the room, but Louis screamed to him, "Cameron, Trife is behind you! Watch out! He's following you! Cameron!"

Cameron stopped. He didn't hear Louis's warning but he could feel it. He looked around his brother's room.

"There he is. Do you see him? Look at him!" Louis said.

Cameron knew something was trailing him. He even thought he sometimes caught quick glimpses of it. Now, for the first time, with Louis's help, he could see a faint image of Trife. They were both bold. Trife stared at him and Cameron stared back. He was facing his own personal demon. The sight chilled Cameron to his soul. It also made him certain that he was doing the right thing by leaving. If not to escape, at least to take whatever this was away from his family. Maybe Louis would even get better if he did.

Cameron would leave home that day.

Louis didn't know it, but Trife would be bound to Cameron for a good while. That was an adventure within itself . . .

Louis turned away from the mirror. That exchange had exhausted him.

While Louis was communicating with his friends and family, Cyndi was looking at her own mirror. Oddly it showed a news program. Behind the newscaster was a photograph of Cyndi with her name printed under it. What startled her was the fact that the word MISSING was stamped in red across her picture.

Missing? she wondered. *Since when am I missing?* Then she realized that if she was here, she was obviously not there.

"All I want is for my daughter to come home safely. I know it's standard procedure for parents and family to be looked at first, but I can assure the authorities and everyone who's lending my daughter their support from around the country that I, my wife, family, and extended family, especially Jason Alan, whom Cyndi considers her brother and I consider a son, have nothing to do with Cyndi's disappearance," said Mr. Chase.

The picture zoomed out to reveal two in-studio reporters.

"The case has captivated the nation. All eyes are following this child abduction, the details of which sound like something out of a fantasy bestseller. So how do you call this?" the host said to the guest commentator.

"First of all, the authorities are looking very closely at Mr. Alan Chase and Jason Alan, who Alan Chase tried to exonerate during the press conference. It sounds terrible, but this could not have happened at a better time. Mr. Chase was already a wealthy man. His company is about to go public. Now, with so much attention on him, everyone on Wall Street is buzzing about his company. It's the hottest pick, and he and his partner, who is Jason Alan's father, stand to make an astronomical amount of money.

"That's not all. Cyndi Victoria Chase is partners with Jason

Alan. We always hear about these teen start-up Internet companies that provide user content, but with her going missing, the traffic to their site has rocketed, driving advertising rates sky high. The country has named Cyndi their lost child, and advertisers are paying to get a piece of it any way they can on her company's site."

"Why has she been labeled America's lost child? Why is she so different?" the host asked.

"This case has captured people's imaginations because it has everything: the rich child who's gone missing, the powerful family that was already in the media, a company that's been making huge waves about to go public. We've seen all of that before in some shape or form in other cases, but what's given this one something that no other has is the X factor."

"You are of course talking about the surveillance footage," the reporter said as it began to play on-screen

"Yes, of course. Here we see Cyndi Victoria Chase, whom people are calling Vicky C, in the house of a close family friend— her father's business partner. She considers him her uncle and his son her brother. Watch closely as Jason Alan walks out of the room to get help. Here it comes; watch closely. What can only be classified as a phantom or ghost races in and takes her body away. It's spooky. Nothing can move that fast. Digital experts who analyzed the video footage have found that it has not been digitally altered in any way and is authentic. The authorities have no clues and are simply baffled by this case. They have no choice but to look at the family."

* * *

Cyndi was deeply absorbed in her story as Perilynn found his own mirror. Its images took him to his first memory.

Limitless snow stretched in every direction. It circled Perilynn's young CE body as it fell carelessly from the sky. He had no idea what the snow was or who he was. He appeared with no memory, name, or purpose. He might never have moved if the red and purple lights streaking in the sky hadn't seemed to call to him. It didn't occur to him that he might not be able to fly, so he tore upward, following them without thought, only instinct.

He could never catch them but they led him over the wondrous landscapes of Midlandia. There were mountains, waterfalls, valleys, oceans, and rivers, but there was no one like him.

"Where are we going? Who am I? What am I? Where am I from?" Perilynn yelled at the lights, but they offered him no answers. Perilynn was not angry, only frustrated as he tumbled from the sky to land in front of a pond whose water was still as glass. He hunched over it and saw himself for the first time. He stared at his image wordlessly. He'd traveled far and knew no more than before. He sat there until he was not alone.

"Perilynn. I've been looking for you," said a voice from behind him.

"Perilynn? Is that my name? Who are you?"

"Perilynn is your name if that's what I want it to be, and you're my brother if I desire that too."

Perilynn turned to see another child. He said nothing but he smiled because this person had rescued him from his solitude.

"My name is Arminion and you must come with me. We're going to find Myth. He's waiting for us."

Arminion took off into the sky and Perilynn followed him. Soon Perilynn was among other eNoli, and Myth showed Arminion and him favor and others none. Perilynn learned the ways of battle and the answers to some questions, but even those were limited. Time after time he was told that the Olivion held the answers that he and others sought and the Olivion was no friend to the eNoli and held them captive in this hellish place known as Midlandia—

"We'll have to move soon, right?" Louis's voice startled Perilynn. He looked away from the mirror, and when he turned back, the image was gone.

"Yes, we should. Where should we go? Where's the last child?" Perilynn said as Cyndi joined them.

Louis thought for a moment. It had been natural to find Cyndi, but right now he felt like they shouldn't leave this place. Cyndi didn't say anything but she felt the same. Maybe the kid was going to turn up here.

Louis began to doubt his feelings, though, when he heard hundreds of footsteps running toward them.

"Again?" Louis asked, looking to Perilynn.

"Again, we have to move now!" Perilynn said.

Perilynn ran back down the passageway but it had become a dead end. Such was the way of Midlandia. He tried to force open an exit. Any place would be better than here. The wall. The floor. The ceiling. Nothing was working.

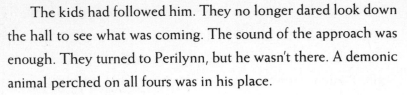

The kids had followed him. They no longer dared look down the hall to see what was coming. The sound of the approach was enough. They turned to Perilynn, but he wasn't there. A demonic animal perched on all fours was in his place.

They screamed in crystal terror.

"No! No! No!" yelled the beast in Perilynn's voice. "It's me. I'm going to get us out of here."

They stared at him, still heavily frightened. He realized the problem and shook himself so that smooth luxurious fur grew to cover his rough hide and his claws retracted. He looked friendlier.

Mind your appearance, Perilynn. Mind your appearance.

Perilynn gathered Louis then Cyndi by racing between their legs to get them on his back. They clutched his fur as there were no seat belts. They had no idea what awaited them around the corner, but that was the only exit. Better use the element of surprise to blow right by whoever was there. Run!

Perilynn stopped. They would not be met by an army but by only one person.

"Hello, Perilynn. Hello, Louis. Hello, Cyndi."

Hello, Mister Orenci.

Chapter **Thirteen**

There were many secrets on Midlandia. Everyone had a part to play. Some did so blindly. Arminion didn't know everything, but he knew more than many.

Arminion played his part in exchange for the liberty he was experiencing right now. Even after living on Midlandia, he was still amazed by the sights that the cosmos offered him as he soared among them. He was searching for something that could bring about the beginning or the end of all things known and unknown. This was why he hadn't gone to Earth. This was his secret. Many were right not to trust him, but for the wrong reasons.

Could it be?

Arminion looked over there, far away, and nearly out of sight.

Had he found what he was looking for?

Yes, he had. His heart filled with a deep and immeasurable thrill.

Chapter **Fourteen**

"Children, you can get off. We're in no danger. Orenci chases no one," Perilynn said. As the children heeded his words, he again took on the form that they'd grown accustomed to.

"No danger? Antithesis of truth. Your situation is archetypal danger. It's a lovely poetic danger, the most beautiful I've ever seen. It's singed with a bit of tragedy, but that adds to the flavor. So what, all of Midlandia seeks these children? So what, your own kind seeks to destroy you? Perilynn, it's amazing to me how you could inspire so many people to become bent on your downfall. Amazing," Orenci said. He was a sturdy yet thin man dressed in stylish blue and white clothing.

"Orenci, I haven't managed to make an enemy of you, or have I?"

"Perilynn? An enemy of me?" Orenci smacked Perilynn with the back of his hand, then immediately followed it with a punch to the face. Perilynn didn't respond, as he'd expected as much. Such was Orenci's trademark.

"Mind your words, Perilynn. My kind have no enemies. It's much more interesting that way.

"Louis, my boy. You're finally here. Cyndi, you too. Let

me take a look at you both. Such lovely children in your own ways, inside and out. Well, of course you would be. You are Favorites.

"Perilynn, you'll need a major plan to get to the third child. The child is very safe—much safer than with you, but that's no fun, is it?"

"You're talking as if you know where the third child is. Tell me—there's no time for games, Orenci."

"No time for games? Well, then, he's in the iLone City of Chance," Orenci said.

"Of all places! How am I going to get to him there? He's surrounded by iLone, and it's nearly impossible to find," Perilynn yelled.

"No, Perilynn, there could be worse places; it's a matter of perspective. All that matters is they arrive at Olivion's Gate together. How they get there, who brings them—these things aren't important. But of course they matter to you. What you're doing would be honorable if it were for them and not for yourself." This strange man paused.

"Two minutes. Your time," he said to Louis and Cyndi.

"What?" Louis and Cyndi said.

"A bit less than two minutes your time. Pay attention." He walked around, looking at the Celestial Drifts as if he were not really talking to Louis and Cyndi.

"As far as you two go, you don't know enough to ask me a question, so what would be the most important thing for me to say? So many bits of information I could tell you. Ahh, I'll tell you this: Don't let everything that happens pass you by. It will make my job easier. When you get to me, I'll help you realize what you already know. Be sure you visit DiVarion before you finally make your way to me; no sense in coming without your Alonis. You'll each know when you need to find me.

"Perilynn, your allies are those who're so driven by destruction that they'd actually want to be in the middle of a war against their own kind and the iLone. There aren't many. Friends of yours, they may take up arms with you and help you enter the city. They're even wild enough to take on a Favorite."

"You can't mean eLynori and the Lost, can you?" Perilynn said.

"Not even you are in enough trouble to seek them out. I said friends of yours."

"Friends of mine?" *Of course! Maybe they would help,* Perilynn thought. He'd have to get to them.

"Less than one minute." Orenci continued to walk around the room. "I'll help you. I'll open a door. Perilynn, that was a good choice of form. You should go back to it and get the kids out of here. But if I may make a suggestion . . . go a bit smaller. It'll be easier to navigate." With those words, the wall began to reconfigure into a passage. On the other side there was a huge opening that led to nothing but darkness.

Orenci was gone. He'd said they had two minutes and that time was over.

"There they are!" aZRon shouted to the hordes of eNoli behind him, who were pouring from the entrance where Orenci had first appeared. He wasn't leading them, only directing them

to the children. He had a knack for finding them. Perilynn immediately spotted Eynd and Gaimek. They were extremely fierce
eNoli; beating them would be a challenge.

Perilynn gathered Louis and Cyndi as he had before. "Hold
on," he yelled.

He wanted out. There was only one way out. Perilynn jumped
into the air. They fell through blinding fog. The kids held on
tight, hands fisted in fur, scared witless. *Thud!* They hit something
solid but couldn't see any ground around Perilynn. Instead, he
seemed to be on a crystal-like path that was about four feet wide.
There were many such paths surrounding them, all twisted and
interwoven together, leading downward.

Perilynn had to gather himself to figure out where he was.
Thud! Crack! Pow! eNoli soldiers were landing all around them. He
took off down the path, half running, half sliding.

The eNoli leaped from every direction, trailing energy. They
were dead set on destroying Perilynn and the children.

"Hold on tight and put your heads down!" Perilynn shouted.
He leaped at an eNoli CE and then spun like a drill, tearing
through him. He landed on another path and immediately jumped
back in the direction he'd just come from while spinning to tear
through another one. He left streaks of light in the air each time.
Leaping high and springing from path to path, Perilynn avoided
the eNoli attacks.

aZRon, higher up on one of the paths, was clapping and
yelling, "Get them!" It was unclear if he was rooting for Perilynn
and the children or the eNoli. Knowing his sick and twisted

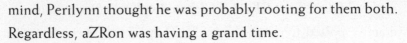

mind, Perilynn thought he was probably rooting for them both. Regardless, aZRon was having a grand time.

Some of the paths began to break under the weight of the eNoli, and it became more dangerous to run and jump on them. Perilynn wouldn't be stopped, though. When a path broke under him, he bounded to another, and he continued to attack the eNoli while avoiding their blades. He tore them apart, but there were so many. There was no way he could defeat them all.

We've got to get out of here. There has to be a way, Louis thought, raising his head.

"That way," Cyndi shouted, gesturing toward a path that was building itself in the direct center of all the other ones. It seemed to be sturdy and strong. Perilynn leaped to it as more and more paths crumbled. The eNoli, caught up in the confusion of the tumbling paths, couldn't immediately follow—except for Eynd and Gaimek. The chase was on. They flew while Perilynn ran on the center path, carrying the children away.

Perilynn found that this path had a traction that the others lacked. He ran and it led them by twisting and winding as they went, so that Eynd and Gaimek had a hard time following and attacking them. Soon they were out of the hovering Celestial Drifts and miles above snow-covered mountains and Midlandian ground. Massive flying beasts soared overhead, and gigantic beings that resembled elephants but were much bigger walked below. These were CE but not eNoli or iLone; they were eLebrions. eLebrions were driven by instinct and learned behavior. Some were much like animals. For now they minded their own business, only adding to the wondrous landscape that was Midlandia.

The combination of the height, the wandering eLebrions, and the snow-touched landscape was breathtaking. Perilynn, Louis, and Cyndi couldn't see where the path would lead because it was still being built. All they could tell was that it was going downward. And now Eynd and Gaimek were blasting at them. The sound was deafening and the heat of the glowing red and yellow blasts was eerily close as they whizzed by their heads.

"Have you enjoyed your time here? Have you enjoyed the quiet destruction you've brought to this unshakable place?" Eynd shouted as she pulled a blade from her back. She plunged down and struck the blade into the path with such force that the crystal shook, cracked, and then crumbled until it was no more.

Perilynn tried to leap from the disintegrating pieces of the path but it was no use. Cyndi and Louis toppled off his back and were falling. Eynd and Gaimek sped up to destroy the children, trailing glowing red energy as they flew. They were only yards away!

Perilynn changed form into a sleek flying CE with wings. Gaimek pulled a blade out and was ready to sever Louis's head from his body in midair. Louis ducked.

"Louis!" Cyndi shouted as she too plummeted. Eynd was about to do the same to her.

Just as Gaimek raised his arm to strike, Perilynn hit him, spinning him away. Then Perilynn swooped under Louis. Louis grabbed the feathers on Perilynn's back and held on as Perilynn rescued Cyndi without a millisecond to spare. They were on Perilynn's back and flying away.

Eynd and Gaimek regrouped. Their blasts were coming often and close.

"Fly into that mountain!" Louis yelled, seeing an entrance open up. Perilynn did, and Eynd and Gaimek followed. They continued to shoot energy bursts, and Perilynn flew erratically to avoid them.

Barrel roll into the mountain's entrance. Suddenly, the sight was amazing! They'd found a city inside. There were tall buildings. CE were gazing up at the flying spectacle of Perilynn and the children.

No time to explore, though, just time to flee. Eynd had been able to follow. Gaimek was nowhere to be found.

On the far side of this city, Perilynn could see sunlight. There was an exit but it looked as if something was moving outside of it. Perilynn sped up. As he flew out, he had to dodge quickly to avoid a massive eLebrion, who was about to sit down. It sat, blocking the mountain's exit and preventing Eynd from following.

Perilynn landed. After the children dismounted, he changed back into his normal form, and they walked side by side.

It's dangerous to have the children in such an open area. Not even the huge wandering eLebrions can offer adequate cover. No sooner had Perilynn thought this than they were surrounded by iLone. They rained from the sky as energy. Upon impact they sprang up into their flawless humanlike forms. The children were awed by their majestic stature, even as they shivered from another threat. The iLone had a quiet force that was imposing and alluring at the same time.

Their leader, Garick, spoke. "Perilynn, you've rescued and guarded these children. Very curious. You must know something the others don't. What might that be?" Garick was fishing to see if Perilynn knew that one of the three children was eNoli. Perilynn did not.

"I know many things and one of them is that your numbers don't intimidate me. I've defeated my own ruthless kind for the children's safety. These two are my means to an end, and along that path they've become a part of me. You won't take them," Perilynn said, meaning every word. Meanwhile, he was calculating an order of attack.

He was sure he'd be able to rip right past them as he had before. He was becoming quite good against the odds and now had great faith in himself. His only problem was the children. He couldn't move the way he wanted if he had to hold them in his arms. And there was no chance to change form and have the children ride on his back.

"Means to an end? Of course they are, but what's your goal? Children, you belong with us. We'll usher you to the Olivion. Perilynn is eNoli and he can only be trusted to serve himself," Garick said.

"There's no way we're trusting you," Louis said.

"Let's get out of here!" Cyndi yelled.

Just as quickly as these iLone had appeared, they were attacked. Eynd and Gaimek had escaped the mountain. Their arrival was such a surprise that Gaimek was able to grab Cyndi. Eynd had thrown Perilynn asunder, leaving Louis on his own.

Perilynn regained his footing and looked to Garick. For this short time they'd have to join sides to save the children. There was no plan, just action. They charged at the two eNoli.

But Gaimek put a blade to Cyndi's throat. "Mind yourselves."

Both Perilynn and Garick stopped.

Reign and his troop came across this sight from above.

"Eynd and Gaimek have the children. Do we attack our kind?" one of them asked.

The decision was upon Reign. Eynd and Gaimek would surely destroy the children, and access to the Gate without all three kids was questionable. It was maddening. This attack would make him an enemy of the eNoli just as Perilynn was.

So be it.

Reign dove in with a precision that Perilynn didn't have and pierced the bodies of Eynd and Gaimek. The two were severely injured and fell to the ground. Perilynn didn't yet realize what had happened, but he changed into animal form and scooped the children up on his back. Just as he did so, Garick fell.

The iLone attacked Reign and his crowd. And hordes of eNoli who'd been told to fall back now swarmed in too. They couldn't believe Reign had turned on the eNoli.

Reign raged. His attack had been for naught. He could see Perilynn fleeing. And he had to deal with countless eNoli and iLone.

But Helenia and Octavio were watching. They appeared with their own legions of eNoli. The battlefield was evenly matched.

Helenia's red orbs were not just for show. She threw them at the enemy, blasting great numbers of eNoli. The civil war had begun.

Utter chaos! Of course, in the midst of this, Perilynn easily escaped with his two friends.

eNoli vs. eNoli vs. iLone. Who could make heads or tails of it?

War makes a bunch of sense, right?

For the first time Louis and Cyndi realized the magnitude of what was going on. They were at the center of a massive war.

Perilynn, do not forget, you still need help . . .

Chapter **Fifteen**

Thoughts of his family hung around Devon's neck like a ton of dead weight. There was so much going on in their lives. He needed to be with them, and they needed him.

He was in a magnificent room. It had no windows; instead, the room itself was made of glass. He could see everything: Trees. Flowing rivers. Tall, intricately designed buildings. The brilliant, beautiful people of the city. Young CE were playing games and running about. Older CE were walking from place to place. Everyone radiated joy, confidence, serenity even. He couldn't imagine sickness or heartbreak here. The iLone City of Chance seemed untouched by tragedy of any sort.

This room, this place, was amazing, but he couldn't enjoy it as his mind raced ever homeward. If he could bring his family here, he'd be happy. That was impossible, so he clung to Vivionya's statement that he would have the power to do anything. He'd use that power to free his family from the threats that had been plaguing them. All he needed was for the other kids to arrive and then to find some gate home. Easy. Except they didn't come.

He couldn't wait. But he had to. So he sat. He paced. He stared through the glass at the city. He tried not to think of home. His family filled his head. And he waited.

Chapter **Sixteen**

By now you surely know that in Midlandia you can only go where you're supposed to go. So you'd better hope and pray that the place you *want* to go is where you're meant to go.

Perilynn, Louis, and Cyndi evaded the iLone and eNoli and found themselves right where they needed to be.

They stood at the foot of a massively long, ghostly white bridge that extended upward at a forty-five-degree angle to a place hidden in deep mist. It was so very eerie that it unnerved Louis.

"This is their bridge, and wherever it resides, they lie on the other side. We'll have no luck in the City of Chance without their help," Perilynn said.

"Perilynn, are you sure we need their help? You've been doing great all by yourself. I mean, you haven't gotten hit or anything. I think we could do it!" Louis didn't want to go on that high, eerie bridge unless he were barging along it on a roller coaster.

"If we can get help, I think we definitely should," Cyndi said. The bridge made her uneasy too, but they were in a war. They needed reinforcements. So be it.

They strode into the sky on the white bridge with no end in sight.

"Perilynn, I've been meaning to ask you this. It's an obvious question. What is the Olivion?" Cyndi said.

"Honestly, I don't know. What I do know is that the Olivion is the answer to any question you can ask, including that one. I hope that after we find the last child, we'll all find out."

The end of the bridge led them to a clearing covered by a fog that welcomed them with an aura of loss and sadness. Dim pulses of light flickered through the mist.

"Mind where you walk. This is a graveyard of sorts," Perilynn said.

"People are buried here? We're walking over graves?" Louis asked.

"Graves? You don't have bodies like we do, so why would you need graves?" Cyndi said.

"You're right. We don't have bodies and we don't die. Our energy dissipates, then takes on a new form. I said a graveyard of sorts." Perilynn made a gesture, and the fog cleared. A plethora of capsules could be seen littering the area. Some were planted in the ground, some were standing, some were lying here and there. There were many, and they were aware that they had visitors. They were glowing with light that soon took on form. eNoli CE now fought violently to free themselves from their prisons.

"Don't be afraid, children. They're eternally trapped inside those Alonis Capsules. The capsules are made from the same powerful material that encases the energy of the Midland Isle inside Alonis Medallions. There's no way for a CE to escape. Only one fate is worse than this: to be trapped in an Alonis Capsule *and* thrown into the Infinite Abyss."

"Eternal? But no one should be imprisoned forever. Who put them in there?" Cyndi said.

"The iLone have trapped them."

"The iLone? They don't want the eNoli to have freedom, and they hand out eternal sentences." Cyndi stared at the captured eNoli. Some were horrid. Some were beautiful. The sight of them caused her Celestial Infection Rate to spike, allowing her to see tiny glimpses of the actions that had led them to this never-ending torment. They quested to be free from this place and they couldn't even rely on freedom via death. Their rage and dark sorrow rushed over Cyndi.

"Let them out! Let them out!" she yelled as she began to bang on the capsules. With each blow, she became more like a CE until she began to glow. Her fists flared up and her hits left streaks in the air.

Cyndi Victoria Chase's Celestial Infection Rate = 45%

Louis may have been on Midlandia, where the impossible was normal, but he knew that a girl from Cali was not supposed to be glowing like that. What if she were to go supernova or something?

"Cyndi, stop! You're going to hurt yourself." Louis reached for one of her arms, but she forced him away, and he fell to the ground.

"Cyndi, stop! There's absolutely nothing that can be done."
Perilynn grabbed her, finally stopping her.

"Perilynn, let them out. No one deserves to be trapped like
that. Death is better than that!" Cyndi yelled.

"There's no way these capsules can be broken—they never
have been. I know it's terrible. I have friends here," Perilynn said.

"Let's go," Louis said.

Perilynn lovingly carried Cyndi away.

Cyndi was a child of privilege; her family had money and
she could do anything she wanted. But what was she doing with
her diamond- and platinum-laced opportunities? She decided
that when she got back home, she and her friends would live
without regrets or boundaries. She would never be imprisoned
in any way.

Living as such is worse than death.

They didn't speak as they continued past this place. Their
destination was just up ahead. Those they were about to see considered this graveyard their garden, and they were an extremely
twisted bunch.

Chapter Seventeen

"Perilynn, what's this? We came here for this?" Louis was looking at a red cube etched with faded gold markings and beaten and worn with age. It was about the size of a small cake box, and it hovered four feet off the ground.

"Oh yes, we did. Stand back!" Perilynn said. Using a forceful but reserved motion, he spun the cube around. Perilynn then moved many yards away, ushering the children with him. As it turned, the cube began to grow and the etchings began to flicker and glow. Now it was a massive red building with no windows. They could hear tons of yelling inside.

Perilynn knocked on the front door, which instantly became clear. Behind it was a girl who couldn't have been more than thirteen years old. She looked happy to see him.

She opened the door. Five younger kids ran outside past the other girl and Louis and Cyndi, all speaking at once.

"Perilynn, you're here!"

"Word of you has spread."

"Did you bring the war with you?"

"Is it in our yard?" Then the children ran back into the building to line up beside one another. Excited, they began to speak as of one mind, completing one another's sentences.

One wore yellow, one blue, one red, one green, and the one in the center was in white. The colors were muted, as if they'd killed these colors and this was all that was left. This didn't seem to fit their upbeat demeanor. There were three boys and two girls.

"Awwww, there's no war out there," White said.

"That's exactly why I'm—" Perilynn started to say.

"Can we please come?"

"Can we please go to war—"

"—with you? We want to fight."

"We'll be able to destroy so many."

"eNoli or iLone, it doesn't matter."

"Battle them all. Such fun!" the Five said.

Perilynn hadn't even had to ask for their help, but he'd soon learn why.

"And we've heard that the—"

"—third child is in the iLone—"

"—City of Chance."

"Yes, that city hides—"

"—from us."

"We've even tried to follow—"

"—iLone there, but you know—"

"—how wretched this place is. No matter—"

"—what we do, we can never get there. It's—"

"—so frustrating."

White deviously smiled at Louis and Cyndi. Then the Five continued.

"We'll come with you because—"

"—you're with the Favorites. It is—"

"—undoubtedly their destiny to find that city. Their—"

"—destiny will become our own. We'll wreak—"

"—havoc on that city on your behalf. So that you may—"

"—be safe and the children will reach the Olivion! Yes—"

"—all for you guys!" This idea was so outrageous for an eNoli that they all fell on the ground laughing.

When they'd recovered, they all said, "Perilynn, we *will* go to war with you!" They sounded a bit sinister, as if a "no" would send them into a frenzied attack. It freaked the heck out of Louis and Cyndi.

"Please come in," they said as the older girl led Perilynn, Louis, and Cyndi inside.

Various weapons were piled everywhere in the room.

"Grayci, you'll stay here—"

"—and you'll continue—"

"—with our research."

"Tend to the garden, if needed," the Five said.

"I can work on my own? Are you serious?" the older girl exclaimed.

"Yes, you may work—"

"—on your own," said the Five.

Perilynn knew he was opening up a can of filthy, disgusting, slithering worms with the Five, but there was no way he'd able to

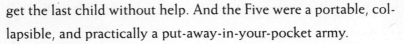

get the last child without help. And the Five were a portable, collapsible, and practically a put-away-in-your-pocket army.

"We can go now," the Five said, poking Louis and Cyndi in their sides.

"Did that—"

"—hurt? We know that—"

"—didn't hurt. You're—"

"—Favorites! Toughen up. We won't—"

"—hurt you. They won't chase—"

"—us if you're dead! There'll be—"

"—no war if you're dead!" They were all smiling.

"We might poke you—"

"—but we won't hurt you!"

"Yet!"

"Guys, keep your hands off the kids," Perilynn said.

The Five just laughed.

The three were now eight in search of one more.

Devon, they're coming for you; you'd best be prepared.

Chapter **Eighteen**

Without a doubt the eight were supposed to go to the iLone City of Chance.

Without a doubt Perilynn had chosen the right people to help him in his cause.

Without a doubt Cyndi and Louis had a good chance of being reunited with the third child.

Why, you may ask? Because when the eight opened the door to leave, the City of Chance was visible in the distance. They wouldn't even have to search for it.

It looked to be a sturdy, confident city, but a quaint one as well. The buildings were high but not too high. However, it stretched far and wide. Countless iLone must inhabit it.

They were almost upon the city when a voice behind them said, "Oh, I've picked the perfect time to drop in."

"aZRon! You—I ought to end you now! You've been leading everyone right to me. Who have you brought this time?" Perilynn said.

"You've brought—"

"—people with you?"

"Who?"

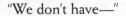

"We don't have—"

"—to play nice, right?" the Five said.

"Oh, it's just me and my sisters. I don't need to bring anyone else. Where you're going, you need no instigation from me. This is nowhere near as good as the War of Myth, but it's been pretty decent fodder. There's even a civil war going on. That's ridiculous because you're nowhere near it and it's over you. But this part right here is going to be exciting. Well, I'm off to watch. Carry on!" aZRon said, dashing away with his sisters to find a good vantage point.

Poke. Poke. Poke. Poke. Poke.

The Five left too, but not without putting their pokes in. That was their way of saying good-bye to the Favorites. Silently, they went ahead to begin their war against the city. Just as they'd expected, Midlandia let them in this time.

Perilynn said, "They're going to destroy everything in sight. While they battle the iLone, we'll find the last child, and then exit. Olivion's Gate will no doubt appear soon after that. We'll cross it and that will be that. I wish I had a better plan, but so far our quick plans have been working . . ."

Four of the Five claimed positions on different rooftops: North. South. East. West. Then White took his place on a tall building in the exact center.

These eNoli were fierce.

These eNoli would bring carnage and no mercy.

These eNoli were going to fight so that Cyndi, Louis, and Devon could be reunited and delivered to the Olivion.

No, not really. They just wanted to destroy. They could have cared less whether the kids reached the Olivion.

It is okay to cause destruction, pain, and death for a good cause, right? Right?

It was dark. But the Five wanted all to know who they were and what they were about to do. They desired light, and it came as the Midlandian night broke into a glorious day. It seemed that Midlandia believed in their cause and was with them now as it had been opposed to them so many other times.

A calm came over the city with that light. Do you feel the sun? Such a great feeling, right? You're sitting on your porch sipping the perfect mix of raspberry iced tea and lemonade. Could it be that a car just drove by playing your favorite song? That's the way it felt right before countless iLone would meet the ends of their lives as they knew them. The car has driven out of sight and now the song is fading away. There it went, and with it your respite is over.

White remained perched high in the center of the city. The other four jumped, landing in unison, and the entire city shook. That would be the only warning. But what was a warning when you never had a chance?

* * *

Blue split into millions, flooding the city and tearing clumps of energy from everyone he encountered.

Yellow literally tore all she saw in half.

Green skipped along, wielding blades of destruction. Each blade ripped through whatever it touched. The blades' energy made CE forms unstable, and they quickly broke apart.

Red spun and flipped gracefully. She left trails of light in her wake that seemed alive as they strangled and cut through the iLone.

Bless the little children,

But curse these little monsters.

They were masters of murder seeking to leave no iLone CE untouched.

Many had fallen but it was time to stop because it was now White's turn. As he sank to the streets, the others rose to perch on their original rooftops. There they sat dormant as if they were vacant shells.

White called a name.

."Vivionya. Vivy! Where is the child? Why would you send so many to search for the others? Did you think you'd be enough to protect the child because you're a Favorite? Where's Kiyonrae? Where's the Young Armada? Overconfident, are we?"

White was focused only on Vivionya. Perilynn had no choice but to battle the remaining iLone, although he wanted to follow the children. He had to trust that if the Gate appeared when they found the third child, they'd keep their word and not cross without him.

As Vivionya emerged for battle, she was at ease because Devon was in a place where only a Favorite could find him.

The city was in chaos, and in the midst of this destruction Cyndi and Louis easily went unnoticed.

It was a perfect plan.

Chapter **Nineteen**

For the first time Louis and Cyndi were on their own. As they ran through the city, they saw iLone who'd had their energy disrupted. The CE were losing their forms, rising into the sky to rocket away. It didn't seem painful, only uneasy and sad. However, it shook Louis and Cyndi, for they hadn't realized that this would be the consequence of their attack.

"Perilynn said they couldn't die, but this sure looks like dying," Louis said.

"I've never seen anything like this, so I don't know what's happening to them," Cyndi said.

Louis stopped as one called to him. Cyndi tried to nudge him to keep moving, but instead he walked up to a beautiful woman who'd been separated from a massive part of her energy. Only her upper torso remained. It wasn't gruesome, though, because it just looked like her lower half had been erased. She was being pulled away. She was about to experience the Reazrion Ascension, as all fallen CE do; their energy returns to the Midland Isle to be born again.

"You're a Favorite. Tell me your name quickly before I leave here." The iLone CE stretched out her hand as she began to fade, and Louis grabbed and held it.

"Louis. Louis Proof."

"A good strong name for a good strong boy," she said with a smile. "No matter what, iLone or eNoli, follow who you are and you will—"

Suddenly she was gone and Louis's hand was empty. He felt empty inside too, as if he'd lost something dear. Cyndi felt the same, especially as they realized that nearly all the iLone had faded away. This lovely city was now almost vacant because they needed to find the third child.

"Louis, we have to go!" Cyndi said. They ran until they came to the foot of a great water fountain. Hidden in the sound of the splashing water was a song that only Favorites could hear.

Say your name first. Say your name second.

For you are the Children of Midlandian Legend.

A hero of lore will mark an infinite path.

Walk opposite ways and you will find the Favorite at long last.

The song's message was simple enough, they thought, but Midlandia is a funny place.

They could hear the sounds of the battle among Vivionya, White, Perilynn, and the few remaining iLone.

"This place will soon to be flooded with people looking for us," Louis said.

"They wouldn't have it any other way. Cyndi Victoria Chase!" She said with confidence.

Louis instantly replied, "Louis Proof!"

"So happy to see you again," a familiar voice said, making them jump.

Mister Orenci was standing directly behind them. "Have you been paying attention? It'll make my job much easier."

"What job?" Louis asked, turning toward him.

"Where did you come from?" Cyndi asked.

"Where did I come from? You obviously have *not* been taking it all in. You have *not* been learning the ways of Midlandia. Aren't I supposed to mark your path?"

"That's what the song said," Louis replied.

"Well, for now I guess that's my job. Here we go!"

He clapped his hands and a ring a centimeter thick, a foot wide, and fifty feet in diameter appeared under their feet. Immediately, it swooped upward, carrying them high and far until they were balanced precariously in the sky. The circle hummed and spun, and they threw their arms out to keep their footing. Then it stopped moving and was perfectly balanced, though it seemed that a mere raindrop would have drastically tilted it.

Louis and Cyndi were standing back to back while Mister Orenci was exactly opposite them. They were above a massive battle. It was eNoli vs. eNoli vs. iLone; it was the civil war they'd left behind.

"You must learn to be a team. Your well-being is dependent on how you regard each other. You cannot think of yourselves as two. You only exist as one. That's how you must navigate the arduous path before you. Are you ready?" Orenci said.

They were petrified. They held each other's hands even though they were back to back, not moving at all. They knew that if they lost their balance, those CE would kill them even before the fall did.

Orenci moved a tiny bit and the circle tipped before he slid back into position. "I said, are you ready? This is serious. Did you think you'd be able to find the third child just because? Oh no!

"You must make your way around to the spot where I'm standing now, acting as the balance for each other on opposite sides of this infinite ring. Are you ready?"

They said nothing.

"Maybe this will help!" He snapped his fingers and Reign noticed them far, far above him in the sky. While the others continued to battle on the ground, the lower portion of Reign's body turned to pure energy, and as if he were a rocket, he raced toward them.

Orenci leaped from the circle. It began to tilt downward, as the weight of Cyndi and Louis no longer had a counterbalance. Instinctively, they both ran on opposite sides of the circle.

Reign was nearing them.

"Louis, too fast!" Cyndi yelped.

Louis forced himself to think about Cyndi's weight and about how much he had to slow down to accommodate that. Cyndi sped up and he stepped more deliberately in spite of the fear pulsing through him. It was tricky.

Meanwhile the energy of fallen CE kept whizzing by. Then one hit the circle and unbalanced it. Louis's side went up and Cyndi's tilted drastically down. She lost her footing and only just managed to catch the edge of the circle with her fingers.

That's when Louis spotted Reign. He was almost on top of her—a few feet away.

"Cyndi!" Louis yelled.

Instantly, Kiyonrae soared into Reign, forcing them both many yards away. They began a wildly intense airborne fight. More were on their way, iLone and eNoli alike.

But Cyndi was still dangling and yelling for her life. Louis had an idea. It was wild and risky, yet he didn't know what else to do. If he was wrong, both he and Cyndi would die. He had to try it though. There wasn't time for Cyndi to struggle back up.

"Cyndi, get ready!"

"Oh no!" she yelled.

Louis jumped. When he landed, he crashed into the ring with such force that Cyndi flew into the air. He immediately jumped again. With no weight on it, the circle balanced itself. Cyndi and Louis then came down on it, firm and solid. As of one mind, they began to run to the spot where Orenci had stood. It was impossible for the ring to balance with them doing that, but they knew this was right. The circle didn't tilt downward with their weight as it should have. When they reached the other side together, it rebalanced. Mister Orenci stood opposite them once again.

He snapped his fingers and they found themselves in front of the fountain.

"Risky! Risky! Risky! The Olivion must surely have been with you," Orenci said.

The fountain turned itself into a stairway.

"There you go. Collect your friend and have a safe journey to the Olivion." He couldn't help laughing as he said that.

A safe trip to the Olivion?

The audacity!

Chapter **Twenty**

Nothing was as Louis had expected it to be. Not the city. Not this building. Everything was graceful, elegant, in perfect harmony. Louis walked slowly, goggling at arched doorways, inlaid floors, and colorful walls that glowed under the skylights. All of this made Louis think that the iLone must be quite different from the seemingly bloodthirsty eNoli he'd met.

"He's in here somewhere. Stop gawking. Let's just get him and go," Cyndi said.

"Yeah, but I just don't get it. How could these people be so bad? I mean, look at the artwork, the furniture—everything."

"That's naive, Louis. You can't judge people by the stuff they own. You know how many people think they know me because of the things I have and the car I get driven around in? To me it just looks like these people are rich. I know tons of rich people with great houses who are just terrible. You should meet my mom. Sometimes people are right to think the worst," Cyndi said with a laugh.

"I don't judge people by what they own. I was just saying . . . And I don't know your mom, but you shouldn't talk about your mom like that. I'm just saying, what do we really know about any of these people, I mean CE, other than Perilynn?" Louis asked.

"What I know is that we need to get home, and Perilynn has been doing a pretty good job of leading us there. That's all I'm concerned about," Cyndi answered.

They turned the corner to find four CE hovering in the air and doing the oddest thing. Well, what they were doing wasn't odd; it was that they were doing it right now during a battle in which so many iLone were meeting their end.

They were painting with wild beams of light. The portrait was so vivid, Louis wondered for a moment if he'd seen the person smile at him. The painters looked at Cyndi and Louis, nodded, then went right back to their painting.

Louis let out a deep breath. Even though the painters had seen them, they seemed not to care that the Favorites were there.

Cyndi wouldn't be distracted from their goal. She was drawn as if by a magnet to a door. She was sure that the child they sought was on the other side. She pushed and the door swung open.

Devon was a bit scared to see strangers in the doorway until he realized they were kids like him. They had to be the children he'd been told about.

Louis laid eyes on Devon, and he immediately remembered his trip to the JunkYard JunkLot. He'd seen this kid after the waterless waves swept in and the two objects sped right through him. When Louis lost the race, this boy was the one who toppled a food stand and ran to the elevator to escape.

"You were there when we first got here," Cyndi said.

"Yeah and I remember you! You were at the JunkYard JunkLot when all of this started!" Louis exclaimed.

"The JunkYard JunkLot! You know about that?" Devon said, looking carefully at the boy who stood before him. "You're that kid! Larry Proof! You drove the car. You were about to win and then that crazy stuff happened . . ."

"No. I'm *Louis* Proof. It's even on my name tag." Louis pointed to his name tag. "Who are you? Where are you from?"

"A name tag? My bad, Louis. I'm Devon Alexander, and I'm from Chicago. Where are you from?"

Louis loved this question. "East Orange, New Jersey."

"Never heard of it. I mean, I know where New Jersey is, but I've never heard of East Orange. What about you?" Devon turned to Cyndi.

Cyndi was looking at the two, flabbergasted. "What? Are you kidding me? We don't have time for this! We've got to go. The Olivion is waiting for us."

Devon straightened. Yes! The Olivion meant Olivion's Gate, which meant home. "Okay, let's go." Devon was totally on board.

"Follow me," Cyndi said. As if she were a bloodhound, she navigated through the building, finding an exit within earshot of the battle between Vivionya, White, and Perilynn. There were no other unharmed CE left in the city.

"No! What did you do to this city? The iLone . . . what did you do to them?" Devon froze, stunned by the destruction around them.

"We didn't do this. We just came here to get you. We didn't hurt anyone," Cyndi said, knowing it was not entirely true.

Devon didn't want to move. It was as if someone had killed all happiness.

I know they did this, but I have to go with them. Vivionya said if I didn't find the children, I'd never get home. I'm a Favorite. I need those powers . . . , Devon thought.

"Come on! We need you!" Cyndi said, and she pulled Devon along, making up his mind for him.

"Vivionya!" Devon shouted. He could now see her in the midst of battle.

His cry caught her off guard, and White punched her, propelling her right through the wall of a building. She lay stunned inside.

"I would've thought more of a Favorite. But it's been fun. Next time?" White said before turning to Perilynn. "Gather your children and let us be gone."

White darted straight up to his rooftop position in the center of his team. The others became alert as the energy that had flowed into White was once again spread among the Five.

So many were coming. Celestial rain hit the buildings and each drop turned into an iLone soldier. It was time to flee.

"Children, lead the way. Just run; the Gate will guide you," Perilynn said.

They ran. They had one advantage. Midlandia wouldn't allow *anyone* to get between them and Olivion's Gate. It's a lot easier to run when no one is fighting you head-on.

What's more, Midlandia wouldn't allow all to follow them. The landscape changed, their path was concealed, and many followed false trails. Soon only about a thousand iLone were in pursuit and they were far behind.

Eventually, the children, Perilynn, and the Five found themselves running over a barren, hard, cracked tan surface. The sky turned red, shifted to amber, and then their view ahead was blocked by the sudden appearance of a solid black wall not far from them.

They halted. The wall's mere size created fear in all who saw it—CE included. No one had ever seen anything that big even on Midlandia. It was literally millions of miles high and wide.

"We've come the wrong way. What now?" Devon asked.

"No, we haven't!" Louis said.

"He's right. There's nowhere else to go." Cyndi said.

"That's IMPOSSIBLE. Midlandia knows no limits! MIDLANDIA KNOWS NO LIMITS!" Perilynn shouted.

Their iLone pursuers were far distant but still were closing in. They had no time.

MIDLANDIA KNOWS NO LIMITS.

MIDLANDIA KNOWS NO LIMITS.

MIDLANDIA KNOWS NO LIMITS.

MIDLANDIA KNOWS NO LIMITS.

"MIDLANDIA KNOWS NO LIMITS."

The phrase repeated small inside the children until they found themselves saying it out loud. Then, as if of one mind, Louis and Cyndi said: "We know no limits!"

They walked up to the wall and gently pushed it. It moved.

"This is surely the end of everything we know," Perilynn said, amazed. What seemed unmovable was toppling over, but it didn't crash. They were standing near an abyss, and the wall was floating, level, parallel to the ground only a few feet away from the edge.

Now they could hear music that was soothing and comforting, yet at the same time somehow ominous. "The Lullaby of Olivion's Gate," whispered Perilynn. The Gate itself was so far in the distance that they couldn't see it.

It seemed clear that they should leap from the edge of the ground to the black wall, but then it broke apart. Pieces of it became spinning blades that whirled through the air. Larger blocks flew about, crashing into one another. And in the midst of these obstacles, paths built themselves, twisting and weaving together, appearing and disappearing behind one another. Some led straight into one another and exploded upon contact.

As if a spirit had passed by all of them and whispered in their ears, they heard:

"You each must find your path. Three paths. One result."

Chapter **Twenty-one**

"Midlandia is surely broken, because I can't see the path. It's changing too rapidly. I don't know how to get you across," Perilynn said.

The three children stood before the seeming chaos. Cyndi was the first to hear the Gate calling to her. Then she was able to see what was really there. There was chaos but there was a way to navigate it. The children had to be beyond the chaos. They had to move with and ahead of it.

It was easy. Kind of . . . sort of . . . no, not really. They could move through it though.

"Louis. Devon. Can you see the way? Look very hard. Can you see it?" Cyndi said.

"No, it's crazy in there. There's no way through," Devon said.

Louis, though, paused and it seemed almost as if he went into a trance. He stared at the chaos until he could actually read it. "Cyndi, I can see it. I can see what will happen."

Then Louis turned to Perilynn. "Perilynn, I can see the way."

"You can? If you can do it, I'll find a way. I'll keep the iLone away to protect you, but I beg of you, don't enter the Gate without me. Do you hear? You all trusted me and I kept my word and

I'll continue to do so. But don't dare cross that Gate without me. Swear to me! Swear!" Perilynn demanded.

"I swear! But we won't go without you. We promised to stay together. We're safer that way!" Cyndi said.

"I know, but this is different. Louis! Cyndi! You whose name I don't know. Go! I'll meet you on the other side. Wait for me," Perilynn said.

The iLone were nearly upon them.

"Go!" Perilynn and the Five yelled in unison.

The three turned and headed for the edge of the abyss.

Perilynn stood with his friends the Five.

"We're in deep." Perilynn said.

"Oh, yes—"

"—we're crap out of luck—"

"—and we couldn't be—"

"—happier. Thank you—"

"—for bringing us here," the Five said.

That may have been a great attitude to have, but six vs. a thousand were terrible odds.

"Are you ready? We charge on three," Perilynn said.

"No—"

"—we—"

"—charge—"

"—on—"

"FIVE!" the Five said.

But no, it would be a thousand vs. ten. aZRon and his three sisters had decided to join the fight. They'd no longer be spectators.

They'd take advantage of the fact that they were the only other eNoli that Midlandia had allowed to successfully follow.

"aZRon, I never expected you to join in," Perilynn said.

"Oh, Perilynn, you did put on quite a show, and I thank you. But now I can't deny my sisters the chance to destroy so many iLone. And I can't let my sisters go into such a battle without me. So, this is the day I get my hands dirty once again," he said with a smile. His sisters also smiled, clutching their weapons and ready to fight.

"Uniting the children so you can cross the Gate with them to destroy the Olivion. Clever," Kiyonrae yelled.

"I've never even considered destroying the Olivion. That's not what I'm after. You failed to unite the children while I succeeded. I deserve to cross with them and become a Favorite," Perilynn yelled back.

"A Favorite? Do you lie or tell the truth? Your kind can't be trusted. All of this is happening because of an eNoli Favorite. There mustn't be another one. We will never let you cross the Gate!" Vivionya said.

"Then so be it! I've come this far and we shall fight. I *will* be victorious! I *will* become a Favorite," Perilynn said. He had three qualities on his side—three strengths that had allowed him to fight as hard as he had and get this far.

Passion.

Resolve.

Ambition.

He thought about having learned the ways of battle from Myth. He thought of Louis and Cyndi and of how much he cared for them. He thought that without answers he had no purpose. He thought of how he'd be rewarded for delivering the children safely to the Olivion and crossing the Gate with them. He thought of what he would ask the Olivion. He thought about all of these things and dissolved his fear of battling a Favorite.

Perilynn was not sure what it felt like to be a Favorite, but he was sure this had to be close. His forgotten mask reappeared and he held his hands low and clutched two blades. The blades hummed; they too were ready. And then, as Midlandia began to howl, the cries causing painful vibrations, Perilynn charged without even counting to five.

Fire-written sky
Acrid, cracked ground
Violence in the air

It was on . . .

Chapter **Twenty-two**

Devon's path was not the same as theirs. He was to bring
balance. All he had to do was run along the path meant for him.
Louis and Cyndi would have to navigate through the chaos by
leaping from block to block. For the first time the children would
catch a glimpse of what they actually were. They'd unknowingly use
the celestial energy growing within them to get to Olivion's Gate.

Louis Proof's Celestial Infection Rate = 61%
Cyndi Victoria Chase's Celestial Infection Rate = 59%
Devon Alexander's Celestial Infection Rate = 39%

Cyndi jumped first, landing on a flying piece of the wall. Louis
leaped second to come down on the same piece, flinging Cyndi
forward. Soon Louis was sent flying in her direction when a burning piece of material collided with the wall. Devon began to run,
spurred on by the promise of power when he returned home.

Louis and Cyndi had to be in perfect sync for this to work.
Every move that Cyndi made, Louis had to counterbalance. They
needed to make their way across the abyss by jumping from one
piece of Midlandian matter to another, and they had to do so

quickly, because the pieces began to crumble soon after the children landed on them. Would another piece come within jumping distance in time? Would they be able to land safely on each one? It was like a maze, and you had to know just where to leap. Sometimes when Louis landed behind Cyndi, she'd fly safely between two spinning objects only moments before they crashed together. They acted intuitively, and Devon, running below on his path also played a role. If Devon fell too far behind, Louis and Cyndi would drift too far apart. Devon would have to speed up to bring Louis and Cyndi closer together.

Jumping, flipping, balancing, and avoiding flying projectiles, Louis and Cyndi eventually reached a monstrous piece of Midlandian matter. As they stood on it, it dipped low, crushing everything in its path. It destroyed anything that might have collided with Devon, but it was also on course to crash into Devon's path. Cyndi and Louis simultaneously figured out what they had to do.

They stood as far as they could from each other while still holding hands and stomped on the behemoth piece of Midlandian matter until it split in half. Letting go, they began to coast away from each other. The two halves blew by on opposite sides of Devon as he raced along the path. The sheer size of the matter frightened the heck out of Devon, so he ran faster. Still, though, Louis and Cyndi were beginning to drift way too far apart.

"Put your arms out!" Louis yelled.

"What?" Devon asked, as it was hard to hear over the collisions around them.

"Put your arms out like you're flying!" Cyndi yelled.

He did it. Louis and Cyndi were drawn closer to each other and closer to Devon. Now the entire path Devon was running along began to crumble behind him. Cyndi and Louis stretched toward him, each grabbing one of his hands to lift him from the quickly corroding path. Devon became their rudder as they navigated across the abyss, the matter they rode on steadily breaking apart, becoming smaller and smaller. Ahead was a gargantuan waterfall. It seemed to be forty stories high and as wide as the wall had been. But where were they supposed to go?

They flew to the top of the waterfall. As they crested it, waves of blue light sped along the water. They headed toward the source of those lights: perfect round stones floating solidly in the river. The circular lights were set in the center of the stones. Devon was first to touch down, then Cyndi, then Louis as the last bit of the matter they were standing on crumbled away.

You are almost there. Great work!

The round stones formed a path that led to land a good ways off in the distance. They walked confidently on the stones across the streaming water. A light fog crept in, hugging the river, and the blue lights gracefully danced through rapids. It was simple. It was perfect. The three were silent.

Reaching land, they finally saw the Gate far ahead. It hovered a few inches above the ground. It was plain, made of a smooth white stone, and was as perfect as Olivion's Lullaby, which filled the air as they approached.

"Olivion's Gate," Louis said, almost tearing up. Cyndi felt the same way and smiled at him. They pressed their fists together. Finally.

"Come on, let's go. We made it," Devon said. He hadn't endured as much as Cyndi and Louis had, so arriving here didn't mean as much to him.

"No, we wait for Perilynn," Cyndi and Louis said in unison.

"But he won't make it. I mean, it seemed impossible," Devon said.

"Impossible? You think that word means anything here?" Cyndi snapped.

"You're absolutely right. All we have to do is cross that Gate and go home. Tons of people are trying to kill us and could arrive any minute, but let's wait right here." Devon abruptly sat in front of the Gate.

Louis and Cyndi dismissed his attitude. If they'd been him, they'd probably have felt the same way.

They waited and waited and when they were done with that they waited some more.

What was that?

Oh, nothing.

"You know, what we did back there was amazing," Louis said. He kept thinking about the maze they'd threaded. He could still almost feel the pieces of wall shifting under him as he landed.

"Spectacular!" Cyndi agreed.

Devon laughed.

And they waited a little bit more until . . .

"Louis, Cyndi!" called a lone unarmed and masked figure in the far distance.

When he neared them, Cyndi ran to hug Perilynn. "You made it! I knew you would. Where's everyone else?"

Louis and Devon crowded close as the mask disappeared.

"Guys! Okay, guys. Okay! There's no time for hugs. We need to cross that Gate," Perilynn said with a laugh, although he hugged Cyndi back. He'd done it! He'd brought them all this way. He'd fought just about all of Midlandia, and there was Olivion's Gate. It didn't even matter if Louis and Cyndi were iLone; they were his children and safe.

"Where's everyone else?" Louis repeated Cyndi's question.

"They couldn't make it across. Only I could. It was the funniest thing. It was like a part of me had made it here with you, and I was able to follow that part." Perilynn looked at the silly name tags that Cyndi and Louis wore. He'd used a bit of his energy to make them; a tiny bit of him *had* made it across with them.

"I'll surely know your names for eternity. No need for those any longer," he said as he touched Cyndi's and Louis's tags. They disappeared, returning his energy to him.

"Let's go. You have to go first and I must enter behind you," Perilynn said. The three pressed their hands to the Gate and it opened, welcoming them. Perilynn was about to become a Favorite. For the first time since all of this began, he let his guard down.

"Perilynn, you will not cross with the children. I won't let you threaten Olivion." The children had breached the threshold of the Gate, and Perilynn was now only a few feet away. But instantly crystal cuffs swallowed up his hands, and a chain spewed from them, binding him to the ground. Kiyonrae had stopped him.

Perilynn had fought hard to come so close.

Fury burned in Perilynn, but he couldn't break free. It burned even deeper, because he could actually see beyond Olivion's Gate. His struggling didn't matter, though, as his entire body was encased in an Alonis Capsule. This was his reward for letting his guard down once. He was now beginning the worst punishment imaginable.

As Perilynn watched the Gate close, he could hear the children screaming his name.

Thank you, Perilynn.

You have brought me My children. You have brought me My Favorites.

Bravo.

Marvelous World

A.K.A.

The Marvelous World of the Supposedly Soon

to Be Phenomenal Young Mr. Louis Proof

Book 1.5: Olivion's Favorites

Level III

Chapter **Twenty-three**

Finally, they'd made it to the one place most people would wish, pray, dream, live, die, lie, hope, wonder, and even kill to reach. But what was here? Who was here? Would you be ready for such a place if you suddenly found yourself here? Better yet, were our three kids ready?

Cyndi and Louis didn't even look at their new surroundings. All they could think about was their champion and friend Perilynn, whom the rotten, conniving Kiyonrae had robbed of what he rightfully deserved: the chance to become a Favorite.

So never mind that they'd crossed Olivion's Gate.
So never mind that they stood in Olivion's Domain.
So never mind that the Olivion was, well, the Olivion.

Devon only thought about getting home, while Louis and Cyndi looked for a Gate that was no longer there and yelled for someone who couldn't hear them. In fact, there was no sign of where they'd previously been. Instead, a bright sunless sky beamed a rich glorious blue as far as each of them could see. It contained clouds that were perfectly outlined with solid lines and no wispy edges. They seemed to have been drawn and arranged by the wisest person. At any other time, the sight would have captivated the three.

"Look at those," Devon said, pointing to pathways similar to the one that they were standing on. They stretched out as far as they could see, coming from many directions.

One came from water. Another came from a dark cave far in the distance. One came from the sky. Another came from what seemed to be a place of fire. Yet another came from an exquisite mountain range. All of these paths led to a simple-looking house that rested in the center of this endless place.

The three were not far from this house. The door was opening. A middle-aged woman poked her head out, and her entire body followed when she caught sight of the children. She had a pleasant, relaxed demeanor as if nothing could ruffle her. Her hair was bouncy and her clothes fit as if tailor-made yet had a relaxed fluidity about them.

"*There you are! Louis, Cyndi, and Devon, come on. I haven't all afternoon. Well I do . . . but we still have to get things going. So if you please,*" she said, motioning for them to enter the house.

"Maybe she can help Perilynn," Louis said.

The children ran along the path to the house, but inside there was no woman to be found. They were alone in a living room. There were no other rooms—no kitchen or anything else—just an ample living room with a stairway leading up. The only sound was the ticking of a clock. Cyndi noticed that the clock had no numerals or symbols of any kind on it, and it seemed to be going backward as if counting down.

It was only for a second, but Louis could have sworn that he had something on his wrist. It was like the shadow of a silver watch with numbers going backward. He wondered what it could have been.

"I'm upstairs. Come on, you three," said the woman. This time Cyndi led the way. When they got to the top, they found a long hallway with many closed glass doors. Each one seemed to lead to an extraordinary world. Louis, Cyndi, and Devon were drawn to different doors and were about to open them to get a better look at the wonders just beyond—

"There's no time for that. I'd think you'd already had enough adventure. Come down the hallway. I'm waiting," said the woman as double doors opened wide. A bit disappointed, the three looked at one another and walked quietly to the open doors.

They found themselves in what seemed to be some sort of observatory. A massive window offered a panoramic view of the wondrous sights of Olivion's Domain. In the center of this observatory a pulsing orb of light was hovering and rotating. The light seemed to wash them clean of everything bad they'd encountered on the way here. They didn't forget any of it, but they felt rejuvenated and refreshed. The tension in Cyndi's face faded away. Louis's back loosened, so he felt limber enough to do a million consecutive backflips. The butterflies in Devon's stomach flew away.

They turned to the woman. They'd first seen her only minutes ago, but all of them felt they knew her—not from another place or time but like you know your mom when you're first born.

"Louis, you're iLone. Devon, you're iLone too. Cyndi, you're eNoli. Well,

now that that's out of the way, what do you say I show you guys out of here? Use the door right over there," said the woman abruptly. She didn't even turn to look at them. She seemed absorbed in the view of Olivion's Domain through the panoramic window. She merely pointed to a door that appeared out of nowhere and hovered a few inches above the ground. Its knob turned and it opened, revealing a path suspended in total darkness that led to a glowing blue light. They recognized this as the first place they'd visited when they arrived on Midlandia.

"What? Wait! The Olivion? Is that who you are?" Cyndi asked.

"Is that who I am? I would have thought the answer to that question would be obvious to you all. You have crossed my Gate. Everywhere is my domain but this especially is my Domain, and you are my Favorites. I know I've chosen correctly, so act as if you have some sense. How about it? Are you ready to go home?" She finally turned to them.

"Okay, fine. So that's it? We can just go home? We had to go through so much to get here and now you're sending us home just like that?" Cyndi questioned.

"Well, did you come here to see me or did you come here so you could go home? Or better yet, how would you like it if I said you'd made it this far just so I could tell you that you're not ready to leave and you should go back out into Midlandia with no one to protect you?" the Olivion said.

"No, thank you. We came here so that we could go home," Devon said.

"Exactly, you're not here to see me. You're here to go home and I'm here to oblige. This way please . . ."

"But we were told that we were important—that you're the Olivion and we're Olivion's Favorites," Cyndi said.

"First of all, if you're going to call me something, let's just make it Olivion. You can drop the 'the.' As far as the other matters go . . . both eNoli and iLone have left Midlandia, and many things have been put into motion because of that. Or maybe it's the other way around.

"Galonious and Trife are on Earth. Things aren't going quite as well as they'd expected. They got themselves stuck in an alternate dimension. You'll have a great time dealing with that, Louis. Let's not forget Arminion. He's everywhere seeking his desire. That's all there is to know as far as the eNoli are concerned.

"As far as the iLone go, Timioosiyon is on Earth and is the reason you're here, Cyndi. When you return home you'll find your own way to deal with all that is to come. If you couldn't, you wouldn't be a Favorite. The same is true for you too, Louis and Devon. You'll find your way. That's what you're supposed to do and why you're important—my Favorites. Okay, I think we're done. This is the way." Olivion directed them to the door.

"What? What does all that mean? We were told you had the answers," Cyndi said.

"Excuse me, Ms. Chase, you asked a question and I answered it. So stop stalling and go. Elliot and Jessica miss you, Devon," Olivion said.

Hearing those names cut through Devon. He had so many responsibilities to his family, and he couldn't imagine what had been going on since he'd left. Even here, all he cared about was his family.

Louis, on the other hand, was only wondering why Olivion was insisting they leave so quickly.

"Well, I have another question. What are you?" Cyndi said.

131

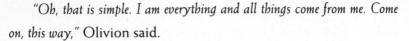

"Oh, that is simple. I am everything and all things come from me. Come on, this way," Olivion said.

"What does that mean? You are everything? How can you be everything?" Cyndi asked.

"You see that window right there? You see the sky? You see that door?" Olivion asked.

"Yeah," they all said.

"Well, there you go! That's all me. Come on, let's go."

"Olivion, Galonious, and Trife . . . how can I do anything to stop them? And what is coming? After all we've been through, I know things are serious," Louis said.

"Louis, you're right. But if I told you, would it matter? Would it give you the ability to deal with it? Are you ready for such things? What you do know is that all of you need to go home and that's what I'm trying to get you to do."

"You're saying I . . . we're not ready and yet you're going to send us back home? That's really messed up," Louis said.

"Is it? But you all need to get back home. You know it's not safe for you here, and if you're dead, there's no possibility that you'll be of any use to anyone."

"I guess . . . but . . . ," Louis said.

"You guess?" Olivion said to Louis before turning to Cyndi.

"I know you understand. Your disappearance has created trouble for your dad and Jason. You need to get back."

Olivion was right, Cyndi had caused all sorts of trouble for her family. But she had so many questions . . . yet somehow she couldn't think of any of them. *After all I've studied, learned, and*

wondered about, how can I not have a question? I need an important one,
Cyndi thought.

Cyndi, I am right here and you're not ready.

"Well, that's that. Come on," Olivion said, ushering them through
the hovering open door and along the path.

Home. Home. Home. Its call was making them quickly forget all that they may have been wondering about. Cyndi thought
about clearing everything up for her family. Devon thought about
his family and how he'd use the power that Vivionya said he pos-
sessed. Louis thought about . . .

"Wait! I can't go back home! My friend is in trouble," Louis
said.

"What do you mean? Lacey was in trouble, didn't you see her? Plus,
Brandon is bored. Angela still wants to hear from you. Oh, and let's not forget
your mom, dad, and brother. Yes, Cameron has gotten himself into a perilous
situation since you've been gone."

"I know, but I can't go home. I, no, none of us, would even be
here with the chance to go home if it weren't for Perilynn. We'd
have been killed. Cyndi, you were about two seconds from death!
I saw it! Perilynn saved you! I would have been killed as soon as I
got here. I'm not turning my back on someone who saved my life
just so I can enjoy the rest of the summer," Louis said.

Olivion looked at the child who was one of her Favorites. He was
exactly who she knew him to be. He always thought about others

and wanted to help. She couldn't have picked anyone better.

Louis, you have the heart but not the strength.

Not yet anyway . . .

"Louis, enjoy the rest of the summer? It's more like enjoy your life. I told you that if you die here, you'll no longer have the powers you need to face the future. That goes for all of you and that would be calamitous for everyone. You cannot risk that. So go home to your families and have fun while you can. There's a hard road ahead of you," Olivion said as she led them down the path to the Midland Isle.

"Olivion, I won't go home. Please don't force me to. I made a promise and I broke it. I have to make it right. You see, after what he did for me, if I don't try to help, it will eat at me forever. I'll always worry about him. That's who I am," Louis said.

Olivion could see it. There's much he'd have to learn, but he was well on his way.

"Louis, that is indeed who you are and I will not stop you," Olivion said, and a new door appeared. It folded itself out from the air and stood about four inches from the ground. It opened, revealing a path back to Midlandia.

"Thank you. We'll be back and then we'll return home! Come on, guys," Louis said, never doubting that they'd follow.

"Wait! Louis, you know how dangerous it is out there! Olivion, Midlandia is screaming. Perilynn said that has never happened before. What does it mean? Is it our fault? If we all go home, will it stop? If Louis doesn't go home, will it continue?" Cyndi asked.

"Cyndi Victoria Chase, that's more like you. Those are excellent questions. Louis, hold on—don't leave just yet. You need to hear this too. No, it's not your fault and it'll continue whether you leave or stay. The only thing that will stop it from getting worse is if you all are successful. The crying is a symptom of a danger that is coming. Something that none of you or any CE has ever encountered. Well, would you listen to me? I told you more than you asked. Okay, now you can go ahead, Louis."

"Wait! Olivion, you can't be serious. What kind of danger?" Cyndi asked.

"Hold on again, Louis. If you want to know what the danger is, this is the answer:

I am everything.
All things come from me.
But there is only one thing I cannot be.
That is the key to everything.

"Say it with me," Olivion said.

"I am everything. All things come from me. But there is only one thing I cannot be. That is the key to everything," all four repeated.

"Exactly. That's the answer. Louis, you can go now. Actually, you can all go now," Olivion said.

"That's not an answer. That's a riddle," Devon said, finally chiming in.

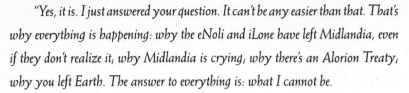

"Yes, it is. I just answered your question. It can't be any easier than that. That's why everything is happening: why the eNoli and iLone have left Midlandia, even if they don't realize it; why Midlandia is crying; why there's an Alorion Treaty; why you left Earth. The answer to everything is: what I cannot be.

"Now I've said too much and I'm not going to say any more, except for this: if you decide not to return home now to search for Perilynn, you won't be able to safely find your way home until you solve the riddle," Olivion said just as a loud chime sounded.

"See, I have other things to do. Look, children—but you're all teens now, I bet you don't like being called children anymore." Olivion laughed.

"I'm a teenager? My birthday has passed?" Louis asked happily.

"Time isn't the same here as it is in other places, but in a nonlinear way, of course, your birthday has passed. Happy birthday, Louis!"

"Thanks!" Louis said.

"You're very welcome. Okay, that's the way to the Midland Isle, which is the only safe way home." She turned to Devon. "Devon, that's the only safe way home. Do you hear me?" Then she addressed them all once again. "That other door leads back to Midlandia and to your friend Perilynn. He was captured, you know. What are you going to do about that Alonis Capsule? You may be going back for no reason. Have you thought about that? But in the end it's up to you. You didn't come here to see me. You came here so you could go home. So go!" Olivion walked back into the observatory, slamming the door behind her.

Cyndi ran after her, opening the door. It lead to the color blue. She had to catch herself from falling from the doorway into bottomless red. She quickly closed the door. No more answers would be found here.

Louis stood before the door leading back to Midlandia. "You guys are coming with me, right? Cyndi, you promised Perilynn too." Surely he wouldn't have to do this alone, not after what Perilynn had done for all of them.

"Louis, Perilynn sacrificed everything to get us here. If we get killed, it'll have been for nothing. Do you think he wants that? And how long have we been gone? I want to go home. I miss my dad and my brother. I even miss my mom . . . a little. And have you forgotten how dangerous it is out there?" Cyndi said.

"Yeah, I know how dangerous it is. People trying to kill me, people trying to kill you. But it's for our friend. Devon, he saved you too! You coming with me?"

"Louis, I'm sorry, but I just don't know him like you do. I don't even think I really spoke to him. I don't even know either of you. Do you know what you did in that city? It was such a wondrous place and what you did was just . . . why does everything have to get messed up for me? Forget it! I'm not going back with you! I have a family to get back to that needs me. Vivionya said that if I made it home safely, I'd have the power to do whatever I want, just like her. I need to use that power now. You wouldn't understand," Devon said.

Louis knew that what had happened in the city didn't feel right, but the iLone were the enemy and they'd had no choice. "Those were the bad guys. We had to get you so you could have the chance to go home. And what do you mean 'wouldn't understand'? Are you crazy? You think you're the only one with family? Like no one else has a mom, dad, brothers, or sisters that miss

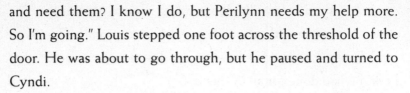

and need them? I know I do, but Perilynn needs my help more. So I'm going." Louis stepped one foot across the threshold of the door. He was about to go through, but he paused and turned to Cyndi.

"Cyndi, one last time: Are you coming with me? We owe him our lives," Louis said. She didn't move or speak. She just looked at him with eyes that said, *Sorry.*

"Fine." Louis went through the door that did not lead to the Midland Isle and home.

Louis, it looks as if this time you'll have to be both the hero and the sidekick.

Chapter **Twenty-four**

It was one thing for Louis to find himself stranded on Midlandia with countless iLone and eNoli CE chasing him. He'd had no choice about that. To willingly turn his back on a free and safe return to East Orange, New Jersey, to endure Midlandia on his own was a different story—a crazy story at that.

Why would he do that?

Just like Brandon, Angela, and now Cyndi, Perilynn was a friend, and friends can't let one another down. His soul would be forever stained, his life would be forever changed if he didn't at least try to help Perilynn.

Non sibi, sed Perilynn!

He'd gone through the door, and Olivion, her Domain, Devon, and Cyndi were no longer behind him. He stood high within Midlandia, probably far above the Celestial Drifts, alone on a barren aerial island about ten yards in diameter with his thoughts, soul, and body embraced by the Midlandian night. He looked down and noticed he was no longer dressed in the clothing that he'd worn on the last day of school. He now had on crisp blue jeans made of an unique material like denim but not, a white shirt, and a black fitted leather jacket that had a light pattern impressed upon it. As fresh and clean as he looked, it did nothing to lessen his fear, but he did feel a bit better.

Never mind that fear walked heavily with Louis. It felt powerful to be scared, so he used it. Even though Olivion had said he was iLone, he was sure he was eNoli like Perilynn. He thought of all the times he'd jumped with Perilynn and Cyndi to an unknown fate, only trusting that death wasn't on their horizon. This time he was self-reliant but his faith was still strong. Too bad Cyndi wouldn't experience this . . .

"Louis, you think I'd let you do this all on your own? Without Perilynn, who's going to save your butt? I'm a black belt; I bet you didn't know that!" Cyndi said, realizing she'd had a wardrobe change like Louis. Stylish!

Louis, overjoyed to see his friend standing beside him, tried to hug her. Cyndi protested but then lovingly hugged him back. She wouldn't let him return to Midlandia alone. She had made a promise, plus she was sure there was much she could learn from this and she couldn't pass up such an opportunity.

"Where's Devon?" Louis asked.

"Where do you think? I left him there, but we can't be mad at him. He doesn't know Perilynn like we do," Cyndi said. "Okay, so what now?"

"Look where we are. There's no way for us get down other than to jump."

"Of course. It's not like we haven't done it before. It always works out . . . I hope," Cyndi said, trying to hide the fact that she was majorly scared. "Running jump?"

"I don't think it matters." Louis grabbed Cyndi's hand, taking her with him as he suddenly leaped.

They fell so fast they turned night into day, snow into rain, and all back again. Midlandia trembled around them. As if of one mind they remembered that they were supposed to do something about the crying, but they had no idea what to do. They'd have to figure it out later. Right now saving Perilynn was their most important goal.

They still held hands, but Midlandia had different plans for them and their grip grew slippery so that when a wind buffeted them, it tore one from the other. They continued to plummet, separately and alone, with no destination in sight.

You are both risking everything for a friend . . .

Louis and Cyndi, you're foolish but truly my Favorites.

However, just what do you plan to do when and if you find Perilynn?

Chapter **Twenty-five**

What would have happened if Perilynn's desire to become a Favorite hadn't been enough to make him do the unthinkable and take on all of Midlandia?

What would have happened if the children hadn't been delivered to the Olivion?

What would have happened if the children had been killed?

In the end those questions need not be asked because Perilynn did bring the children safely to the Olivion.

Perilynn's motives would never be their own, but both Kiyonrae and Vivionya respected him for his accomplishments. Out of that respect, they decided to turn him over to his own, so that they could deal with him as they saw fit. If he was lucky, maybe he'd wind up in the Five's garden.

Vivionya and Kiyonrae led a small convoy with Perilynn in tow in search of Lefton Rack. It was surely their destiny to find it because it was soon in sight. The eNoli were discussing the children's successful journey to the Olivion. They would surely be marked iLone and return home hoping to destroy the plans of Galonious, Arminion, and Trife. The eNoli's chance for escape had been greatly diminished. They also had much to resolve because, thanks to Reign, they were now in a civil war.

As they approached Lefton Rack, Perilynn shouted and banged on the Alonis Capsule. Pointless. Not even sound could escape. He was truly trapped.

Vivionya and Kiyonrae grabbed the capsule and thrust it through the wall of Lefton Rack. The wall shattered and crumbled at the point of impact. The capsule then slid across the floor, gouging it, until it came to a complete stop at the center of the great hall. As soon as the capsule halted, Lefton Rack rebuilt itself.

Vivionya and Kiyonrae had delivered their cargo and were sure they'd hear of its fate. Not wanting a conflict, they left.

Everyone whom Perilynn had battled was there. Seeing him in the capsule, they booed and screamed in disappointment because they'd been robbed of their chance to attack him. At least the capsule kept him safe. Without the prospect of becoming a Favorite to fuel him, Perilynn wouldn't have survived such a fight.

Perilynn spotted aZRon. No one knew that he'd helped Perilynn in battle not long ago. But he'd been fighting *against* the iLone not *for* Perilynn. Still, aZRon had lost his sisters in the fight he'd joined simply for entertainment.

For aZRon there was only one thing that might make it worthwhile. Perilynn had agreed that if he failed, aZRon could cast him into the Infinite Abyss. In fact, ". . . if I get caught, you can be the one to throw me into the Infinite Abyss" had been his exact words. Had he really meant it? aZRon winked at Perilynn and then began to speak above the crowd.

"Because of Perilynn the children have crossed Olivion's Gate. They've been marked as iLone to return home to defeat our brethren! Need I say that will make your efforts to leave this wretched place nearly impossible? He must be made to suffer in the Infinite Abyss!"

His words were met with a cheer that shook Midlandia—oh wait, that was just the effects of Midlandia calling out once again. aZRon gathered himself, then quickly smiled at Perilynn as only he could.

At that moment Perilynn knew that aZRon was going to throw him into the Infinite Abyss.

All agreed on Perilynn's fate, and if the Abyss was truly his fate, it would appear before them. There were no words spoken; there was only anxious anticipation. The eNoli cleared from the center of the floor and stared at the circular pattern as it began to spin and open. What would it reveal?

Cheers! Shouts! Applause! What they saw could only be one thing: the Infinite Abyss. It *was* his fate to be sent there. The eNoli went into a ravenous frenzy.

"The tyrant! The traitor!"

"Perilynn will sink for a Midlandian eternity!"

"Always aware. Always deprived of everything!"

"The worst fate imaginable!" various eNoli yelled.

Holliston was about to kick Perilynn's prison into the hole. No! No way would aZRon let Holliston or any other CE do that to his friend Perilynn. Perilynn had delivered the most excitement aZRon had seen in a long time. And on Midlandia long times are notoriously long. So, with an odd feeling of gratitude, aZRon forced Holliston out of the way and kicked Perilynn into the Abyss. Such was his prize alone.

Do not fret, Perilynn; it seems you do have a few friends left . . .

But you are in the Abyss. Not even Louis and Cyndi can rescue you from there.

That is a promise.

Chapter **Twenty-six**

Maybe she had only experienced an unusually vivid dream.

Maybe she had never even been to Midlandia.

Maybe she had not been near death or saved by Perilynn.

Maybe she had never met anyone named Olivion.

Maybe she had never jumped from the heavens with Louis Proof.

Cyndi wondered these things, because she awoke on a beach and was welcomed by what had to be a gorgeous California day. She was home. It was not her room, but this would do. The sun was high in the sky, and she could see a marina with tall and medium-size boats in the distance.

She began to stroll, not realizing that as she walked the sand quickly filled in her footprints so that it remained perfectly smooth. It was the first time she'd been on a beach alone, but she didn't mind even though that was a bit odd. When she reached the boats, she noticed that each one looked new and the designs were flawless. There was not a hint of dirt or wear on them. The sails had no wrinkles. The metal gleamed, free of any water spots. It was all too flawless. It was all too perfect.

She was not home. She was still on Midlandia. Where the heck was Louis?

"Louis!" Cyndi shouted.

Midlandia began to tremble. Sand rose up as if it were water, making a powerful wave. It crashed no more than a few yards from Cyndi. There was so much chaos in the crashing sand behind her, it was an easy decision to head for the peaceful waters ahead.

She ran toward the water, and when she turned back to see how much distance she'd put between herself and the wild sand, she realized that it had calmed. The billions of grains of sand began to glow and sparkle. They swayed and did a cordial waltz in the air as they built a glittering white building right in front of her. It was as lovely as the Midlandian Ocean was wide. She walked up to the tall curved entrance and two large doors opened. . . .

Louis was still falling. This was one of the reasons why the eNoli were so frustrated with this infinite place. His fall wouldn't end until Midlandia wanted it to. He could have fallen for years or for a matter of seconds no matter where he'd jumped. And of course where he'd land also would be anyone's guess.

He wasn't worried about himself; he was worried about Cyndi. He imagined that she was alone and it was his fault. Was she still falling? How long would it take him to find her?

Finally, he crashed into the surface of the sparkling Midlandian Ocean. He sank many yards into the water. It was calming, as if he were being baptized after a new Midlandian birth. He was here because he wanted to be, not because of some crazy circumstance.

Louis started a carefree swim toward the surface. It was all love until he felt a sudden pressure and then a pull on his leg. Now he was being dragged deeper below. He struggled to look at what had him . . .

Cyndi stepped into the building to find a white marble floor and an elegant glass stairway that branched off to many floors, which were sprinkled with additional stairways, as it climbed into the distance. The building seemed to get wider and deeper with its height.

A fit man wearing a tailored vest and expensive-looking pinstriped pants crouched on one of the higher levels. He was putting glowing cases onto shelves that stretched as far as Cyndi could see.

Cyndi noticed that the letters CVC were meticulously inlaid in platinum in the floor a few feet in front of her. She felt compelled to stand on them. As soon as she did so, the many levels lit up, not all at once but in an upward sequence, creating a wave of light. Locks unlocked and glass walls and cases rose into the ceilings, exposing what was protected behind them.

The man turned to see the girl he'd been waiting for.

"Cyndi Victoria Chase! I'm so glad you found your way here. I thought you might leave. I'll be right down." He was obviously excited that she was here because he began to rush to reach her. He tripped and fell over the illuminated railing, tumbling past floor after floor, clumsily flailing his arms. Cyndi cringed at the thought of him hitting the ground. When he was about ten feet from the bottom, he miraculously turned the right way up and gently landed on one foot.

"Fooled you. Ha! Ha!" the man said in a cheerful voice.

"That wasn't funny. You know who I am, so who are you?" Cyndi said.

"I'm sorry if that was in poor taste. I thought it might be fun for you. Mistaken! Let's move on as friends. I am Avery Rush, the Librarian, and this is of course a library, but not just any library. The Olivion created this place. The Olivion created all things, but still you'll find this place special. Everything you need to know is here. Stay as long as you want. Learn whatever you want to learn. Learn everything!" said the Librarian.

"This has to be the best library I've ever seen. But I have to find—"

"Knowledge, right? And here you are!" he said, flourishing his hand toward the great library. "The last person to visit this place was Emyli FyneStory. She learned much but she had to stop because she couldn't handle it. Nor was much open to her. But she wasn't a Favorite as you are. You've met the Olivion, so nothing will be off limits to you.

"That's where you want to be. Nowhere else." Avery pointed way up. Cyndi could see a vibrant red light at the top of the library. Its call tickled her brain.

"Cyndi, the answers to everything you can imagine are in this building. But up there are the questions you never thought to ask and the answers you never thought to inquire about. The sum of Olivion's knowledge is in that light. Go and claim it," the Librarian said.

She'd always been cavalier about her quest for knowledge, but now something scared her.

Knowledge is what she'd come back for, though. Shaking off her sense of foreboding, she began to take the glass stairs upward, and Avery walked beside her. It would be a long, long climb. . . .

They were horrific. They were not mermen but merbeasts. They were aquatic eNoli CE, to be exact, but as far as Louis was concerned they were demons. They all seemed to have humanoid but gray-blue scaled torsos, with oversize arms and extended fingers. Their fingers had to be over ten inches long. The lower portions were webbed, and the upper portions were like claws that were fully functional as fingers and not hindered by the webbing. Some of them had lower bodies similar to squids. Some had lower bodies similar to dolphins or whales. Others had lower bodies like eels. They were varied but all equally terrifying. They surrounded Louis, laughing and taking swipes at him. One jerked him, using all of its force to throw Louis through the water to get hit by one of its cohorts. Another grabbed Louis by the shoulders, rushed him to the surface, and leaped sixty yards out of the water. It screamed in Louis's face and shook him from side to side. At least Louis was able to breathe. At the apex of its jump it threw Louis down violently.

* * *

Cyndi suddenly felt an urgent need to find Louis and help him.

"Wait. I can't stay. I have to find Louis and Perilynn first. Louis needs my help," Cyndi said, stopping on the stairs.

"You can't stay?" Avery said as some of the lights dimmed and some of the doors locked.

"All of the doors are . . . were . . . open to you and you're going to turn your back on this? No, eNoli child! All will be lost if you don't take these steps." Avery didn't seem angry but rather upset and scared.

"I'm sorry. I have to find Louis. I can feel that he needs me!" Cyndi turned to head for the door. The library went totally dim and all the doors locked except for the one by which she'd entered.

"I understand. Really, I do. I guess you're not yet ready. Maybe not today, maybe not tomorrow, but hopefully someday you will be and you'll find what you're looking for so that you may save us all. Go back out into the chaos that is Midlandia and get Louis. He's not far from here. Take one of those boats. Hurry! Oh . . . remember . . . NO SHORTCUTS. You really need to find your way back here!" Avery said.

Cyndi thanked him and left the library to collect one of the smaller vessels. Her father had taught both her and Jason how to operate a boat but this one was so intuitive that it didn't matter. She set off into the seemingly calm waters for Louis. . . .

To Louis's surprise all of the CE surrounding him were pushed aside by a CE who seemed much more human in form than the others. He even delivered a violent blow to the face of one CE. He was either not pleased with the way Louis was being treated or he wanted to claim the kill for himself, Louis thought.

Right before this unique CE reached Louis, elaborate patterns of light lit up the Midlandian Ocean from below. All of the CE scattered, leaving Louis alone in the water.

Thankfully, some paths are inevitably intertwined. Cyndi Victoria Chase was cruising the Midlandian Ocean without a set destination, only a feeling that she was headed in the right direction. This reminded her of sailing with her family off the Greek coast three years ago. She loved going on trips with Jason and her dad; if her mother had to tag along, so be it.

This was not exactly like Greece because she was of course in Midlandia and the fact that there was nothing in sight but water was beginning to worry her. Oh, wait . . .

Cyndi could sense something in the distance. She sped up, creating a wake behind her that was quickly absorbed by the water so that it could be perfect once again. Spying Louis, she cut the motor and jumped into the water to pull him out.

To Louis's surprise he was once again snatched from behind, but this time he was swiftly carried to the surface. "Climb into the boat. I can't get you up there. You hear me? Climb into the boat!" his captor shouted.

Louis did as he was told and lay on his back in a boat that sure as heck hadn't been there when he'd been taken under. He coughed and spat out water. He opened his eyes. There was only one person standing over him. It was Cyndi Victoria.

She could tell he'd been through a lot as he silently looked up at her. This was not the Louis she knew. Louis was usually all smiles when he saw a friend. Cyndi thought about what she'd given up by leaving the library as Louis was pulling himself together. She wondered what she could have learned. She wondered if she was going to be able to find her way back. It didn't matter. She'd found Louis.

"Hey, you know I didn't mean to let go. You know that right?" Louis finally said.

"Of course. I don't know what happened. I just found myself on a beach. I don't remember landing. I bet you do," she said.

They were in a boat floating atop the bluest water imaginable. It glistened as if it had diamonds floating on its surface. Cyndi breathed deep and noticed that the air was refreshing, with no hint of salt or anything else she'd expect to smell on an ocean.

"Do you have any idea where we should be going?" Louis asked Cyndi. She didn't but wouldn't look unknowledgeable because she would be robbed of the chance to answer. There was no warning! The perfectly tranquil water became turbulent as a huge blue metallic structure pierced its surface. This behemoth object spat out glowing spheres that circled it like satellites or, better yet, moons.

"Hold on to something!" Cyndi shouted.

Louis was about to jump out of the boat. Cyndi, surprised by her own strength, grabbed him and pulled him toward her as she held on to one of the boat's railings.

"Are you crazy? You're so quick to jump! Hold on!" Cyndi said. Louis obediently clutched the railing. They were being carried upward. Louis and Cyndi trembled not because of the height but because they didn't understand what was happening.

Cyndi, Louis, and the boat they were in were on top of the huge object, but not for long. It was not flat, and the boat began to slide down the side until it was in the water once again. This object was bigger than a skyscraper and towered over them. It was a floating city. It was made of what seemed to be lustrous metals that were engraved with patterns of brilliant light. This light was so stunning that it could turn the darkest, most horrific patch of hell into a celebration of heaven's wonder. Whatever this object was, it was bigger than anything Louis or Cyndi had ever seen, here or where they were from, except for the incredible black wall. It was a true phenomenon, and it had become nearly motionless after it completed its ascension from the depths of the water.

So small. So miniscule. Louis and Cyndi were the equivalent of the buttons on a video-game controller in comparison to this marvel. They looked at it, then at each other. One of the lights left its orbit and transformed into an elegant airship that zipped down to the two kids. Without hesitation Louis and Cyndi got in and were flown high in the sky to a large docking bay that had not been open before now.

The panels of a colossal door parted ways. A man walked out with his hands behind his back and greeted them.

"Hello, Cyndi. Hello, Louis. I did not expect you both to get here at the same time. I'm DiVarion Alonis, which of course would make me the Alonis Maker . . ."

Who is the Alonis Maker, DiVarion Alonis?
What *exactly* is an Alonis?

Chapter **Twenty-seven**

It was a punishment: not one of living, not one of suffering, simply the punishment of being. Perilynn would drift for a Midlandian eternity in the Infinite Abyss.

He was conscious of everything as he stared through the clear Alonis Capsule. The Abyss was not nothing; it was something. It was dark murky water with only the faintest light. All that could be seen were a few air bubbles every now and then. If he was lucky—and he'd have to be extremely lucky—once in a quarter of a millennium he might catch a glimpse of someone else who'd been cursed with the same fate.

Perilynn reverted to pure, formless, brilliantly glowing energy and exploded its power outward. He'd been strong enough to defend Louis, Cyndi, and Devon, but he couldn't break an Alonis Capsule.

Eventually, Perilynn calmed himself. There really was no way to escape and it *was* the worst punishment imaginable for a CE. The Infinite Abyss now extinguished a determination that had once been immeasurable. He sank to the bottom of his capsule, let go of his form, and glowed as shapeless energy.

He had no idea how long he'd been here. There was no day or night, only forever. But to his surprise there was suddenly something he'd never expected . . .

Chapter **Twenty-eight**

Cyndi and Louis looked at the man who called himself DiVarion Alonis, the Alonis Maker. He appeared to be in his late thirties and was wearing an off-white leather jacket that had an elaborate pattern lightly embossed across it, much like Louis's and Cyndi's. The pattern was almost unnoticeable; it showed up mostly when it caught the light.

To his surprise Louis noticed that DiVarion's shoes had laces and one was untied. After seeing so much perfection, this welcome aberration made Louis smile. DiVarion spied what had caught Louis's attention and crouched to tie his lace.

"No, Louis, I'm not a CE, so I do have faults," he said with a laugh.

Cyndi's face took on an expression of bewilderment.

"You look surprised, Cyndi; not everyone here is a CE. Have you met Orenci—" DiVarion was interrupted by a shimmering electrical form that had stealthily made its way up through the docking bay toward its target. Before striking, this silent assassin took on its preferred form and raised unsheathed blades.

"Kiyonrae!" DiVarion shouted, snapping his fingers and lifting his hand in one swift motion to create an electrical energy barrier that protected Cyndi. It sparked and shimmered, forcing

Kiyonrae back. Louis could see that it came from a device attached to DiVarion's wrist.

Cyndi whipped around to face the assassin, her eyes blazing and her hair practically standing on end, not from fear but from anger. This CE had taken Perilynn and now he was attacking her.

"You're so ill-advised! I will not have any of the children hurt in my presence. Where were you moments ago when Louis was attacked by SysRic and his clan? Your efforts would be better served by finding out what SysRic knows. Play nice! Do you hear me!?" DiVarion shouted.

Kiyonrae knew he was out of line to attack here, so he turned to leave the ship. But Louis rushed at him. "I'll show you what'll happen if you attack my friends! You took Perilynn. Where is he?!"

DiVarion motioned with his hand and once again used his mysterious device. This time it lifted Louis off his feet, halting him in the air. This angered Louis even further, and to DiVarion's surprise, he had to use more power to keep Louis at bay. Louis was growing very strong; this pleased DiVarion.

Kiyonrae turned back before leaping off the vessel. "Louis, I'm not your enemy. Cyndi, you are a serious threat, so I am yours. It's just how it all worked out. You'll both understand that in time. As far as Perilynn is concerned, I've gained a tremendous amount of respect for him, but yes, I did capture him. However, his own kind dealt him his final punishment, so your quarrel about that should be with them and not me." Then Kiyonrae jumped out the still-open docking bay door toward the seemingly endless Midlandian

Ocean. He swung his Alonis Medallion around his neck and an electric-blue vehicle built itself around him just before he hit the water. It carried him into the ocean's depths.

"Louis. Cyndi. First let me say that even in the face of what just happened you are both totally safe here, so I want you to relax and enjoy your time in my city." DiVarion laughed as he heard his own words. "Relax . . . enjoy your time here . . . listen to me. What a funny thing to say in these circumstances. But I mean this, and I cannot stress enough that you're safe. Within these doors is a Midlandian sanctuary untouched by the Midlandian War." He led them to the door of the vessel. Just as it opened, a massive deafening sound roared throughout all of Midlandia. DiVarion grabbed the two and hurriedly ushered them inside.

"This is serious. They're getting louder and louder and can be both heard and felt throughout Midlandia," DiVarion said.

Louis and Cyndi weren't listening. How could they be inside a place that seemed more like a floating country than a city?

You surely remember the JunkYard JunkLot, right? With all of its rides, games, monstrous-size hi-def screens—oh, and the roller coaster and racetrack? Not to take anything away from that extravagantly fun place, but it was nothing compared to what Louis and Cyndi saw now. Sadly, an Earth marvel, even one built by the Magnificent ProliFnGlitcH, just can't compete with a Midlandian marvel.

They stood on a high platform overlooking countless CE, all of whom seemed to be cheerfully moving about like regular people. There were many levels to the vessel. What was oddest, though, was the fact that there seemed to be no outer walls. Louis and Cyndi were sure they existed because they'd seen them from the outside. But here they could see Midlandia. The walls were see-through. Cool.

"Hold on," DiVarion said. A portion of the platform they were standing on broke away, and all at once they were traveling through the city.

"This is incredible! What's the name of this place?" Cyndi asked.

"Oh, forgive me. This is DiVarion City. I know it's a bit egotistical, but the city *was* my idea," DiVarion said. "I can't tell you how happy I am that you made it here. We were all worried that once you reached the Olivion, you'd end your journeys. You wouldn't have been any use to anybody had you left then. You hadn't even claimed your Alonises. But I always say that on Midlandia things work themselves out."

"We just want to rescue our friend. That guy Kiyonrae captured him. Do you know Perilynn?" Louis asked.

"Of course I do! He's quickly become a Midlandian legend."

"Do you know if he's safe and where he is?" Cyndi asked.

"Well, the good news is that he's safe but that's also the bad news since the reason no one can harm him is that he's in the Infinite Abyss," DiVarion said.

"Yes! He's alive! I knew it! Whatever this abyss is, we'll rescue him from it," Louis shouted.

"That's a lofty goal. Not even the most battle-tested CE

would dare attempt to rescue someone from the Infinite Abyss," DiVarion said.

Louis didn't want to hear this. He turned his attention to the sights of the city as they traveled upward. There were buildings but there also seemed to be full-blown Midlandian lands. Both Cyndi and Louis were tempted to explore; however, there wasn't time for that.

Finally they reached the very top. Consider it the penthouse suite. The platform docked itself to a landing, and DiVarion led the way to a door, which opened as soon as he got close to it. The children followed to find themselves in a control room with many people. Each one was doing something in front of a screen. It seemed a bit like an office on Earth.

Cyndi looked around: screens, chairs, people, devices, more devices, Devon Alexander. Wait! Who? Cyndi grabbed Louis and led him over to Devon.

"Devon, you didn't go home," Louis said when they reached him.

"Uhhh . . . no . . . I decided to stick around and make sure that Perilynn guy was okay. I mean, he did save me too, right?" Devon said.

"How did you get in here?" Louis asked.

"And how long have you been here?" Cyndi asked.

"I just showed up here not long ago," Devon reluctantly said.

"Well, I jumped and fell into the ocean. It was kind of fun until these things attacked me. I wasn't lucky like you," Louis said.

"I had to turn my back on what I was doing to save him."
Cyndi only regretted this a tiny bit. Louis was more important.

"You didn't save me. Those lights did," Louis said.

"I didn't save you? What do you call getting you out of the
water when no one else was around?"

"Fine, Cyndi." Louis smiled. "You saved me. Thank you."

"You're very welcome, Louis. But I won't always be around to
rescue you." Cyndi jokingly pointed her finger in Louis's face.

Before Louis could say anything more, he saw something
familiar on one of the screens—something he'd never expected
to see here.

"Hey, that's the JunkYard JunkLot!"

"Of course it is," said an attractive woman who was hovering
on a platform. She came closer to the children. She had caring
green eyes and gave them an irresistible smile.

"Louis, Devon, you're going to need help and a safe place to
go. We've made sure that you'll have both," DiVarion said.

"Yes, the JunkYard JunkLot. Brendan and Stacia—or as
you'll come to know them, Prolif and Glitch, or the Magnificent
ProliFnGlitcH—built this for you," said the woman.

"You know them?" Louis asked.

"Well, yes and no. We guide them but they don't know who
the information is coming from. Maybe you can tell Glitch when
you get back. I'm sure she'd like to know, especially from you,"
the woman said.

Louis stared at Glitch; he was drawn to her just as he had

been when he first saw her in the JunkYard JunkLot. Talking with her was a *must.*

"What about me? I've never been to that place or seen that girl. Am I supposed to go there too? Amusement parks aren't really my kind of place," Cyndi said.

"Not your sort of place? Of course not. Cyndi, when you return home, demand that your beloved, Kimber Lime, take you to meet the sisters. You'll find them to be very helpful," the woman said as she pointed to one of the screens, where they could see three lovely women talking with one another in a unique kitchen.

"Yes, you'll all have help when you return. Now, you three, come with me. You'll have plenty of time to get acquainted with Lynda. Oh, what am I doing? This is Lynda, my second in command in some things and my first in command in many more things," DiVarion said.

Lynda laughed at his words. "I'm Lynda Alonis, DiVarion's wife."

"Now follow me. I have something to give all of you." DiVarion led them toward the back of the control room.

They took an elevator up to the *real* penthouse. The doors opened onto a peaceful quiet. They'd have sworn that they were outside if it hadn't been for the transparent barrier that protected the vessel from water when it dove. They walked along a pebbled path that led them past gorgeous flowers and shrubbery. The flowers weren't like any they'd seen before. Some sparkled like stars in the sunlight. Some sang lovely multipart music as a gentle breeze blew through their petals and reeds. The garden surrounded a magnificent house. But they walked right past this house to a smaller one.

"This is my lab, where I do much of my thinking and creating. You've seen one of my lesser creations. It's handy for many things, as it helps turn my thoughts into reality," DiVarion said, referring to the device around his wrist that Louis had noticed earlier.

"Can we get one of those?" Louis asked.

"One of these? Of course not! I have something much better for each you. You'll need them to survive Midlandia. You know, I love this place; it upsets me that it's in danger," DiVarion said as he opened the door to the smaller house.

They entered a workroom packed with tools and devices, some on tables, others hanging from hooks on the ceiling. DiVarion saw amazement and curiosity in the kids' eyes.

"There's no need for any of this here—my tools or my inventions. Not even for my city. Here you could simply be. But what's the fun or purpose in life if you can't create things? Here there's no limit to what I can create. You know, the CE don't need anything, not even bodies, but they desire them. It makes their lives interesting," DiVarion said, leading them down a stairway to the basement.

"Who'd just want to be? That'd be so lame," Devon said.

The basement was cozy. Countless medallions hung from curved shelves and from an elaborate rack on the ceiling. The medallions had different-colored stones: some blue, some red, some green, some diamond white, some yellow, some purple.

However, each stone actually displayed every variation and shade of its color when it shimmered in the light. All of the stones were set in shiny platinum, which was partly woven over the face of some of the stones. Each medallion was unique and stunning.

"We're allowed to take one, right? This is what you meant when you said you had something for us? I know that one is mine," Louis said, not out of greed but familiarity.

"If you're sure, Louis, put it around your neck," DiVarion said.

The one that Louis had identified glowed brighter blue with each step he took toward it. Louis shielded his eyes as he lifted it from its hook with one hand. Once he put it around his neck, it stopped glowing, and he noticed that the words eNoli and iLone were inscribed on the metal surrounding the stone.

"My mom wears this around her neck. Hers is smaller but it's the same. That's how I knew this one was mine. I've always loved it," Louis said.

"Of course. Each one of these represents one that's in your normal lives that you may or may not know about. Louis, yours has been with your mother, keeping her safe and strong so that she may watch over you. When you say to her, 'I believe you are holding something for Olivion's Favorite,' she'll know it's time for you to claim it. Now repeat those words."

Cyndi thought the words as Louis said them aloud. Then Louis asked, "My mom knows all about this?"

"Yes and no. She knows that you're very important and that you'll have a great responsibility, but she knows nothing of Midlandia or of any details," DiVarion said.

Cyndi and Devon were now looking for their Alonises. Neither had seen any of these before. As she neared one, though, Cyndi began to feel the same way she felt whenever she entered her father's home office. She'd first felt this way when she found in her father's desk a mysterious blue box that didn't seem to have any opening. She dared not ask her father about it because he'd know she'd been snooping. Instead, she snuck in to try to open the box every chance she got. She'd been young when she did that and she'd forgotten about the box, but she never forgot the feeling she had in her father's office. The medallion that was creating this feeling called to Cyndi and she touched it. It was like Louis's but the stone was like a diamond. It didn't glow nearly as brightly as Louis's had, but it glowed. Cyndi knew it was hers.

Devon wasn't having any luck. Was his that green one? Maybe. Was it that yellow one? Maybe. Was it that amber one with the metal weaving? Nah. That wasn't his style. Finally, he looked at the many Alonis Medallions in front of him and then he closed his eyes. At first he could still see them all and then they faded away until there was only one left. It was to the right of him. With eyes still shut tight, he walked over and took it. As he placed it around his neck he thought about his family and it glowed just as Louis's had.

"There are so many. Who are all the rest for?" Cyndi asked.

DiVarion knit his eyebrows together seriously. He sat in a chair in the middle of the room and invited the others to do the same. The Alonises shimmered in the background, catching the light and reflecting it back. They swayed back and forth, tapping one another to create a mellifluous song; it was almost as if they too were excited that these particular Favorites were here.

Each one was alive.

Each one was important.

Each one had a story.

Each one *would* have an owner.

"Well, where should I begin? The Alonises are for all of the Favorites, iLone and eNoli alike. You'll each wear one. They don't give you power, they only help you focus your own strength, just like this invention on my wrist helps me—but the Alonis will help you even more. I honestly don't know all of their abilities. You see, they contain energy from the Midland Isle, and that's the most powerful form of energy there is—"

"It has no limits—" Louis interrupted.

"Just like us . . . ," Cyndi continued.

Limitless. I just have to learn how to use it and I'll be able to do anything when I get back home . . . , Devon thought.

"Kiyonrae has an Alonis. So he's like us—he's a Favorite—" Louis said.

"So why is he trying to kill me?" Cyndi asked.

"He believes that by killing you he'll destroy the eNoli's chance of being called to Earth," DiVarion said.

"What does the eNoli coming to Earth have to do with me?" Cyndi asked.

"It has everything to do with you, Cyndi, and with you too,

Louis and Devon. The CE can't escape unless the Olivion permits it, but you have the unique ability to call your kind to any location, including Earth. That's why you're so very important. It's lucky that Perilynn wanted to become a Favorite so badly that he got you to the Gate safely."

"DiVarion, it wasn't just about him becoming a Favorite. He's our friend and he'd have gotten us there safely no matter what," Louis said.

"Louis, why does anyone do anything? It's always complex. Who is really selfless other than the iLone? Yes, I'm sure that after spending time with you, Perilynn began to care about you, but it was an undying desire inside of him that allowed him to deliver you safely. It fueled him so that he was able to claim powers that hadn't always been his to fight much of Midlandia. Understand that the eNoli are the epitome of self and that's from whence a true darkness can spring. That said, Perilynn did save your lives. I harbor no ill will toward the eNoli. I aid them just as I'll aid you, Cyndi. I have no desire or right to make any judgments. I only observe and help."

"Olivion and you say that I'm eNoli. How am I eNoli?" Cyndi asked.

"Cyndi, only you can understand what it means to be eNoli. It's your own truth, and I'm sure it'll reveal itself in time. The same goes for you, Louis and Devon. You know yourselves and what drives you. However, you can never be purely anything, including eNoli or iLone," DiVarion said.

Cyndi thought about the way Perilynn had accomplished the

impossible to lead them to safety. Never mind finding the answer in herself, Perilynn was no joke. And Kiyonrae was trying to kill her, so stuff the iLone, present company excluded. She was proud to be eNoli.

"What about the iLone? I hate the iLone! They're trying to kill Cyndi, and I can't let that happen. They're the bad guys. Both sides were after us, but it was only an eNoli that defended us. I don't want to be iLone. I'm myself and that's enough, but if I had to choose, I'd want to be eNoli like Cyndi and Perilynn," Louis shouted.

"I can see why, but, Louis, you don't know all there is to know. Neither do you, Cyndi. Hey, neither do I. All I know is that I have a job to do and I'm doing it. Both sides are important. Midlandia is shouting. Something is wrong and something is coming. This will affect us all: cat, dog, mouse, human, eNoli, and iLone. I don't think anything will be safe," DiVarion said.

"What is it? What's coming?" Cyndi asked.

"The Olivion didn't tell you? You're Favorites! I was going to ask you," DiVarion said.

"No, she didn't. She just gave us a clue that we have to figure out," Louis said.

"What is it?" DiVarion asked.

"I am everything.
All things come from me.
But there is only one thing I cannot be.
That is the key to everything."

Louis, Cyndi, and Devon recited together.

DiVarion thought silently about the riddle. Three times he motioned as if he were about to speak, then hesitated, before finally speaking. "Sorry, children. There's nothing I can think of, nothing at all. It sounds simple but it seems it's not. Such is the way of the Olivion—simple but complex. If I figure it out, I'll let you know. In the meantime, there's someone else who may be able to help. Her name is Emyli FyneStory. She resides in a place we call Quicker Cove. You'll love her. She's a historian of Midlandia and is writing a book that my wife and I have been helping her with. Usually I can find Quicker Cove when I look for it. Who's up for a trip?" DiVarion asked.

"A trip within a trip. I'm up for it," Louis said.

"Me too. Why not?" Cyndi said, remembering that Avery had mentioned Emyli FyneStory too.

"Well then, me three," Devon said.

"That settles it. Let's go," DiVarion said, and they all stood.

"Hey, DiVarion, do you think she'll know something about Perilynn?" Louis asked.

"Possibly," DiVarion said as he led them toward the door. Louis, Cyndi, and Devon took one last look at the brilliant Alonis Medallions before leaving.

Soon they reached the control room. "Lynda, we're going to go see Emyli," DiVarion said to his wife.

"That sounds like a plan. Make sure you give her this. She's been waiting for it." Lynda pulled from her pocket a metallic disk. It was a little bigger than a quarter and had a glowing blue edge and patterns on it. She tossed it to her husband.

"No problem. We'll be back as soon as we can, and then I'll show the children to their rooms." DiVarion kissed his wife good-bye before leading the children through the city to a massive hangar.

The hangar was round with extremely high light-blue walls that had very large paintings on them. Each painting was of a different person. Louis and Devon recognized two of them: One was of Kiyonrae and one was of Vivionya. Their names were printed on shiny silver plaques on the bottom center of the picture frames. Some canvases were blank. One was currently being painted.

Louis was drawn to a painting that seemed a bit more important than the others. It was of a man and a woman. Walking closer, he saw that their names were Myth and eLynori. The legendary Myth and eLynori!

Myth. eLynori. Where are you? Are you coming back? Louis wondered.

Cyndi and Devon were at first too absorbed in the twelve airships to notice the paintings. Each ship had a different stunning design, yet all were equal in their creativity and beauty. They were arranged on a metal circle. This seemed more like a museum or an exclusive showroom than a hangar.

They all felt small in this huge room. Then Cyndi noticed something. "Hey, are they painting Perilynn over there?" Four people were working on separate sections of a large canvas with different colors of light.

"Yes, indeed. These paintings are of Midlandian legends," DiVarion said as the painters—two men and two women—stopped what they were doing to begin walking around the children, speaking to themselves. They seemed to be taking mental notes and measurements. After they were done, they nodded to DiVarion and returned to their work.

"We call them simply the Painters," DiVarion said.

"I remember them. They were there when we went to get Devon," Cyndi said.

"Oh, yes. They get around. They don't speak much. All they want to do is paint." DiVarion led the three to a midsized ship near the back.

As they climbed a stairway into the aircraft, Cyndi said, "Shotgun."

"Oh, man, why didn't I think of that?" Louis said.

He and Devon sat in the second row of seats while Cyndi settled beside DiVarion. She wanted to watch him control the vessel. Actually, she wanted to learn everything she could while she was here.

The platform now rotated until the ship was at the front of the hangar. The walls opened, and without warning, the ship rocketed off into the blue Midlandian sky.

When they'd been flying for a while, they reached a place where there were only sandy dunes as far as they could see. "This is where it usually is. I wish things would stay put. But I'm sure we'll find it," DiVarion said to the children and to his wife, who could be seen on a small screen.

"Maybe you should come back. I don't want you out there for long. There's no telling who you could run into," Lynda said.

"I guess we have to have faith that we'll find it," Devon said.

"What does faith have to do with it?" Louis asked.

"Yeah. This place is crazy and unconventional. It has nothing to do with faith," Cyndi said.

"I can't believe you two are saying that. I mean, you decided to come back here without anyone to protect you. That was the most faith I've ever seen. Everything has to do with faith," Devon said.

"Not at all. I made a decision to come back," Louis said.

"So did I," Cyndi said.

"Well, sometimes all we have is faith that everything will be all right," Devon said. His Alonis began to quietly glow. He was sure they'd find Quicker Cove. It was just a matter of time.

Devon Alexander's Celestial Infection Rate = 52%
Cyndi Victoria Chase's Celestial Infection Rate = 69%
Louis Proof's Celestial Infection Rate = 70%

Chapter **Twenty-nine**

They soared between twin cities suspended in the sky.

They navigated through massive caves.

They zoomed above the clouds into the night, only to dive back down into the day.

They darted through wondrous multicolored rain.

They flew until they reached Quicker Cove. . . .

"We're here," DiVarion said as they neared an extremely large cove. It was so wide that it had room for an island in its center, where there was a five-story circular white building that seemed to be constructed of a material similar to porcelain. It had large blue windows all around it that reflected the light.

They landed on the far side of the cove and crossed the water on a bridge that extended toward the island as they stepped forward. When they reached land, the bridge retracted again. They entered the building through a clear glass door. The white lobby was lit by blue light from the windows and by a violet light that outlined the top of the ceiling. There was a high desk but no one behind it. Soon, though, a woman strode in.

Emyli FyneStory was unique to say the least. She was in her

late twenties and quite attractive. Actually, very, very attractive.

"Hello, Emyli, I have some important guests with me," DiVarion said.

She stared at the three children wearing Alonis Medallions, and then abruptly said, "You're Favorites. You've crossed Olivion's Gate; you've met the Olivion. My information is inconclusive on both; please tell me all that you can about them."

"Emyli, Emyli, Emyli, there'll be time for that. You haven't even been introduced. Where are your manners? Not to mention, they've traveled here to ask *you* a few questions," DiVarion said.

"Ask me questions? What I know is nothing compared to what they must know. They've met the Olivion! The Olivion knows all," Emyli said.

"We're sorry to disappoint you, but we don't know much," Devon said.

"Everyone goes on about the Olivion and how we're Favorites, but it doesn't seem to be all that," Cyndi added.

"Yeah, but hey, do you know Perilynn? Do you know how I can get to him? He's in the Infinite Abyss," Louis said.

"Wait a minute! I know we've shown up unannounced, but can we have a few chairs? Seriously, there's no need to do away with the simplest of pleasantries. I'm one for the pleasantries," DiVarion said, turning to the children with a smile. He was a good, kind man, Louis thought. Emyli was good in ways but not nearly as good as DiVarion. Louis didn't know much about her, but he knew that.

"Oh, of course. Follow me. I just got caught up in the moment," she said as she led them through the building. "Well, I'm Emyli FyneStory, as I'm sure DiVarion has told you. You there, who is the perfect shade of brown, what's your name?" Emyli said, looking at Louis.

"I'm Louis Proof. Nice to meet you," Louis said.

"Likewise, Mr. Louis Proof. iLone of course. You there, lovely girl with the golden blond hair, what's your name?"

"Cyndi Victoria Chase. Nice to meet you," Cyndi said.

"Likewise, Ms. Cyndi Victoria Chase. eNoli? Curious. Well, and you there, oldest of the bunch, may I ask what your name is?"

"Devon Alexander. Happy to meet you," Devon said, and unlike the other two, he extended his hand to the lovely Emyli FyneStory. They shook. Devon smiled, and Louis laughed because he saw his friend Brandon in Devon for a second.

"Mr. Devon Alexander, iLone. Happy to meet you also," Emyli said.

"How can you tell what we're supposed to be?" Louis asked.

"It's simple. You're marked in a way that most cannot see, but we on Midlandia can. You can't hide or disguise it; it's part of who you are like the color of your eyes. Unlike the eNoli or iLone, you can't ever be entirely one or the other, but you clearly have an affinity for one," Emyli explained.

"True, Emyli. Oh, this is for you. I came with the children but not empty-handed," DiVarion said as he handed her the disk.

"Oh my! Oh my! Is this what I think it is? I'm going to look at it right now. Follow me!" Emyli said. "The information on here is going to be a great addition to my book."

"What book is that? I bet it's fascinating," Devon said, winking.

"Yeah, does it have a name?" Louis asked, laughing once again as Devon reminded him of Brandon.

"May I have a copy?" Cyndi asked, eager to learn all she could.

"The name of my book is *The Book of Midlandia for the Non-Midlandian Mind* by myself, Emyli FyneStory, with contributions by DiVarion and Lynda Alonis. It is quite a great work. Thank you, Devon," Emyli said, smiling at him.

"How did you gather the information? This place is endless and not everyone is friendly," Cyndi said.

"Plenty of CE are friendly at least to DiVarion, me, and others like us. We have no problems with even the worst kinds. Both iLone and eNoli speak to me. iLone can be a bit pompous, but the eNoli—they're a hoot. They love to talk about themselves—a very self-centered and interesting bunch. I really like them," Emyli explained.

"What are the CE? The iLone and eNoli? I mean, what are they exactly?" Cyndi said. She was ready with questions this time, not like how she had been with Olivion.

"Well, they seem to be composed of the oldest elements: Dark Matter and Dark Energy. They cannot get sick or die. They have no form; therefore, they have all forms—or any form they choose. There's also something else; I just don't know what it is. It vexes me like something that's caught in your teeth that you can't get out. What I do know is that their actions influence all things . . ."

"What? They influence all things?" Devon asked.

"Their wars influence your world. And have you wondered why things seem familiar here but are far more complex and advanced? It's because Earth objects are just the tiniest echoes of what you've seen here," Emyli explained.

"How can that be?" Cyndi asked.

"You know, I was hoping I'd be able to ask you—"

"Wait, you said CE can't die. That's not true; I've seen them die," Louis interrupted.

"You're mistaken. They can't die. Their energy is sometimes dispersed during what's known as the Reazrion Ascension, and then many things can happen—like they can take on a new form but—"

"Energy cannot be created or destroyed," Devon said.

"Yes, Devon! It's the only truth that can be found here that corresponds to all other places," Emyli said.

"A universal truth," Cyndi said thoughtfully.

"Yes. Energy also provides a pathway between places. The Midland Isle is a gateway; its energy connects all places and things. What's more, the Midland Isle is the source of all of the energy throughout all things known and unknown, so of course everything is an echo of what you find here. You know, energy carried the purest part of you here; I guess you'd call it your *essence*." DiVarion said.

"What exactly is the Midland Isle?" Cyndi asked.

"You crossed the Gate and you met the Olivion. I can't believe *you* aren't educating *me*." Emyli sounded a bit frustrated as they reached their destination. The room had to be the entire height of the building. Neat shelves, seven inches high and shielded with glass, were set into the walls, and on those shelves were countless disks similar to the one DiVarion had given to Emyli. They were organized by color—all the blue ones were together, all the green ones were together, and so on. It was like a library of disks. At the center of the room was a silver object that looked like a narrow, elaborate cylindrical device.

Cyndi realized the room had been modeled in part after the library she'd abandoned to find Louis.

Emyli led them toward the silver object. "The most sacred secrets are those of the Olivion and the Midland Isle. Quite simply, they are the answers to everything that can be wondered. There are also iLone and eNoli secrets, some major, some much like the secrets you or I keep. There are a few important eNoli secrets. One is why Myth abandoned Olivion's Gate after searching for ages to find it. Another is . . . well—"

"Who crossed Olivion's Gate when Perilynn failed," Louis said, cutting her off. So much had happened that he'd forgotten to ask Perilynn. How could he be so stupid!

"You know less than I thought. I know who crossed the Gate, but you're close," Emyli said. "Events become part of the energy that exists in the place where they happen. Once that energy is gathered, this machine can read it." Emyli rested her hand on the silver object. She looked at Cyndi as if she were speaking to her alone.

"This is a very important instrument. It can read all types of energy. All energy holds a story." Emyli began to operate the machine. Once she'd turned it on, she placed the disk in its top, where it floated, glowing, as beams of light traced its surface. Then, all at once, the room was overtaken with images. They didn't seem like projections; they seemed real. There was Olivion's Gate and Myth. He looked perfectly imposing: a threat to be respected. Louis was surprised at how well the painting in DiVarion City had captured his likeness.

Everyone in the room could move throughout this space and see the image from any angle. There was Perilynn. There was Reign. Louis was shocked to see the being that Perilynn had said was named Trife, the one he'd encountered at his school. There were others too, trailing behind Myth, but Louis didn't recognize them. eLynori was nowhere in sight.

As Myth strode toward the Gate, Louis said to Cyndi, "That's Myth."

"The great Myth?" Cyndi walked up to his image. He moved with a confidence and strength that reminded her of her father. She could read a lot in his face. He'd been through much more than the war to reach this point. He'd also conquered something inside himself; perhaps that had allowed him to find the Gate.

She watched him reach Olivion's Gate, extend his hand, and touch it, palm open and fingers spread. The expression on his face altered. It was not one of fear. It was not one of disappointment. It was one of shock and amazement. Then it changed to deep understanding, and then to terror. He took off into the sky.

"See, he knows something. He didn't cross the Gate, but the Olivion revealed something to him," Emyli said to Cyndi.

"Louis, Cyndi, Devon, that one over there is Arminion. That's Galonious and that's Trife. Those are the eNoli who escaped. The other three are Reign, his brother Kyll, and Fury." DiVarion identified the CE as events continued around them.

"White!" Louis and Cyndi said together. Fury didn't look exactly like White, but the expression on his face, the way he moved, and the intensity in his eyes all reminded them of White when the other four had gone silent and gathered into him!

"Myth, are we supposed to follow?" Trife shouted.

"What is this?! There's no way I'm leaving this Gate! Open it!" Fury yelled to the other eNoli.

Louis watched Arminion and Perilynn charge for the Gate. They looked so young—thirteen or maybe fourteen. Before they could reach it, Reign and Kyll threw them from it.

That's how it happened. So who crossed the Gate? Louis wondered.

"You may have come this far, but you'll never see what's beyond the Gate," said Reign.

"Myth is gone and you have no favor with either of us. Be thankful that we're letting you live," said Kyll. He and Reign both touched Olivion's Gate, expecting it to open for them. But Olivion's Gate neither opened nor revealed any secrets; such was not for the likes of Kyll and Reign. It simply threw them back far more violently than they'd thrown Perilynn and Arminion.

If Olivion's Gate was not here for Myth or either of them,

Who was it here for?

Kyll and Reign were gathering themselves to try again when Trife shouted, "Look!"

Trife was pointing upward. He was the first to spy in the crystal blue midnight Midlandian sky the countless iLone closing in on them.

Cyndi glanced at Arminion. She realized that this was the perfect opportunity just as Arminion did, and she was frozen by the look in his eyes.

It was a determination that was not unlike her own.

It was a courage that was not unlike her own.

It was an abandonment of consequence that was not *like* her own.

That abandonment of consequence was the same she'd seen in Perilynn when he'd protected them. It was the same she'd seen in Louis when he'd left Olivion's Domain. She'd had to second-guess her actions and Louis had had to drag her with him when he jumped.

She wondered if she could master such a thing. No fear of consequence. No fear. It would give one a tremendous advantage . . .

Arminion ran to the Gate and placed his hand on it, and Olivion's Gate welcomed him. It was here for *him*. He looked beyond the Gate and saw a pathway he would ravage with destruction.

"I'll end this on my own," Arminion yelled, pulling two sparking, glowing blades from his back. They dropped low in his hands, tearing radiant streaks in the Midlandian ground as he ran through the Gate. Before anyone could follow, the Gate closed and disappeared.

"No! You can't be serious!" Cyndi said, realizing that she couldn't follow him.

Of course it was Arminion who crossed the Gate! Who else could it have been? Louis thought.

"Arminion! Don't leave me!" Perilynn shouted. Not only was his brother gone but Perilynn would never find the answers he sought. If Arminion were to destroy the Olivion, Perilynn would be left to wander aimlessly and exist pointlessly for an eternity.

Kyll and Reign cursed the fact that Arminion was the one who'd crossed the Gate. They wanted to take their frustration out on Perilynn but the iLone were a threat.

"No Gate. No Olivion. Then there's only war! I see thousands against us, so let's get to it!" Fury shouted. Some eNoli are driven solely by a lust for destruction. Reign, Kyll, and Fury happened to be three such. Destroying the Olivion alongside Myth would've been the ultimate kill; now tearing apart countless iLone would have to do.

They rushed into the sky. Kyll and Reign took the lead, spiraling around each other to create a flaming double helix. Fury flew in the center a few yards behind.

Louis was amazed. Their formation was spectacular and they were bent on carnage. They tunneled through the iLone. They

seemed unstoppable. Their attack was so small and well organized, it was hard for the iLone to target. Louis wished he could
fight like them.

Devon was not amused. All he saw were eNoli butchers who
didn't value life. Then Vivionya arrived. Fury broke ranks to seek
her out. He wasn't afraid to challenge a Favorite. He sped toward
her, and Vivionya raced toward him in her Alonis vehicle.

You really should not challenge a Favorite.

They swept past each other. They stopped in midair with
their backs to each other. Then Fury's head fell from his body. It
sparked and shimmered before dissipating.

"Whoa!" Louis said.

Only two eNoli remained in the sky. They continued to tear
iLone enemies apart until they saw that the great Fury had fallen.
Now they flew high above the battle. "You don't want us to leave
Midlandia, so we will forever be at war! When this one ends,
a new one will begin! If I fall, I'll return to continue this fight,"
Reign yelled.

"Kiyonrae! Vivionya! Spare your ranks to fight us alone," Kyll
challenged.

The challenge was accepted and all iLone, even the ones on
the ground battling Perilynn, Galonious, and Trife, stood down.

Vivionya and Kiyonrae's vehicles dismantled to become glowing, impenetrable body armor. The four CE met in battle, darting
through the sky as if engaged in a sacred dance of death. They

had only danced a few steps when Vivionya pierced Reign's form. He fell hard to the Midlandian ground. Kyll wouldn't be so lucky as to be injured. Kiyonrae used his Alonis to trap Kyll in an Alonis Capsule, and Kyll too dropped to the surface.

It seemed that only a miracle could save the remaining eNoli.

Cyndi watched as Olivion's Gate reappeared right where it had stood before. She waited as it opened. The person who exited wasn't the same as the person who'd entered, or at least he didn't seem to be. Arminion had gone in as a child and came out as an adult wearing an Alonis Medallion around his neck.

"He's a Favorite!" Cyndi said.

"What?" Louis turned his attention from the battle to Arminion.

"You all see what hangs around my neck! You all know what I've become! With that authority I say this war is over! The Olivion has created a new age: the age of the Alorion Treaty. Neither iLone nor eNoli will seek to leave Midlandia. I, on the part of all eNoli, accept this as law, and I will go unchallenged," Arminion said, shocking everyone, especially Galonious and Trife.

Vivionya and Kiyonrae instantly stood before Arminion. "So be it," Kiyonrae said.

"Fury is gone but what's to be done with Kyll and Reign?" Vivionya said.

Fury was a psychopath but a loyal friend as long as you laid the potential to create carnage in front of him. Arminion wished Fury had survived instead of Kyll and Reign. He was happy to see them in their present conditions. It served them right.

"There's no way for Kyll to be released, so you might as well throw him into the Infinite Abyss." Arminion smiled vindictively at Kyll.

"No! You traitor! You've betrayed us all! I swear you will fall, Favorite or not. If I pass, no matter how I return I will seek to end you," Reign shouted as Arminion turned to him.

"You protest for your brother? For that and for all other matters for which you believe I have betrayed the eNoli *you* may challenge me—that is if you can pull yourself together. I will make an example of you." Arminion looked deeply into Reign, and Reign shuddered. Arminion was in no way the child he'd easily thrown aside not long ago. He was to be feared even more than Myth.

"No one will touch or help him. If he lives, he lives. If he passes, he passes," Arminion said, then laughed.

Reign closed his eyes and lowered his head in resignation.

"Well, I guess that's all, then, so excuse me! Clear out of my way!" Arminion said to the hordes of iLone that stood in front of him. Because of the newly formed Alorion Treaty, they obliged. "Galonious, Trife, Perilynn, you will follow. Question me and you'll find out just how much I *have* changed."

Cyndi, Louis, and Devon could see that the energy that raged within Arminion was unique and dangerous. Arminion didn't put fear into Vivionya and Kiyonrae, but somehow it seemed as if they all should have bowed to him in awe. No one did such a thing, though the eNoli *would* follow and the iLone *would* let them pass.

"Perilynn, I know you seek answers. All in good time. You won't have them soon, but you'll have them before never. I will have much for *all* of you to do," Arminion told his brother, Galonious, and Trife. A devious smile crossed his face. The past faded away as the projection ended.

"It seems laws and treaties were all made to be shattered, and this one was no different. Arminion went beyond Olivion's Gate to destroy the Olivion. He returned as a Favorite and announced the Alorion Treaty. That was a complete three-sixty. That's why many question where his allegiance lies. No one can exit via the Midland Isle unless the Olivion wills it. I think Arminion knew the exact time when the Alorion Treaty would be broken and that he would be the one to break it. *He* started the Earthbound Celestial Wars. That's why all three of you are here," Emyli said.

"That was amazing! I had no idea that's what happened. Now I understand why Reign hates Perilynn and Arminion so much," Louis said.

"Yes, but the biggest mysteries are still unanswered," Emyli said.

"Why Myth fled and what was said between Arminion and Olivion to bring about the Alorion Treaty," Cyndi said.

"Yes, Cyndi, I believe that once those secrets are revealed, everything will make sense," Emyli said.

Devon recited:

"For each iLone and eNoli CE to leave
A child will endure a Midlandian quest for matching
power to receive.

If the children die before they return

They will go home robbed of all they have learned."

"I've never heard that. It's true, but who told you that? Was it the Olivion?" Emyli asked.

"No, it was Vivionya," Devon answered. Vivionya was a sweet memory.

"It's funny, there are three of you, and Cyndi is eNoli. This is all wrong. That would mean the iLone also have broken the treaty. There are so many things I don't understand. You were in the presence of the Olivion! How could you not have asked? Cyndi, how could you have squandered such an opportunity?" Emyli said.

"I wasn't ready. I couldn't think. But it's okay. We'll return. I know my time will come! I'm a Favorite. I'll find out everything I want and need to know. I'll get back to Olivion and then home," Cyndi said with an intensity that was chilling. Her Alonis began to glimmer, although it didn't glow as strongly as Louis's or Devon's had.

"I understand, Cyndi," Emyli said, smiling. Cyndi was exactly whom Emyli had hoped she'd be.

"So how do *you* plan on getting the answers that you seek?" Cyndi asked.

"Energy will tell me what I need to know, just as it's told me many other things." Emyli was staring at Cyndi's Alonis.

If her machine were to read the energy in that Alonis, it would tell her everything. It held secrets beyond Emyli's understanding.

The Alonis wouldn't work for her. She was not even a CE. Plus an Alonis can't be forcibly removed from its owner, and getting one from DiVarion was impossible. But Cyndi brought her new hope.

"What energy, Emyli?" Cyndi said.

"You were there. You could have gathered it: the energy behind Olivion's Gate in Olivion's Domain. That would hold so many answers. The secrets of Arminion would seem like nothing compared to that. Even beyond that, you have the energy of all energies, the energy of the Midland Isle, contained within your Alonis—"

"Emyli, how dare you speak of such things! You swore there'd be no talk of the energy within the Alonis. It's not for us. Some things are beyond our understanding. Need I remind you of what's happened to those of us who've tried? Do you think you'll fare any better? Do I have to remind you of your time with Avery Rush? Tampering with such energy in that manner is its own punishment," DiVarion said.

"Of course, DiVarion. I truly am sorry. Once again I've gotten carried away," Emyli said.

"It's time for us to go," DiVarion said.

"No, wait! Emyli, I have a question. We have to solve this riddle from the Olivion," Cyndi said.

"Actual words from the Olivion? Please let me hear them."

The three recited the riddle together again:

"I am everything.
All things come from me.

But there is only one thing I cannot be.

That is the key to everything."

"What is it that Olivion cannot be?" Cyndi asked.

Emyli thought about everything she'd come to know about Midlandia through her exhaustive research. Nothing came to mind.

"The Olivion is everything; there's nothing the Olivion cannot be. Are you sure that's what you heard. It sounds so—"

"It's simple but it's complicated. Such is the way of the Olivion," DiVarion said with a laugh.

"True. I don't know the answer, but if I figure it out, I'll send word to you."

"Wait. Where's the Infinite Abyss? How can I free Perilynn from it?" Louis asked.

"You must stay away from the Infinite Abyss. If you fall in, you'll never get out. I'm sorry, but your friend Perilynn is lost to you. You can't do anything to save him," Emyli said.

"I don't believe you. I know anything is possible here. This place has no limits and neither do I. So you know what? I will find him. And you can record that for everyone to see!" Louis's Alonis began to glow wildly. He grabbed it in his hands and looked at it wide-eyed. Then the FyneStory device began to vibrate like it never had before as it read the energy flowing from the Alonis.

It projected an undecipherable scene that was nonetheless harrowing. There was an absence that drove terror into everyone. DiVarion rushed Louis out of the room. Devon quickly followed. DiVarion was so distracted that he didn't realize Cyndi had remained. Emyli was amazed; she'd almost read Midland Isle energy right here. Never mind that, though. This was her chance to talk with Cyndi.

"Cyndi, we don't have much time. You can do what Louis just did and read the energy of your Alonis. I can't help it; I just have to know. It may be too much for me to handle, but you are a Favorite. The information is yours for the taking. You know that. What you learn, you can filter for me for the betterment of all." She strode quickly to the energy-reading device. It had immediately stilled when Louis left the room. Emyli pressed a button, and it became a small, slim disk the diameter of an Alonis.

"Did you watch me as I operated it? I saw that you did. Were you able to follow it, though?" Emyli said.

"Yes," Cyndi said.

"This will read the energy of the Alonis—the actual energy of the Midland Isle. You just saw it almost happen. You could unlock everything. So keep this safe and secret, because certain people won't think it appropriate for you to know more than what the Olivion tells you," Emyli said.

"Cyndi, I thought you were following us. We have to go back." DiVarion's voice sounded distant.

"It should attach to the back of your Alonis. No one will know you have it. Cyndi, these are dangerous times. In order for things to be made right, you'll need to know as much as possible. All I ask is that you tell me what you learn so that I can document it for everyone's sake. But you must use the energy reader on Midlandia, because I don't know how to send it home with you. Do you understand?" Emyli said.

Cyndi could see that if Emyli had an Alonis or even were able to operate one, she'd risk her life to learn that which should not be known. Cyndi finally had knowledge above all others right here in her possession. She could do so much with it.

"Yes, I understand, and I can keep a secret. I must go now," Cyndi said.

"Take these. They'll help explain your delay." Emyli gave Cyndi three copies of her book in progress.

"These will be useful to all three of you, but you'll have an extreme advantage. I *will* be in touch. Stay safe," Emyli said.

Cyndi left and in the hallway met DiVarion, still shaken and apologetic for leaving her behind in the confusion. The other two weren't far behind. Louis took the volume Cyndi proffered. "Thanks for the book."

"Don't thank me. Thank Emyli," Cyndi said.

"Did she give you anything else?" DiVarion asked as they walked back through the building.

Cyndi paused. "Of course not. What else could she give me?" If you'd listened closely enough, you could have heard the tainted lie in Cyndi's casual laugh. She felt as if she were about to vomit.

Cyndi, don't feel bad. You're eNoli.

Your secrets are your own.

Chapter Thirty

"Perilynn," a familiar voice called.

Perilynn coalesced into his humanlike form. He heard his name again, once as a whisper, then louder. There was no one there, but the voice was clear and seemed to reverberate both within the Alonis Capsule and outside, in the waters of the Infinite Abyss.

"Perilynn. You did well. It's just terrible that you were caught," the voice said. Perilynn recognized it. "Arminion? How are you here? Where are you?"

"Brother, I am with you of course." Arminion appeared as a shadowy phantom outside the capsule.

"How did I do well? You left me here and I betrayed you so that I could become a Favorite," Perilynn said without remorse.

"Oh no. You didn't betray me. You made it possible for the children to be delivered. They are marked now," Arminion said.

"They will return to destroy you all. How is that not betrayal?" Perilynn asked.

"I'm not afraid of the children. What's important to me is that one of the children is eNoli," Arminion said.

"How is that possible?" Perilynn asked.

"Timioosiyon of the iLone has also broken the treaty. He's on Earth now," Arminion said.

"If you, Timioosiyon, Galonious, and Trife have escaped Midlandia, where is the fourth child?" Perilynn asked.

"There is no fourth child as of yet. I've escaped but I have not set foot on another planet. The fourth child won't be spawned until I do."

"Why have you not—"

"Gone to Earth? Do not question me! My reasons and secrets are my own!" Arminion answered.

"So all that time I was protecting our hope? I should have been a hero. Instead I'm trapped here for eternity!" Perilynn said.

"A hero? Oh, brother, you'll be much more than that. This was always my plan. It was I who gave you the notion to protect the children and cross the Gate," Arminion said. "If you alone deliver the children to me and cross my Gate with them, I will praise you as a Favorite." The words sounded in a woman's voice—in the voice that Perilynn had assumed was the Olivion's.

"That was you? You mocked the Olivion?" Perilynn said, sparking with rage.

"Yes, it was. Did you think Olivion would speak to you when you are not a Favorite? What is more, do you think Olivion would utter the words 'praise you'?" Arminion said with a laugh. "But don't fret; it was all true. I may have delivered the message, but if you'd crossed, you would have become a Favorite. I never lied to you."

"Yes, but I'm *not* a Favorite."

"Perilynn, are you defeated? Is this the end for you? Don't you know there are countless ways for you to become a Favorite?"

"Stop! I'm here now. There's no chance of escape, so it doesn't matter! This is the ultimate torment."

"What? Am I not here talking to you? You think I'm just here for fun? Here to scorn you? . . . Oh, look at Perilynn; he screwed up and now he's on permanent punishment. I have no time for such things," Arminion said.

"Then why are you here?"

"I'm here to free you and send you on your new quest to become a Favorite. It's all you'd hope for it to be. I know the answers you seek. I understand how to be with you now and how to do this . . . ," Arminion said, then he raised a finger and did something that no other CE had ever been able to do. He tapped the capsule, leaving a glowing point of red light right in front of Perilynn's face. He had actually pierced the capsule.

"Do you truly desire to become a Favorite? Show me! Feed upon that desire and escape!" Arminion demanded.

Perilynn thought about becoming a Favorite, and suddenly he could see streams of energy all around him. They spoke to him in lost tongues and fueled him. Were they always there? he wondered. Had he been using them without realizing it? It didn't matter, as they were now truly his. He concentrated on the point left by Arminion. Rage, passion, and focus! Each grew stronger within him, and he turned into pure energy once again. He exploded outward. The capsule shattered. He was free within the Infinite Abyss.

Perilynn floated, reborn, in the water, feeling a new energy that surpassed even that which had allowed him to take on a Favorite and survive. He was ready for any task.

"Yes. See. I didn't ask you to follow me only to abandon you. Seek that light," Arminion said.

A crimson light illuminated the way out of the Abyss. As if propelled by booster jets, Perilynn and Arminion surged through the water. Perilynn passed others who'd been condemned to this Abyss, including Kyll. He paused. He wanted to destroy Kyll. Had Kyll not pushed him from the Gate, maybe he and Arminion could've crossed together so long ago. He wouldn't have had to undergo any of this.

Curse you, Kyll, Perilynn thought. He tried to destroy Kyll and the capsule but he couldn't. Perilynn clearly wasn't as strong as Arminion. He needed to become a Favorite.

Arminion was pleased to see that Perilynn's powers didn't equal his own. "Leave him," he whispered to Perilynn.

Perilynn nodded. What had he been thinking anyway? Why free Kyll from the worst fate imaginable? Just seeing Perilynn free in the Abyss would infuriate Kyll. That was a brilliant revenge. Perilynn threw Kyll a sarcastic smile and thrust himself away.

"How do I gain what I seek? Tell me!" Perilynn demanded. He and Arminion were racing after the crimson path, which twisted and looped in a way that no one would be able to figure out. This was the only way to escape the Abyss.

"It's very simple. You will become a Favorite by killing a Favorite. You'd have a nasty time killing a CE Favorite. Devon and Louis are iLone Favorites, but they aren't CE. They aren't even close to understanding their abilities, which may eventually surpass those of the CE."

"They're surely home by now. Am I to escape and destroy them on Earth? That sounds impossible. May I destroy Vivionya, Kiyonrae, or some other iLone Favorite?" Perilynn said.

"You think you could destroy a full-blown Favorite? Be my guest, but you'll fare much better if you help me by destroying one—or both—of the iLone children who haven't yet laid claim to their powers and abilities. And the children are still here! Find and destroy the iLone children, protect Cyndi Victoria Chase, and guide her home. She is eNoli and crucial to my plans," Arminion said.

"That's too much to ask. I'll find myself against the same odds that sent me to the Abyss inside that capsule," Perilynn said.

"No. You won't be alone in any of this, because the eNoli will support you."

"Why would the eNoli follow me? They sought to destroy me and they'll try even harder upon my return."

"That was all part of my plan. Just believe in my words and do what I ask," Arminion said. "You have the ability to do something I've never been able to accomplish. You'll be able to unify all eNoli CE. They don't need to know that I freed you. You will seem all-powerful and gain their obedience from respect not fear. I told them a leader will make himself known in my absence. You never assumed such a role; that's why I always wanted you. I'll ensure that they dare not deny you."

Arminion's plan was ingenious. Perilynn could never have come up with it himself. No sooner had he agreed to it than Arminion sped ahead.

Perilynn finally broke the surface and hovered above the water. He was in a depressing place. The sky appeared unforgiving in its gray-black darkness. On the horizon it met an endless dark ocean whose surface was perfectly still as if it were an obsidian table and not water at all. Bewildered by the water's dead appearance, Perilynn touched his hand to it. That was a mistake, as ribbons of murky wetness grabbed at him, trying to pull him under even as he tried to shift form. Perilynn struggled, and the water grew more aggressive. It rose around him as if it were a tornado wanting to carry him deep again. And Arminion was gone . . .

A demonic female face formed within the water. Cursing Perilynn, it remained in front of him even as the water spun. It was about to swallow him whole when, powered by an unrelenting passion to succeed, he snapped the water's grip and rocketed straight up into the sky. He still had no idea where he was, but his desire would lead him to his destination. He would seek out the very eNoli that wanted to destroy him.

Chapter **Thirty-one**

Perilynn stood alone at Lefton Rack wearing robes that hid his identity. Lefton Rack seemed to be welcoming him back as it expanded to its greatest extent, draped itself with platinum and gold ornaments, and grew countless rows of seats. Its windows had battles of eNoli lore and legend faintly etched within them. It was as if the Rack was now finally what it wanted to be: a grand hall fit for a king.

The soon-to-be sort-of king waited in the center on an elegantly crafted golden emblem of the eNoli. All he needed now was his audience.

He focused on his desires and pushed his palms out. A glowing mist rose from the emblem. He would stand there no more. He disappeared, only to return seconds later with hordes of eNoli. He hadn't called them; rather he had physically pulled them here. He'd forced them to revert to their natural energy forms and set them along an energy stream leading to Lefton Rack. After about seven trips, Lefton Rack became titanic and was filled. Even those like SysRic, who preferred the water, were present. Only eLynori and the Lost were missing. Perilynn wouldn't call upon them even in these monumental circumstances.

Such a feat had never happened before, and the eNoli shook with bewilderment as they took on their humanlike forms. A few moments passed before they realized where they were. Perilynn stood silent in the center of Lefton Rack. The emblem now rose ten feet off the ground so the thousands of eNoli could see him in the round.

This is serious. I really brought them here! Perilynn thought. What power he mysteriously had at his command!

All battling parties were present and they might have leaped back into their civil war if they hadn't been so busy trying to figure out how they'd been brought here and who the mysterious form in the center of Lefton Rack was.

"Who has called us here! Reveal yourself!" Holliston said.

"As you wish." With those words Perilynn dropped his hood.

The crowd roared. Many of them had seen Perilynn sent into the Infinite Abyss, trapped in an Alonis Capsule.

"Uh-oh," said aZRon as he started to creep out of Lefton Rack unnoticed.

"What trick is this? Who has taken on the form of Perilynn and called us here?" Holliston said.

"I assure you, this is no trick. This is my own form. I *am* Perilynn. I have broken that which cannot be broken and I have escaped that which cannot be escaped. But I haven't called you here. Oh no. I have *brought* you here."

"There's no escaping the Abyss. There's no escaping the capsule. I know not who you are, but for assuming the identity of a traitor, you shall fall!" Holliston said.

"I shall fall? Never! I challenge the strongest, those who opposed my brother, those who support my brother; those who sided with Reign and started a civil war. Act on this—I challenge every last one of you to attack me! Do it together. You will fail. Come on!"

Am I serious? What am I doing? Perilynn thought, but just like when he'd broken the capsule, a power boiling inside him made him feel invincible.

There was no time for misgivings. The eNoli leaped from their seats, charging at Perilynn. They reverted to pure energy for the attack, but none could come within a foot of him. They swirled around, frustrated, until they realized that they couldn't touch the new Perilynn, let alone harm him. There wouldn't even be a fight.

Oh yes, there would be. They couldn't reach him but he could reach them.

Perilynn charged at Reign and punched him in the face to send him rocketing back. Hordes retreated, clearing a path for him to bounce off a row of seats and hit the wall.

Perilynn did the same thing to Helenia, Octavio, and all those whom he knew had grievances with his brother but didn't have the heart to challenge him.

Retaking his position on the raised emblem, Perilynn focused his wishes. Lefton Rack repaired itself. Then Perilynn called those he'd attacked to stand before him. No one moved. They hadn't seen such a threat since Myth (who'd actually done worse things), and he was long gone.

Perilynn looked down, and laughter filled Lefton Rack. It was coming from Perilynn but it wasn't Perilynn's voice. When he looked up again, all fell backward in shock.

"Arminion!" They shouted as they saw Perilynn shape-shift into his brother.

"We knew it was impossible for Perilynn to have escaped from the capsule and the Abyss," Holliston said.

"Then you know nothing! This is indeed Perilynn who just defeated you. I'm simply paying a visit. My powers are far beyond any you can imagine. Listen well because I won't stay long. I have more important things to do. I will ask you a few questions and I want you all to answer me. Who challenged both eNoli and iLone and defeated you all to reach Olivion's Gate?" Arminion said.

There was no answer. "I said 'Answer me'!" he roared, shattering every window in Lefton Rack.

"Perilynn," they finally responded as the glass reconfigured itself.

"Who destroyed an impenetrable Alonis Capsule?" Arminion said.

"Perilynn," they answered for the second time.

"Who escaped from the Infinite Abyss?" Arminion said.

"Perilynn," they answered for the third time.

"Who just challenged every last one of you and triumphed? None of you could even get close!"

"Perilynn," they answered for the fourth time.

"Yes, Perilynn! Are those undeniable feats not proof of his

power? I told him to challenge you all as a test of his worth and he's done it. I demand to hear the voice of the person who can dispute his supremacy!"

There was no answer.

"Many of you do not follow me willingly. Some of you question my secrets and the path that led me to become a Favorite. But you dare not question anything that my brother has done!" Arminion said.

"Lord Arminion, I don't doubt his supremacy, but may I ask a question?" Holliston said.

"Lord Arminion, I like that. So yes, you may ask a question," Arminion said.

"Why did you have him deliver the children to the Olivion? Won't they only seek to defeat you, Galonious, and Trife?" Holliston said.

"Do you think I am not strong enough as both a Favorite and an eNoli? I fear *nothing*! I keep many secrets that are my own to keep and you shall not question me. But I will reveal that one of the children is—" Arminion separated himself from his brother's energy. Perilynn was once again himself.

"eNoli," Perilynn said, completing Arminion's sentence.

"How is that possible? There are only three children," said many voices in the crowd.

"The iLone have also broken the treaty," Perilynn said.

"Why did you keep that a secret? That's greatly in our favor!" Holliston said.

Why did I do anything? Why was it a secret? Perilynn thought. His brother had manipulated him, but he wasn't going to tell them that.

"Would any of you have been cautious enough to deliver all of them to the Olivion so they could be marked? What would have happened if you'd destroyed the wrong child? I underwent the ultimate trial and passed," Perilynn said.

No, you only want to be a Favorite.
But there may be hope for you yet.

"There should have been four children, not three. If one is eNoli, then we've been lied to and one eNoli hasn't gone to Earth, or any other place for that matter. Does Arminion keep secrets or tell lies? Which is it, Perilynn? Are your brother's goals different from ours? This is why I challenged all who followed him! I was right!" Reign said.

"Then do not follow him. Don't trust him if you cannot. He visited but he isn't here. He isn't me. I have no secrets. I made it to Olivion's Gate twice. Who else has done that? I challenged all of you and thousands of iLone and was only stopped by an iLone Favorite. I destroyed the Alonis Capsule and escaped the Infinite Abyss. I brought you all here. I fended you off when you attacked me en masse. I tell you to follow me!

"I seek that which has never been done. I seek unity among all of us under my guidance. You need that unity to escape this place. What say all of you?" Perilynn said.

There was silence. Then, one by one, they raised their glowing hands. It was a unity they'd never seen. They were determined to escape from Midlandia.

There was one holdout: Reign. He looked at the child he'd thrown from the Gate, the brother of the one he hated. There was still hate in his being but he couldn't help respecting Perilynn.

I will have my day, but this is not it, Reign thought. So eventually, silently, he raised his hand.

"Thank you. This is a new day and a new age!" Perilynn said to the loudest cheers ever heard on Midlandia.

"There are three children and none of them has gone home. Two are iLone. We must ensure the safety of the eNoli child, Cyndi Victoria Chase. She is your key to exodus. The iLone will seek to destroy her. We will go to war with the iLone to grant her safe passage home," Perilynn shouted as the eNoli once again cheered uncontrollably. This was a plan they could all support. It was not wrapped in secrecy. It was simple: Go to war to send the eNoli child home. Done deal. Case closed.

"Do not harm any of the children. I want them all brought to me so that I can personally deal with them. I will say it again: Do not harm a single one of them or I will rain my power down on you," Perilynn said.

At that moment Lefton Rack began to reconfigure itself. Its roof blew right off and a sleek black, winding staircase built itself in front of them. An intricate pattern in the steps allowed light to shine through. The staircase led upward to a beautiful castle fortress hovering in the sky. This was a place of Midlandian legend. It hadn't been seen in an eon. Olivion's Gate and Domain were perfect in their simplicity; this was perfect in its complexity.

A pure smile crossed Perilynn's face. All he'd been through seemed worthwhile. His destiny was even now being grandly written. He had never objected to Midlandia as so many of his kind did. In his eyes, Midlandia had a way of working things out.

> Very good, little brother, but make sure you
> remember who fed you your power.

Chapter **Thirty-two**

Back in DiVarion City, DiVarion showed everyone where they'd be staying. Louis was glad to have some time to thumb through the book he'd been given. He knew exactly what he wanted to look up.

DiVarion led Cyndi to her room first. It was even more spacious than the one she had at home. A meticulously crafted, ivory white desk stood on the far side of the room. It had no drawers, only a matching ivory white chair. Drawn to it, Cyndi sat and thought about what to do next as DiVarion led the boys their rooms.

Oh my God. There was a mirror! Was there a place to take a bath? Oh, yes. She'd been through so much, she'd forgotten herself. She'd never before gone a day without at least taking a shower. Jumping into the ocean to save Louis didn't count.

Looking into the mirror, she saw that her face glowed and she suddenly seemed beautiful. She'd always known she was pretty, but now she was taken aback. Either every flaw she usually saw in her face was gone or she was now comfortable with it all. She couldn't tell which.

This room reminded her of home. She missed hanging out with Jason. She missed her father's jokes, which were actually funny. She even missed the verbal tussles she got into with her mom. She missed Kimber Lime and her delectable desserts. She missed reading in her grand tub.

Hey, what about a bath and reading? She could relax with the Emyli FyneStory book. She was about to take her clothes off when she grabbed her Alonis. Wait. She had something to do that outranked her desire to take a bath. She had to try to activate the FyneStory device. . . .

Louis was not concerned with anything but that book.

There were so many things inside it: names, stories, facts, legends.

But he wanted to know . . . there, he'd found it.

eLynori of the Vile

eLynori was Myth's mistress and second in command. No female in the history of Midlandia could rival the destruction she wrought. She was the only one who could reprimand Myth and call him to task.

eLynori and her followers, who would come to be known and the Lost, were separated from Myth right before he reached Olivion's Gate. When Myth left and they couldn't find him, they went mad and isolated themselves from the other eNoli. No CE dared seek them out.

Wow! That's serious, Louis thought as he continued to flip through the book.

* * *

Devon looked at the Alonis around his neck and wondered how he could use its powers. He had no idea.

Gazing at the city through the window in his room, Devon thought of the similarly inventive JunkYard JunkLot. When he'd discovered it, he felt guilty. How dared he enjoy anything when his family was in turmoil? He didn't deserve fun.

His visit to Midlandia changed everything, though. Maybe he could be happy again. Devon's Alonis began to glow; however, Devon didn't notice.

He hardly dared think of being happy, so he began to flip through the FyneStory book until he came across a section on Flying Entities. There were five, multicolored and majestic, and each had a name. He stared at them for a long time. To be able to fly and be free . . .

Cyndi removed the disk from the back of her Alonis and placed it in the center of the room. It took on its original form. Cyndi turned it on.

What would her Alonis reveal? It glowed and lights began to circle around it. Carefully, she removed the Alonis from her neck and placed it in the center of the device. This was going to be awesome! She wished Louis were here to see this. Louis . . .

Oh no!

The Alonis went dark and the device collapsed again into a simple metallic disk.

Cyndia stared at them, disbelieving. Then, slowly, she returned the Alonis to her neck and reattached the device to it. She sat, as still and lightless as her Alonis stone, for a long time. Here she was, safe and protected in DiVarion City in a spacious room provided just for her. And she'd lied to DiVarion and her friends. Most important, she'd lied to Louis. If it were her, not Perilynn, who needed to be rescued, Louis would save her. Deceit and dishonesty were the perfect way to show gratitude for generosity and friendship. She wanted the secrets and the power they'd bring, but there were none. She'd betrayed trust and friendship for nothing. Her dad always told her to be unashamed when lying to enemies but not to your friends. When you start easily lying to your friends, you take the turn in the road to become a monster.

With that in mind, she went to visit Louis. When she knocked, he called, "Come in!" His room was as big as hers and just as special. He had the lights off and was lying on his back, playing with an elaborate racetrack that was hanging near the ceiling. It had loops and tunnels and things she'd never seen before. The track was clear, so the cars could be seen from below. It wasn't her sort of thing but it looked like fun.

"Louis . . . um . . . I want to talk to you," Cyndi said.

"Hey, Cyndi, I was going to come see you. I was thinking about Perilynn. That book doesn't say how we can find the Infinite Abyss. We'll have to wait on more info. And can you believe no one sleeps here? I'm not tired at all. It's weird. So what's up?"

"We'll save him, don't worry. And you're right. I don't even remember what it feels like to get tired. Uhhh . . . you know when you all left Emyli and I stayed behind? She gave me something."

"She gave you one of those devices, didn't she?" Louis said.

"How did you know?" Cyndi asked.

"I didn't. You just told me," Louis said.

"Okay, smartstuff. Very good. I don't feel right about lying about it, not after all we have been through. We're friends . . ."

She lay on the floor next to Louis to see the racetrack from his viewpoint.

"Happy to be considered a friend. You know, I have one of these in my room back home, but this is way better. Come on, try it," Louis said.

"Try it? Sure, why not? I like racing and cars, just not like this."

"Are you serious? You like cars and racing? Okay, let's race," Louis said as he nudged her with the controller for a second vehicle. Cyndi's car was red while Louis's was blue. The cars could run on the underside of the track. They ran all around the room through loops.

"This is fun. I bet you like NASCAR," Cyndi said.

"Yeah! Hey, I race my own radio-controlled cars at home. What do you do for fun?" Louis asked, realizing this was their first relaxed conversation.

"I read, study, and plot the downfall of corrupt people so that I can extort them," Cyndi said.

"Really? You do that?" Louis asked.

"Yes, but only one corrupt person actually. Everything I've done so far is a starter kit. I figure I'm ready for something big. I can't believe I'm telling you this," Cyndi said.

"You can't believe it? After what we've been though? We've

been this close to death, you and me." Louis pinched his fingers together.

Louis's Alonis was glowing. Cyndi's wasn't. She knew that she had Louis totally relaxed and off guard. If she asked, she'd be able to get him to use his Alonis to operate her machine. It would be so easy and she would . . . betray a friend.

"You know, Louis, you have to be careful. You're so nice, people might try to take advantage of you," Cyndi said.

"Thanks for saying so, but I'm from East Orange, New Jersey, and we don't play that. I'm always on guard and usually a good judge of character," Louis said.

"You are? How would you judge me?"

"That's easy. People think you're one thing, but you're another."

"In what way?" Cyndi asked.

"Come on, Cyndi. Look at where we are and what we've done. Do you think that anyone could imagine what you're capable of? On a different note, do you know how much flak I get because I like NASCAR? Like I'm some sort of alien. And my favorite channel is the Food Network. Well, I used to be kind of chubby, so that's not really a stretch," Louis said as he made his car go underneath the track so it could pass Cyndi's.

"Louis, you know that's the key to what I do."

"What do you mean?"

"I know a few things about NASCAR, and I bet you don't know many people you can talk NASCAR with. In a way, even though you have tons of friends, that NASCAR thing makes you a bit like an outsider. If I popped up and was able to talk NASCAR, I'd seem like a glowing ray of sunshine to you. I could get you to tell me anything about yourself because you'd think we had so much in common. You have to find that special thing; it's research, perception, and manipulation." Cyndi said.

"Oh yeah? I just talk to people because I like to talk and I like learning about people and making friends."

"I know, Louis. I don't see you manipulating people like I have. I don't do it to everyone. I tried when I first got here, but they still strapped me to that machine. Back home I've only done it to people who deserve it, like my principal. He's a dirtbag."

"I like my principal. Ali Brocli—now that's a dirtbag! I didn't do it on purpose, but I pushed him into a dirty toilet. You know, I feel bad about that, but that's what he gets for putting his hands on people that don't want hands on them," Louis said, speaking of the middle school terror and the last time he'd seen him.

"Ali Brocli? Is that a real person?" Cyndi said.

"Yeah, Ali Brocli is real. Anyway, why do you learn all that stuff about people and how they tick? I mean, I'd think you'd never be at ease with anyone," Louis said.

Cyndi thought about why. No one had ever asked her why. Jason knew how she did it, and since he knew her better than anyone, maybe he knew the why too. She'd never considered it. As the lights of the cars swept around the room, she came to a conclusion.

"My dad is a powerful person and he got there through hard work and by doing some things he might not be proud about. He taught me that business is like war. You analyze your opponent and attack.

"It's easier since I've been here. I don't have to study people; I'm beginning to feel things. I could feel that there's something a little twisted about Emyli FyneStory. She's not superdark but she could get into some trouble. You aren't like that. You do dumb stuff but not for the wrong reasons," Cyndi said.

"That's funny. I could feel there was good stuff about her. And DiVarion is like a saint; he's a really good guy. You . . . you're great too. I can see it.

"You know what? What are we doing in here? This is crazy. We should search this place for info and for fun. Are you up for a DiVarion City adventure?" Louis asked.

"Actually, I'd love to go on a DiVarion City adventure," Cyndi said.

"Then let's get Devon and have one." Louis put the controllers away, and they set off. They were going to take Devon with them whether he wanted to go or not.

Chapter Thirty-three

After all the talk of the "something" that was coming and the responsibility that our three were supposedly supposed to carry, they found that they *needed* some fun.

There was so much to do within the many lands of the DiVarion City:

They played in snow, sliding down and winding about great mountains.

They hopped from singing stone to singing stone under clouded orange skies to reach what looked like an Aztec temple.

They wandered through white rooms filled with multicolored books that Louis had to literally carry Cyndi away from so the fun could continue.

They explored lands filled with eLebrions that seemed happy to meet them.

They ran through dark rooms where lights frolicked with them, creating bridges and tunnels for them to dash over and through until they found an exit.

There were so many different lands here, brimming with spectacles beyond even a CE's imagination. They could have explored forever. They might have, except . . .

* * *

The three quieted down as they neared a conference room, where they could hear serious adult voices buzzing. Lynda Alonis was speaking with another woman, whom the kids had never seen before. There was also an unfamiliar man dressed in white. Cyndi recognized the stylish Avery Rush. And Orenci was spinning in a chair as if he were a child.

". . . but I've never seen anything like it. The child has a capacity for love like no other person in existence. It's beautiful . . . ," the unknown woman said.

"Yes, the same can be said for the other child and knowledge, but will it be enough?" said Avery.

"That's the question. This is an enemy like no other. Whatever it is, it's actually hurting Midlandia," said Orenci.

"Everything rests upon these children, and I suspect they'll have to sacrifice much for there to be a future. I can't even imagine the magnitude of the trials they will face," Avery said.

"Let's not forget that one of the children is eNoli, and it's just not their nature to—" said Lynda.

"Even now that child is conflicted—" the unknown man in white interrupted.

Orenci caught sight of the children and smiled. The kids knew they shouldn't be eavesdropping and fled from Orenci's sight.

They were still running when Devon hauled his friends out of sight behind a corner. Kiyonrae was walking purposefully, holding something that looked like a head encased in a glass con-

tainer. It wasn't like the capsule Perilynn was in because it had a
black bottom that latched, so it clearly opened.

"Let's follow him," Devon said.

"He's trying to kill Cyndi and now he's carrying a head and
you want to follow him?" Louis said.

"Yeah, we should see what he's up to. You know, keep your
friends close—"

"—and enemies closer," Cyndi finished. Her father hadn't
raised her to cower in the presence of those trying to intimidate
her. He may not have had in mind people trying to kill her when
he instilled that value, but it would come in handy now and in
the future.

"Okay, I'm up for it, so let's move," Louis said.

They followed Kiyonrae through the city, control center, and
finally to DiVarion's residence. They stood outside the closed
door, wondering what to do. Should they try to sneak in? That
second floor window might open . . . but should they be doing
this at all?

Now the door opened slightly on its own. How convenient.
As DiVarion had said, things have a way of working themselves
out here. They slunk through the hallways until they came upon
Kiyonrae and DiVarion; then they found a spot out of sight for
eavesdropping.

"Talk or you'll never see the rest of your body. I'll sink you in
the Infinite Abyss and—" Kiyonrae shook the glass container.

"Your threats mean nothing, Kiyonrae! It seems the Abyss
is not such a curse any longer. Perilynn has escaped. He has

returned." Louis almost made a noise but held himself in check. Could the head be telling the truth? It was gloating. Louis recognized it as the head of the CE who had forced the others away from Louis in the Midlandian Ocean.

"SysRic, you are lying. The Abyss is inescapable. The Alonis Capsules are unbreakable," DiVarion said calmly.

"I speak nothing but the truth. Perilynn has escaped by breaking the unbreakable. He has claimed the position of our rightful Midlandian leader. He will ensure that the eNoli child returns home safely! He's looking for the children and has ordered that they be brought to him unharmed. Kiyonrae, turn me around so I can look at you while I say this," SysRic said.

Kiyonrae twisted the head's container and held it at eye level.

"Yes, Kiyonrae, we know you violated the treaty. The eNoli child will bring about our exodus from this place! Midlandia is shrieking, and it's a sign of what's to come. Perilynn is not a Favorite, yet he must be more powerful than you. I think the Olivion may be turning the tide in our favor!" It seemed as if the volume and tone of SysRic's voice should break the glass.

"Only a Favorite can match a Favorite. You won't forget that!" Kiyonrae said, his hands and Alonis glowing. He made a fist and pulled his arm back to strike the glass.

"Okay, that's enough. Let him rejoin with his body. Thank you, SysRic. Kiyonrae, the next time I say, 'Play nice,' please do so," DiVarion said.

Cyndi, Louis, and Devon didn't need to hear any more. They snuck out of the house.

"Yes! Perilynn's free and looking for us!" Louis said.

"Great, let's find him and go home," Devon said.

"We have to borrow one of those ships. I remember the way," Cyndi said

She was about to lead them to the hangar when she heard a voice. *Cyndi, to your left. The pathway to your left . . .* It was DiVarion.

She didn't see him anywhere, but there was a pathway to the left. Leading her friends down it, she reached a door. It opened to reveal a large room that was inviting and cozy. It had a lush burgundy and gold carpet and deep, rich cherrywood walls. On the walls were three paintings:

One of Louis.
One of Devon.
One of Cyndi.

They were stunned by their likenesses. The Painters had to have done these. Obviously this is what the Painters had taken time out to observe them for.

There was something else even more impressive and unexpected in this room, though: an aircraft. It had three seats, almost as if it had been built just for them. They climbed aboard.

"Cyndi, how did you know to find this place?" Louis asked, looking at the plush cockpit.

"Wouldn't you like to know? I'm driving or flying—whatever." Cyndi had paid close attention to DiVarion and knew what to do to open the outer doors. "Okay, guys, hold on. Or don't . . . ," she said cheerfully as they lifted off and left DiVarion City.

DiVarion proudly watched them trail across the night sky. He would tell no one of their abrupt departure. Their path was their own; it didn't lie in his city. They each had an Alonis and a bit more knowledge. That was the best he could do for them . . . for now.

Chapter **Thirty-four**

The three were on their own, traveling across the Midlandian night sky.

"I'll tell you one thing. I would have gone into that Infinite Abyss but I'm glad we won't have to," Louis said.

"Perilynn escaped it, so it can't be as bad as they say it is. I wonder why everyone is afraid of it," Devon said.

"I don't know, but our boy Perilynn is safe and in charge," Cyndi said.

"Do you hear that?" Devon said.

"Hear what?" Louis asked.

"Listen," Devon said.

It sounded like a wind chime was ringing on and off as if it was being rocked by a lazy midnight tide.

Wind chimes? Maybe . . ., Devon thought.

A Flying Entity rose into view. It was the most beautiful, unique being they'd ever seen. A mesmerizing midnight black, winged, and serpentine, it flew with astonishing grace. They had the sense that it was aware of them and meant them no harm.

"I read about them in the book," Devon said, realizing that he'd left his book back in DiVarion City.

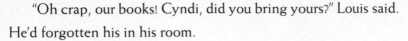

"Oh crap, our books! Cyndi, did you bring yours?" Louis said. He'd forgotten his in his room.

"Yeah, I never took it out of my pocket," Cyndi said.

"The book said these Entities don't mean any harm, and when they're near, you can hear wind chimes. They can guide you to hidden Midlandian locations. Let's follow it," Devon said.

"Are you sure?" Louis asked.

"Why not? We have no idea where we're going and in this place you have be lucky to get somewhere. So I guess this is our luck," Cyndi said.

It made sense. If this wasn't a sign that Midlandia was offering them help, they didn't know what would be. So they followed the Entity over the seemingly endless ocean. It flew in elaborate patterns, twisting and winding agilely in the sky. This amazed Louis and he wanted in on the action.

"Can you do that?" he asked Cyndi.

"Do what?" she asked.

"Do that. Fly like it's flying. If you can't, I'll try . . . ," Louis said.

"Why should I? We're doing just fine," Cyndi said.

"Oh, come on. What are you holding back for?" Louis asked.

"Yeah, Captain, what are you holding back for?" Devon said.

What am I holding back for? This is safe compared to other things we've done. So why the heck not? Cyndi tested her driving skills and managed to follow the Entity's patterns flawlessly. Louis yelled enthusiastically. He always enjoyed a ride. The twists! The turns! The loops! It was like a roller coaster. But he sure wished *he* was driving.

After a few minutes the Entity stopped. It floated in the air, flapping its wings to create wind gusts that disrupted the water.

"What's it doing?" Louis asked.

"I don't know," Devon answered.

"Look!" Louis shouted, pointing at the window.

A perfectly round patch of land was rising from the ocean. It was about eighty feet in diameter. The Entity lowered itself and rested upon it. It stared directly at the children, beckoning with its wings, waving them back and forth as if saying, "Come on." With poise Cyndi landed the ship and they all got out.

"I'm going to say hello," Devon said. He felt an inexplicable connection to the Entity as he approached. It said no words; it just stood on its hind legs, waiting for Devon. Louis and Cyndi were fixated on Devon's actions until they heard sounds coming from the ship.

"What the heck?" Louis said as the ship lifted into the sky, stranding them.

"I didn't even know it could do that on its own," Cyndi said.

Devon didn't react. He knew this was the start of something epic. "You have something important planned for us, don't you?" Devon asked the Entity.

"Yes, you do. Don't you?" Louis could feel it too.

"I sure hope so," Cyndi said.

The Entity flapped its wings only once, and it was lifted high into the sky. It did a graceful back flip before plummeting head-first toward the ground.

"Wow!" Louis said. Cyndi tried to pull him out of the way just as Brandon had during the first trip to the JunkYard JunkLot, but he resisted.

"There's nothing to be afraid of. Watch," Devon said, holding his ground. He was directly in the Entity's path and saw peace in its eyes as it sped toward him.

Devon raised his arm, hand open, fingers wide. The Entity was on course to meet Devon's hand, but it stopped about a foot and a half away, hovering head down in the air.

"Come here. Something's about to happen. Don't be afraid," Devon said. Louis and Cyndi strode over to stand on opposite sides of Devon. They too raised their hands to the Entity.

"See," Devon said as the Entity hovered above them, ever so gracefully flapping its wings. Its body began to shed small flecks of light over the teens. It was a wondrous sight. The children looked into its eyes and nothing else seemed to matter. The light fell faster as the Entity flapped its wings more quickly. Now the Entity dropped down, turning into millions of particles of blue light from its head to its tail, falling like Celestial rain.

Devon could see that the island was greatly expanding and the light was creating elaborate writing everywhere as it hit the ground, but the writing disappeared almost immediately.

"What just happened?" Cyndi asked.

Louis knelt to examine the terrain. Then he shrugged his shoulders and put his hands in the air with a clueless look on his face.

"So how did you know to do that? Was it good or bad?" Cyndi asked Devon.

"All I knew was that it wasn't gong to hurt us," Devon answered. Something caught his eye. There were three symbols left on the ground. He quickly walked over to them, and when he reached the one that he sensed was for him, writing became visible. He was shocked that he could read it.

*Devon Alexander, the first to see
what is to be shown.*

*Your destiny lies ahead
on this path for you alone.*

"Hey, this is crazy! I can read this writing. Even my name's here," Devon shouted. "It says this is my path, but it doesn't go anywhere. It just leads off the edge of the land."

Louis and Cyndi could both see the writing but couldn't make out a single word. When they got closer it disappeared.

"Where'd it go?" Louis asked.

Before Devon answered, he thought about what had changed. It was simple. "I think it's still here; walk away."

Cyndi and Louis retreated and the writing came back.

"It did say the path was only for me. Hey, try standing on one of the other symbols," Devon suggested.

Louis and Cyndi ran to a symbol and stood on it. Nothing happened.

"Not the same one," Devon said. Louis ran to the other symbol. Still nothing.

"Louis, switch with me," Cyndi said.

"Okay," Louis said as he ran past Cyndi to the other symbol.

Writing reappeared everywhere, and the island's outer rim began to glow as a mist flecked with specks of light rose from it. The mist flowed upward as far as they could see into the dark, steel blue Midlandian night, then began to spin, brightening the teens' faces with every color imaginable.

"Here we go again!" Louis said as the light streamed outward and its wake created a full-blown city in every direction. No, actually what it did was *reveal* the city. It seemed ancient and forgotten, yet it was as everything on Midlandia is: perfect. The nearly complete darkness suited it. Mischievous shadows outlined the buildings and pathways, making them foreboding and inviting at the same time.

For each child there was a path of words written in pulsing light that only they could read.

Louis Proof, so far you have come
with still so far to go.

Your truths lie ahead for
you to meet solo.

Cyndi Victoria Chase, so far from
that which you call home.

Your desires lie ahead
on this path for you alone.

"I guess we're each supposed to follow our own path," Louis said.

"Ya think?" Cyndi said sarcastically.

"Oh, Cyndi, I tell ya, one of these days . . . one of these days . . . I'm going to have a good comeback. Just wait!" Louis said.

Cyndi just smiled.

Devon let his eyes drift down his path. He started to say something, then stopped.

"All right, then I guess we do this," Cyndi said.

They looked at one another, hoping it was not for the last time. Cyndi and Devon were understandably hesitant to move forward. Louis, on the other hand, thought that after jumping from Olivion's Domain this would be easy. He grinned at his friends and set off on his solo adventure.

Chapter **Thirty-five**

Louis Proof's path had a bit more light than the others, courtesy of his Alonis. It wasn't a full-blown beacon, but its radiance helped.

The blue words written in the darkness were more than just words. They came with the feelings of the story they told: Louis Proof's story, the summation of a best friend, if the world ever needed one.

He'd be responsible so his brother didn't have to be all of the time.

He'd get into trouble but never too much trouble.

He'd work hard and save his money.

He'd sometimes bend the truth so that it was a new truth but still the truth.

He'd fight for you if you needed someone to stick up for you.

He'd loan you money for the bus if you ever got stuck.

He'd tell you that your fly was undone when everyone else would laugh behind your back.

He'd invite you to meet his friends if you were new to school.

He'd let you borrow his favorite video game if you were a nice person.

He'd try to make his dad proud.

He'd see the good in you when others wouldn't.

He'd cheer you on when you forgot how to cheer for yourself.

He'd risk everything for a friend in need.

He'd be your family when you had none.

He'd rather be judged by his actions than his words.

Louis Proof was heart, strength, and loyalty.

The story went from one of happiness to one of warning that:

He'd have to be the hero plus his own sidekick.

He'd experience great loss and have to shake it off.

He'd have to leave all he knows behind.

He'd fall and face his own death but even then he'd have to fight back.

The writing was fading away as it led him to a plaza whose ground was made from cobblestones of rich bluish and gray tones. In the center of the plaza, an exquisite fountain spouted water that glowed a marvelous blue color much like Louis's Alonis. It was beautiful here but the buildings still couldn't really be seen. They were draped in shadow and only highlighted with a fine blue aura from the glowing water. Louis could just make out some steeples and modest towers—nothing you'd find in Times Square.

When he stepped into the plaza, the words disappeared.

Wandering over to the fountain, Louis found that even though the water was disrupted by splashes, he could see himself in it. He was different: thin and fit. It was a bit shocking.

Is that who I am now? Louis thought. Then he began to wonder why he'd been led here.

"I'm here! What is this place?" Louis shouted. There was no answer other than the babbling of the fountain. No one was here, but there *was* someone overhead. A person was riding on the back of a Flying Entity that looked like a cross between a horse and a bird. The Alonis began to glow wildly as if it was a guiding light for those in the sky.

Louis fumbled with his Alonis. It wasn't that he was scared. Okay, maybe he was, but it was also best for him to be cautious, so he hid behind one of the buildings. He tried to cover the Alonis and turn it around so it faced him. But it protested by moving erratically as Louis tried to grab it.

"You there, come on out. My friend and I just want to meet you," the person said, walking toward Louis.

The Alonis actually began to pull Louis out from hiding as the person got closer. Louis could see that it was a woman, and her eyes lit up as soon as she saw him.

"Oh, mercy on me! Is it time for us to meet already?" She dug into a bag she was carrying. Pulling out a shiny silver pocket watch, she opened and read it. "Oh my! There it is right there. An eighth past the Earthbound Celestial Wars. Well then, I guess it is time." She seemed to be talking to herself.

Louis waited until she turned her attention back to him. She'd been one of the people in the conference room in the DiVarion City, so she likely wasn't an enemy.

"Exciting, so exciting! I've been watching you from afar. How are you?" she said with true wonder and interest.

"I'm just fine, I guess. My name is Louis Proof."

"Louis. I know your name and your heart! I'm Paris and my friend here is France, and I'd have to say I'm fine too. What are you doing here? I've never been here before, but that's how it is on Midlandia."

"Yeah, why doesn't anything stay in one place?" Louis said.

"Stay in one place? Are you kidding me? Do you stay in one place?" she asked.

"No way," Louis answered.

"Of course not! So why should anything else? Everything here is alive. There is nothing dead on Midlandia and it all has a mind of its own. I know you must have sensed that." Walking over to one of the buildings, she greeted it as if it were a person. She put her hand on it and then pressed the side of her face to it, whispering. After a few seconds it began to change shape, turning from a tall building into a quaint, warmly lit cottage. Amid the other dark buildings it looked cozy. Louis could see flames licking in the fireplace. The writing appeared once again, this time leading right into the cottage.

"Come on in." The woman entered and shut the door after Louis. France remained outside but looked in through the window, keeping a watchful eye on everything.

"Now, I'm terribly grateful that you've provided this for us, but we'll need a few more things—places to sit and such—please," Paris said.

With those words, a cozy sofa and burgundy leather chairs built themselves in front of Louis. A luxurious printed rug raised itself right under their feet. A chandelier tinkled into existence to dangle from the ceiling. Louis took a seat and thought that all he was missing was a spot of tea and crumpets, whatever they were.

Wait! Food. Louis had just remembered that he hadn't eaten anything since he arrived here. He wasn't hungry at all. What a strange thing, especially for Louis Proof. He couldn't be concerned with that now, though.

"You have to tell me how you did that. I've seen passageways open and things like that, but they had to be forced and broken through," Louis said.

"Well, here anything is as hard or as easy as you make it. Some try to use force and others just ask nicely. There's a time and place for everything, including force, but I think asking nicely is better," she said.

"Okay, so how do things appear to be there one day and then gone the next?" Louis asked.

"I told you that everything is alive. Things have their own desires. They want to take a trip. Or this house might agree to become something different if it's asked. One more time: Midlandia is alive!"

"Maybe that's what happened when we were at the barrier. Cyndi, Devon, and I couldn't go any farther, but we touched it, and it changed into a crazy obstacle course. We crossed it to get to Olivion's Gate."

"Yes, indeed. Say, do you mind if I look at your Alonis? DiVarion won't let me or anyone else see them, which is crazy since I'm the one who delivers him the energy to create them," Paris said.

That was a pertinent piece of information and it went right over Louis's head as he was wondering if this was a trick to get his Alonis. Relax and then, boom, they try to take it. But what did Devon say? "Have faith," so he quieted his apprehensions, rose, and moved close enough for her to touch it.

"Very nice. Thank you, Louis. Thank you for trusting me. I could see your hesitancy. You do know it can't be taken from you, right? It's more powerful than anything you can imagine. You don't know how to use it, do you?" Paris said.

"Not a clue," Louis said.

"I thought not." Paris laughed. "Well, I can't help you with that, but I can help you with other things. You know what? I will show you how to see things a bit differently."

"You can?"

"Sure I can. Come with me." She extended her hand. She was so bubbly that Louis couldn't resist. He even wondered why he'd hesitated to show her his Alonis. She was definitely a friend.

Paris led him outside. She looked around and then at the sky.

"Louis, black is lovely and darkness is grand but there's nothing wrong with a bit of light and color. It seems this place may not have seen any in a good while. Are you ready?"

"Sure. What are we going to do?" Louis asked.

"I'll show you. Follow my lead. Remember, this is Midlandia. Anything and everything is possible!" She ran up to one of the buildings. She whispered to it and it became a great blue glass building, its color contrasting brilliantly with the black structures around it. She whispered a little more and purple light lit up its interior.

"Now that's something to write home about," Louis said.

"You try one, Louis. Go ahead!" She shouted at him as she raced to another. This one changed into a golden tower.

Louis trotted to a building and pressed the side of his head to it. Before he spoke, he listened. He could hear that it was alive. It wasn't like it was speaking, but it had a voice. It was friendly. This entire place was one entity but it had multiple thoughts at the same time. He didn't know how, but he knew this entity. Yes, he did! It was the Entity that had guided them here. It hadn't gone anywhere. Its energy just changed from—

"Louis Proof! What are you waiting for, young sir?" Paris shouted.

"Blue glass building. The best I've ever seen. Please," Louis requested.

Sure, Louis. No problem.

It changed right before him into a marvel of architectural design. It was utterly modern amid the ancient city. It looked like it had been designed by an architectural genius who still knew what it was like to be a kid. The vibrant color scheme of greens, yellows, reds, purples, and blues seemed childlike, but the technical design of the interlocking windows was totally pro.

"There you go. Come on! And remember, you have no limits," Paris said, and with a single leap she jumped to the top of one of the buildings. She changed it with her touch only, no words.

"See, Louis, if you begin to have just a hint of understanding of this place, you can speak with words, thoughts, and touch. You are your thoughts, which can become words, and they can flow through you. It's all energy," Paris said.

They chased each other through the city, touching down on building after building, changing them all. Louis felt a rush as he propelled himself through the sky. This time there was minimal fear. It was nothing like when he'd dropped from Olivion's Domain. He was beginning to own and welcome his developing abilities.

Each building became something different from the next: some high, some short, some wide, some thin, some glass, some metal, some transparent. As unique as they were, they all seemed to fit together. Well, all but one. This was a special one that Louis created himself.

"You made that building change exactly as you wanted it to, didn't you?" Paris said.

"I did. That's my house," Louis said, thinking about how much he missed home. She ran up to him and gave him a hug that almost made him fall over. Louis hugged her back in appreciation. Although he saw the wonder of Midlandia, he felt lost, as if he had no control over anything. Paris had shown him that he was connected to everything, and with that understanding he did have a bit of control.

"Louis, I think I was a good teacher and you went above and beyond the lesson."

"Thanks. I meant to ask you: Where are you from?"

"Louis, I am from here, there, everywhere, and I must go," she said with a laugh. Sticking her fingers in her mouth, she whistled. This was something Louis couldn't do, and whenever he saw someone do it he always wondered, *How did they do that?*

France scooped Paris up. They were about to leave. But first Louis remembered to ask the question. "Paris, what does this mean? 'I am everything. All things come from me. But there is only one thing I cannot be. That is the key to everything.'" Louis asked.

"That's quite a riddle. Too much for me. There's nothing that I can think of. You're smart. I'm sure you'll be able to figure it out," Paris said to Louis. Then she spoke to her flying friend. "Come on, France. Let's see what else we can get into." With those words, she was off, leaving Louis alone in the marvelous new city.

"Louis!" Paris called, and he turned to see what she wanted. "This is for you!" She blew him a kiss. As she did, the sky turned from night to day. The effect this had on the gleaming buildings couldn't be described. The city transformed into a masterpiece of shimmering light, bathing Louis in bold, vibrant colors.

Louis didn't know where he should go. He'd wandered away from the writing. Or had he? Words soon zipped right between his legs. The writing had trailed him throughout his entire roof-top escapade.

This time the letters wrote directly in front of his face. They were words of learning, power, worth, and accomplishment.

These final words sparked and created a dark wooden door. It hovered in front of him just as Olivion's Gate had not long ago. But this was a door with a knob. He turned the knob with a new confidence that whatever or whoever was behind this door was someone he was supposed to meet or some place he was supposed to be. As always, he was up for the adventure.

> Louis, you've just learned that with power you
> have some control.

> That is great but very dangerous, especially
> without the proper knowledge.

Chapter **Thirty-six**

As Cyndi slowly stepped along her path, the only light came from the writing. Her Alonis still refused to be more than an exquisite piece of jewelry.

So, what were these words saying as they twisted through the city, leading her who knows where? Just like Louis, she quickly realized this was her story.

Cyndi, born Cynthia Victoria Chase, first said hello to the world—and to her parents, Alan and Valerie Chase—in Brooklyn, New York. She didn't cry or fuss at all. Of course it's utterly silly to think so, but it seemed as if she raised her right hand to ask a question. Possibly: Who are you? That guy who was talking to me for all these months? As soon as he spoke, the question was answered. He was indeed Daddy Alan Chase. You see, even from an early age Cyndi was all about discovery. It was as if she was forever looking for something—even if she didn't know what— and she'd be darned if she wasn't going to find it.

Brooklyn was her beloved stomping ground until the age of five, and then it was off to an entirely new life in Cali. Due to the entrepreneurial exploits of her father and his partner, whom she considered to be her uncle, she became a child of the nouveau riche. She grew into a very lovely girl and she learned that beauty had its positives and negatives. But everything could be a positive if you knew how to exploit that which was negative. Cyndi was reserved, but not in a way that was off-putting. It was just that you wouldn't ever see her drunk or acting a fool in public. Even with her reserve . . .

To Cyndi's surprise, a new path of writing appeared. The letters on the alternate path were red, and they flowed in a different direction. These were not words of who she was. They were of other things and places. Cyndi followed them to the right, and only a little farther on they stopped in what seemed to be a dead end. In the dim red light she could see someone standing there. Whoever it was was smaller than her and, unlike everything else in Midlandia, imperfect. It was shirtless, dirty, and its head hung down so hair covered its face. Cyndi was taken aback by its appearance. But since it was a child, she wasn't afraid and said hello.

"You wear that around your neck and you've come. They want to speak with you," the figure said.

"Who are they?" Cyndi asked.

It didn't answer but began to look up. Before its full face could be seen, it moved twice, as if teleporting closer and closer, to stand no more than three feet from Cyndi. At first it only had two arms, then two more sets emerged from behind its back, and it began performing odd hand gestures, clasping its own six hands randomly with an evil grin. It turned its head to fix dead eyes on Cyndi.

It made the hand gestures more and more rapidly. The ground began to shake. Then the child stopped abruptly and bowed before Cyndi. With that, the wall behind it began to crumble and was sucked away piece by piece to reveal a decrepit, modest, two-story house with one bare tree in its sandy dirt ground. There was light there, but not normal light; a red light that came from the sky highlighted everything. Cyndi had no clue where she was. It didn't feel like she was in the city any longer.

She'd been so distracted that she didn't realize the child was now beside her. It grabbed her hand. As if in a trance, Cyndi allowed the freakish child to lead her forward. The words reappeared but they no longer led; instead they trailed just behind Cyndi.

At the door of the house, Cyndi looked down to the child and it grinned and nodded before ushering her in and closing the door behind them.

Inside the tattered house books were everywhere. Cyndi wondered if they contained more information than the FyneStory book. There was no perfection here—unless this was all perfectly decrepit.

From the front hallway, Cyndi could see a stairway to her left in a living room that was dominated by dark colors: a dirty burgundy carpet with a warped gold pattern and dark, battered walls. Ahead of her was a bare room only furnished with stacks of books and a desk. A person was sitting at the desk, reading from a book and writing down things in other books placed neatly all over the desk's surface. It seemed as if his writing was causing waves of words and letters to flash through the house toward him.

He had long brown hair rippling down his back and perfectly tailored pants. His arms were thin and longer than usual, giving him the ability to reach books that normal-length arms couldn't have reached. He was whispering and chattering to himself as the child touched his shoulder. Even when he looked up to stare unwaveringly at Cyndi, he didn't stop writing.

"Cyndi. Cyndi Victoria Chase. Chase Victorious Sin. That's how I always regarded you," the man said.

"Chase Victorious Sin? Sorry to disappoint you, but I do nothing of the sort. Who are you?" Cyndi asked.

"We are just a few who've been watching. We've no time to waste, so let's get to it."

The child had moved to the corner of the room and stood with its head bowed and its back to her. Odd.

"Yes, let's!" another voice said.

Cyndi turned her head to see a man elegantly dressed in all white sitting on a frayed couch. He had flowing white hair, a chiseled face, was of a medium shade of brown, and stood to speak. She immediately recognized him as one of the people in the conference room in DiVarion City.

"It doesn't work, does it?" the man at the desk asked her.

"Yes, it won't perform for you," the other man said.

"The Alonis? No, it won't. How do you know that? Who are you two?"

"Who are we? I, for brevity, shall be the Standing Man. He shall be the Sitting Man," the Standing Man said.

"Oh, good fun!" the Sitting Man said.

"Fine, play that way. Do you know something about why my Alonis won't work? I need it to work."

"Of course it won't work. You haven't committed to who you are yet. You're conflicted! You unlocked the library and turned your back on it! You've no idea how significant that was. Not even the writing on the wall will convince you. As soon as Louis went after Perilynn, he was ready. You, on the other hand, have gone back and forth without settling," the Standing Man said.

"I thought we were marked. iLone and eNoli," Cyndi said.

"Yes, but things can change," the Standing Man said.

"There's always a choice. But eNoli is what you are. So simple to see. You just need a bit of encouragement," the Sitting Man said.

"Choice?" Cyndi asked.

"There's no time. We can only divert her path for so long," the Sitting Man said.

"Cyndi! Victoria! Chase! Give me what Emyli FyneStory gave to you," the Standing Man said.

"She didn't give me anything," Cyndi said.

"You think me a fool?" the Standing Man said.

"No time!" the Sitting Man said, and he kept writing away as if his very writing was keeping her there.

"It's in your best interest to give it to me. You won't make good use of it here and can't take it with you when you leave. I'll send it ahead. You'll be able to claim it just as you claimed your Alonis," the Standing Man said.

"No time!" the Sitting Man said, gravely urgent and writing feverishly.

With a stern look at Cyndi, the Standing Man shifted form. He became a solid light that bolted around Cyndi, stopping periodically to speak in her ears.

"Arminion knows much, but he's not the only one with knowledge. Cyndi, within your reach are all the secrets you can imagine. When you return home you can free the eNoli and be regarded as a queen. You alone can bring about a change in all humanity.

"With knowledge and power whispering in your ear, you'll be able to cure every disease imaginable. You can bring peace where there is war. If you do any of that . . . well, that's up to you.

"You'll be faced with a hard decision. The road will split in two. You must stay true to your kind. You must commit to the eNoli for anything . . . no, everything, to continue.

"Look around you. Things aren't as perfect as they seem. If you hadn't been diverted by the red writing, you wouldn't have seen this underbelly of Midlandia. You think you've seen Midlandia? You've seen nothing! On top of that you know nothing! I'm not offering a deal. There's nothing to be paid. There's no one to be in debt to. We'll be in your debt. Some kind of end is coming. You and the knowledge you can discover are the key to stopping it. Give me the device and I'll grant it safe passage. It must be now because our paths may not cross again on Midlandia."

It wasn't until the Standing Man stopped speaking that Cyndi was able to see two paths. One showed her choosing *not* to be eNoli. There was an end. There was failure. Beyond that there was . . . naught.

The other showed her as an eNoli. She'd do monumental things for many people. She saw friends, adventure, and fame. The fame she could do without but still it was there. There was also massive fighting in a war unlike any seen before. But it was a war that had to be fought. Louis was there, young, strong, and powerful. She was also there, wise and brave. There was a chance.

That was far more than nothing.

She removed the device from the back of the Alonis and handed it to the Standing Man. He took it.

"Give me the book. For kicks I'll send it along too, but if all works out with the device, you won't need it," he said, and Cyndi did.

"No time," the Sitting Man said as two more arms tore from his side and he wrote even faster. Cyndi was now sure that there was a connection between his writing and her presence here.

"Quickly, remember this: your father's office. You know what I'm talking about. You know what you must find. When the time is right, it'll open for you. Galonious will become an ally and even give you a bit of important information. Now he knows nothing, because Arminion hasn't yet revealed any of the truth to him," the Standing Man said.

Suddenly the Standing Man and the child were gone. The Sitting Man slowed his writing and things began to shake and tear apart in a systematic way. The steps. Then each panel of the house's siding. The sand began to blow inside. Cyndi knew she wouldn't be here much longer. She thought quickly.

"Do you know the answer? 'I am everything. All things come

from me. But there is only one thing I cannot be. That is the key to everything,'" she shouted at the Sitting Man

The Sitting Man dropped his pens and slammed his hands on the table, raising himself up. He quickly turned to stand before Cyndi with his head down. "No time!" he yelled as he pressed his right hand hard against her forehead, forcing her to fall backward. She was about to hit the floor, but she fell right through it, doing a 180 to land on her feet, but it was as if the world was upside down and she was standing on the ceiling. She wasn't. She was right side up, back in the dimly lit city. To her surprise, the shining blue words had caught up to her. They began to write in front of her face. They sparked and created a door that hovered before her. So she grabbed the handle and opened it.

Chapter **Thirty-seven**

Devon stood still for a moment before he began to read and follow the words. They told of his life, and each word he read pulled him farther on. He'd experienced so much loss, disappointment, pain, mourning, sacrifice, imposed responsibility, and duty—far more than most children ever have to endure. Those feelings were coming to the surface and he began to shake them off. They were not the total of his story.

His story was also one of strength, maturity, and discipline. It was the tale of a boy who diverted his dream to be a better son and brother. His wasn't a big dream, certainly not as big as many others.

Only a year ago his two older sisters, Stacey and Karen, were in a serious car accident. Stacey had just gotten her license and had taken their mother's car. She was killed instantly, but Karen survived, trapped in a coma. Soon after this, Devon's mother was diagnosed with cancer. His father was strong but constantly occupied with his injured daughter and sick wife. On top of his work, he did hours of research on comas and cancer. His worst fear was that the end would come and he wouldn't have done as much as he could to stop it.

Devon was exceptional at football. He seemed able to run the ball at will. But he no longer felt he had time to devote to his school's team. His dad fought with him to continue playing, but with his mom sick and so many responsibilities around the house, Devon just couldn't.

The school was far from home, but even though he'd chosen it for its football team, he stayed because it was a phenomenal institution. Devon began catching rides with random friends so that he could arrive in time to pick up his younger brother and sister from their school. He didn't like imposing on friends, but Lauren didn't mind at all. Their friendship ran deep. Even when Devon decided he should go back to taking the bus, because his burden shouldn't be hers, she'd show up ready to go. Her interest in him was genuine, plus she knew a million other girls who'd love to drive him anywhere.

The words took a turn and now focused on his little brother, Elliot. Elliot was five years old and addicted to peanut butter and organic cherry preserve sandwiches. Organic cherry preserves were an elusive commodity but Elliot demanded organic and had been known to be able to tell the difference. When it wasn't in stock, Devon would call stores to hunt it down and hope his dad wasn't too tired or broke to pick it up. For Elliot all problems could be solved or at least forgotten when he gripped a peanut butter and organic cherry preserve sandwich. And with so much going on, Devon was happy when Elliot was happy.

The words shifted direction again, this time turning to his little sister, Jessica. She was three and very reserved and soft-spoken.

She'd only raise her voice to tell Elliot to stop bothering her or, infrequently, to cry. She liked her oldest brother but hadn't actually come to love him until the day she'd wandered away from her family in the supermarket. There she was with Doritos on one side and Captain Crunch on the other; they were familiar but they weren't her family. Panic was taking over. Her face was tense and she wore that frown that comes just before the crying starts. She was opening her mouth to yell when someone swooped in and grabbed her from behind. It was the perfect surprise to offset the oncoming cry. She turned to see her big brother Devon Alexander. In that moment she went from liking her brother to loving him, so much so that the next day when he was doing his homework she came over to give him a kiss on the cheek and call him her "big brother buckaroo." She ran away knowing no more needed to be said. Plus she was three and didn't have anything else to say. What a feeling bloomed in Devon . . .

They were both lost and dealing with their losses the best way they could.

The words shifted down another pathway. Devon followed.

Suddenly the words faded, replaced by a scene, blurry at first. It reminded him of the scene they'd watched play out at Emyli FyneStory's house. He could feel his family but he couldn't see them. They were here somewhere. Where were they? Then the image became sharper and he knew this place. This was a hospital.

He turned his head and . . . oh no! His younger siblings were by his mother's side. She was so sick, but even like that she was beautiful to him. No matter what, she was strong. He'd always had faith that she'd get better. With his new self, he gazed upon his mother and saw what he'd never been able to see before. She was close to the end.

Then it happened. He could see it. Energy cannot be created or destroyed. He could see what she truly was and it was slipping away, leaving her body. She was dying.

"No! Mom. Mommy!" Devon's voice trembled. He refused to be helpless even as his eyes welled up. His Alonis began to glow like it was fighting against the dark.

"Devon, you'll never understand or be able to use that power if you don't return to Midlandia." Those were the words that Olivion had spoken to him after Louis and Cyndi had left to rescue Perilynn.

He had the power but didn't know how to use it, so he wished. It was such a loving and passionate wish. He wished that what was leaving his mother would return to her. He wanted her to be alive when he got home. His Alonis glowed even brighter, and because of the wonder of Midlandia, his wish was granted. What had been leaving his mother went back into her body. A calm came over Devon. He'd succeeded but he hadn't won. The cancer was still there. That's what he wanted to destroy. Until that was gone, his mother would still have to fight to hold on.

He wanted to try to tackle the cancer but he could no longer see or feel his family. Frantic, he searched for them. They were gone.

Holding his Alonis, he told it, "Thank you. I guess we bought my mom some time. We have to get home so I can wipe out the cancer and wake my sister up."

The glowing words reappeared and led him to a doorway. He walked through to find Louis and Cyndi waiting for him. Louis was beaming with the prospect of his future. Cyndi was as gorgeous and alert as ever. Devon was excited. For the first time, he knew he could do something to make things better. He couldn't wait to go home.

Hold on, Devon.

You will be home and with your family soon enough.

Chapter **Thirty-eight**

"Have a good time?" Louis asked.

"Hmm. It was interesting, Louis. Very interesting," Cyndi said.

"It was powerful. I have to get home," Devon said.

"We're all going home. But check this out!" Louis touched the walls. They immediately changed to the exact shade of blue as his bedroom. He didn't want to show off, but he wanted to show them what he'd learned.

"How'd you do that?" Cyndi asked.

"It's easy. I'll show you later," Louis said. Eager to get moving, he opened a door he'd noticed directly behind him. The room on the other side was large and drab, lacking color. At its center was a raised circular platform supporting a lone chair with a lone figure slumped in it. As the children approached the person, he looked up, revealing his face.

This was not expected . . .

"I know you. You're Myth." Louis recognized him even though he seemed faded and lackluster like the room.

"You know me, do you? Yes, everyone knows of the great Myth. So you know *who* I am, but you do not know me," Myth slowly said.

"You have a secret that many want to know," Cyndi said.

"As sure as those medallions hang around your neck, I have many secrets, which will no longer be secrets if I choose to tell them. I've held on to them for far too long. In fact, I've been gone for far too long," Myth said as if he was a bit relieved that he'd been found. As he spoke, the room started to liven up.

"Have you been lost or hiding?" Louis asked.

"Lost? No. Hiding? No. But waiting? Yes! Waiting for you. Nothing mattered without you, so I didn't need to deal with anything else. Now you're here, which means it's finally begun and I may return. It will soon be upon us." Myth was becoming more animated, as was the room.

"When you touched Olivion's Gate, what happened?" Cyndi asked. She was in no mood for double-talk.

Myth paused as that long ago day walked across his memory. *Finally*, it was time. So, right in front of the children, he regained his former stature and glory. The colors of the room became richer, and golden highlights grew along the walls.

"I searched for Olivion's Gate for so long. I started a war. I sought it so that I could destroy Olivion and leave this place . . . this place that can't be harmed yet is in pain," Myth said.

"Tell us, Myth, why did you abandon the Gate? What did you learn?" Cyndi demanded.

"What did I learn that caused me to abandon what I sought so tirelessly? Wouldn't you and the whole of Midlandia like to know?" Myth said.

"Yes, Myth. Please tell us. Please," Cyndi said.

"Well, my child. You are eNoli and you two are iLone. You, Cyndi Victoria Chase, seek knowledge of that which should not be known yet must be known. I know a bit about that.

"You, Louis Proof, are protector of the children. Protector of all. You are a warrior above all others.

"You, Devon Alexander, your path is one of sacrifice so that others may know where they truly stand.

"I know all of that because Olivion's Gate showed me nothing, but Olivion was everything and showed me the truth," Myth said.

"Stop playing games. What's the truth?" Cyndi demanded.

"There are many truths, but I'll tell you a few. One is that Olivion can't be destroyed. Olivion is everything. The end of Olivion is the end of us all. We were foolish to think we could destroy the very thing responsible for our existence. Very foolish."

"That's what caused you to leave? That's it?" Cyndi said.

"You think that's a small morsel of information?" Myth asked.

"No. I was just expecting . . . ," Cyndi said.

"You were expecting more. Like myself, you're never satisfied. We eNoli always want more." Myth smiled. "Okay, I'll give you more. Olivion can't be destroyed, but oddly, I saw what could destroy Olivion and all things."

"But you said Olivion couldn't be destroyed," Louis said.

"Yes, and this place can't be harmed, yet it is in a slow agony," Myth said, and as if on cue Midlandia cried out.

"I've seen it. It put fear into even me. It will bring about an eternal end. It will leave zero in its conquered path. Such a lovely thing, if it weren't so absolute in its disregard for all things known and unknown. So, when it comes, what will it matter—to iLone, eNoli, CE, your kind—if it can destroy us all?" Myth and the room were at full glory. The rich reds and blues of the walls were overlaid with gold patterns.

"What is it?" Cyndi demanded with a wild and burning interest.

"All things come from me. But . . . ," Devon whispered to himself.

"There is only one thing I cannot be. . . . Yes, I too know that riddle, but I don't know the answer. It makes no sense even though I've seen the threat. We can't face what we don't understand. There's no way to understand what I saw," Myth said.

"If you don't know that, tell me why the eNoli want to leave this place," Cyndi said.

"Leave this place? We are *not* to leave this place. We have no place but here. You're from the finite and flawed and we're from the eternal and perfect. We make no sense where you come from. We would destroy all that you know. But we long for what we've left behind. We're never satisfied, even here. We serve ourselves without regard for the consequence to others. Yet still we are to leave this place. If we don't, all will be destroyed."

"What about the consequences? For each of you who leaves, there will be a child with the ability to fight you back," Louis said.

"Yes, with both the ability and the power, but the duty? Is it your duty to do so? Maybe we assume too much. You, Young

Louis Proof, stand in front of me and I have both the ability and power to destroy you." Myth was immediately in Louis's face, seemingly half-solid with streams of energy floating about him.

"But duty? Is it my duty to do so? Is that what the prophecy says? You'll be much better off if you don't assume, but then again, maybe you did get it right," Myth said.

You long for what you've left behind. Left what behind? Devon was turning Myth's words over in his head. He also thought about what he'd seen leaving his mother's body. No wonder Olivion didn't answer many questions. She spoke through others and through the journey she'd sent them on. He'd learned much, and he finally believed that he'd figured it out. He believed he knew who the eNoli and iLone were.

"Myth! I know—" Before Devon could continue, there was a massive commotion outside.

"We're not alone. It seems you won't be the only ones to find me after all this time," Myth said, leaving through a corridor that opened up right in front of him.

Chapter **Thirty-nine**

Myth stood on top of a tower. He could see his eNoli brethren coming in like a swarm. They were led by one of his former generals, Reign. Myth pulled two white sabers from his back and plunged them into two silver slots in a panel in the front of the tower. Instantly, the city came alive with countless tentacles of light that slapped at the would-be intruders. Myth held the sabers and left an impression of himself there, so that it looked as if he were still holding them even as he leaped forward and snatched Reign out of the sky. Streams of lustrous energy connected the two. If Reign were human, he'd have crapped his pants. He'd never seen this place before and surely didn't expect to encounter Myth—never mind two Myths—here or ever again. Not even in an eternity.

"Boy, don't think that in my long absence I've lost the skills and desire to fight. I remain as I was, and I have even managed to build upon that," Myth exclaimed as he landed on the ground.

"Lord Myth . . . I . . . I . . . I . . . thought I'd never be in your presence again. I come with no desire for destruction. My numbers are not meant to be intimidating. I only seek the children. Perilynn has done much since you left, and he requests that the children have safe passage to him," Reign explained.

"Perilynn? You serve Perilynn? How is that possible?" Myth asked.

"He challenged all of Midlandia in order to deliver the children to Olivion's Gate. He was captured before he could cross it, was condemned to the worst fate possible, and escaped it."

"Worst fate possible? He was trapped within an Alonis Capsule and thrown into the Infinite Abyss?" Myth asked.

"Yes, and he broke that which cannot be broken and escaped that which cannot be escaped," Reign said.

"Then much has come to pass. The possible end is immediately upon us." Myth let Reign go. His self on the tower flew down to join again with his self on the ground.

"There's one last thing: We that cannot be united have been united, have we not?" Myth asked.

"Yes. Perilynn demonstrated a power that we can't deny. He's brought about eNoli unity."

"Then we must destroy the order of all things to leave this place. Does Perilynn have a plan for this?"

"He's working with his brother, who already escaped with Galonious and Trife. The eNoli girl that we seek must return home safely. She can call us all to Earth and we'll be free," Reign said.

"Free? We know not what that means and we know not what we are to do. Very well, I'll release the children to you if Perilynn wants their safe delivery," Myth said. "But what of the iLone?"

"They've been searching for the children. They seek to destroy the eNoli child and are preparing for a war to prevent her from returning home," Reign said.

Olivion! What a dangerous tapestry you've created! Is it by your divine design or purely for your amusement? If we fail, you'll come to an end! All will come to an end! Myth thought as he looked aimlessly into the Midlandian sky.

Myth was correct; it had *all* come to pass.

It's about time Myth got back into action. Don't
you think?

"Children, it's time for you to leave this place. They're waiting for you outside," Myth said, leading Reign to them.

Cyndi shook with terror at the sight of him.

"Relax. I know who you are, but we haven't been properly introduced. My name is Reign. Much has changed since I last saw you. I mean you no harm. Perilynn requests that you be brought safely to him," Reign said.

"Children, he speaks the truth. I can promise you that. Perilynn awaits, and I'll accompany you," said Myth.

"Yeah right. You're going to take us to him? The last time we saw you, you were trying to kill us!" Louis said.

"As I said, much has changed. Perilynn has shown us a power not even I can deny. He wishes to see you all. I won't force you. I'll just report that you wouldn't come. I don't know what he'll do to me when I tell him that, though, so I'd like you to come," Reign said.

"Where is Perilynn?" Cyndi asked.

"He's high within Midlandia, in a city that most can only wish to see, waiting for his three friends. He's promised us much, but he won't do anything until you arrive. Will you come?"

"How will we get there?" Louis asked.

"I said I'll take you," Reign said.

"No, *I* will take them," Myth said, opening his shirt to reveal a secret: Around his neck was an Alonis.

That's why he knew so much, Cyndi thought. She'd suspected this.

"How are you a Favorite? You didn't cross Olivion's Gate," Louis said.

"Cross the Gate? You say that as if there are set rules here and as if you know every one of my actions. There are *no* unbreakable rules, and you don't know what I have or haven't done during my absence. What adventures I may have been on. There are many ways to become a Favorite, none of which are guaranteed," Myth said.

Reign broke in. "Myth, I can't believe you're a Favorite. When did you become a lap dog for the Olivion?"

Myth charged at Reign, grabbing him by his neck and forcing him to the wall so quickly that not even CE eyes could've seen it.

"It seems you've forgotten yourself. There are many things you don't know. You think Olivion favors the iLone over the eNoli? Olivion takes no sides. It's beyond belief that we can be all that we are and do all that we do yet be so ignorant as to what we are, what this place is, and most important, what Olivion is."

Myth's words. Myth's understanding. The streams of light that circled Myth's body. The rage and strength that pulsed quietly within Myth's form. Reign could see that this Myth was far more powerful than the one he'd known ages ago. He dared not challenge him.

"All I care about is getting free from this place. I look into your eyes and know that's going to happen. Maybe I've been mistaken about what it means to be a Favorite," Reign said. Once he left, he'd be a god among those not of Midlandia.

"Maybe you have. Lead the way and we'll follow," Myth commanded.

"No, I'll follow you. You have the children and I'd bet Midlandia wants them to be reunited with Perilynn. You'll lead us directly to him," Reign said.

"Very well," Myth agreed as Reign left to gather his troops to trail Myth.

"Well, children, it seems we are to lead," Myth said, sitting down in his chair. His Alonis began to glow and the walls of the room became transparent and began to spin. The three could see that the room was flying. Louis looked back. Hordes of eNoli were following. Mighty airships that looked ready for war brought up the rear.

More than ever Louis knew that he wasn't iLone; he was eNoli. They didn't seem selfish; it had to be a misunderstanding. Perilynn was safe and had been looking for them. Reign had changed from foe to friend.

We found Myth and we're going to be reunited with Perilynn. I've learned so much and am sure to learn far more. Cyndi thought of the Standing Man and inadvertently shivered. Soon she'd be home.

Devon felt the power he was going to use to save his mother. He noticed the smile on Louis's face. He wanted to join in, and for the first time in a while he genuinely smiled, and hope touched his heart.

A complete calm came over the dark city after they left. The Entity rose from the writing, leaving only the small island that the children had first landed on. The Entity stood on the island until it began to sink back into the Midlandian Ocean, then the Entity flapped its wings, rose high into the sky, and flew away.

It was just about time for the beginning of the real war.

Chapter **Forty**

Midlandia has a mind of its own. It wasn't until now that it wanted the children to truly be found. They had to be, because a crucial time was about to begin and all players had to be on their proper teams, which they were not.

eNoli and iLone. None of us is perfect and we may coast between both sides but Louis, Cyndi, and Devon each have a proper side. If you cannot choose the right one, maybe something will happen to force you to.

They found a wondrous ethereal city. Its buildings shimmered like pearls. At the center of the farthest portion of the city was a magnificent palace. The children landed on a lush field and exited the flying room to find their friend. Running up the palace steps, they yelled Perilynn's name, and they could've sworn they heard Perilynn calling all of their names at the same time. It sounded as if he were in three different places, reachable by three separate stairways. The calls were hypnotic, drawing them toward their distinct paths just at the writing had in the dark city.

The stairways seemed to lead to the same upper level. However, looks can be deceiving; they did not. Such is the way

of Midlandia, and each child arrived at a different room at the top
of their stairways.

In Louis's room he found the Five. He hadn't expected to see them;
it was unsettling. Wait, they were no longer five but four. White
had been defeated and lost his form. The four remaining were no
longer able to function properly. They sat in the room, listless,
floundering, with inconsistent forms. Louis spoke to them and
they tried to answer but they were incoherent. All Louis could
make out were the words "lost," "gone," and "Kiyonrae."

Kiyonrae? Kiyonrae did this? The iLone seemed to be the
root of all things wrong here.

Cyndi found herself in a room with Eynd.

"I remember you! You chased us when we escaped the Celestial
Drifts. You almost killed us!" Cyndi said, backing up.

"Cyndi, don't worry. I'm no longer your enemy. You're safe
here. Perilynn is waiting for you," Eynd said, kneeling to Cyndi
out of respect and appreciation for her abilities. Cyndi was taken
aback by the gesture but could sense the honesty in it.

"Please get up. Where is he? I can't wait to see him," Cyndi
said.

"He's here. He just has to handle something. I'll take you to
him when he's finished," Eynd said, standing again.

Devon hit pay dirt. Perilynn had his back to Devon, but it was
Perilynn all right. He was looking out over the city through a

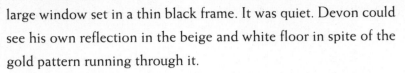

large window set in a thin black frame. It was quiet. Devon could see his own reflection in the beige and white floor in spite of the gold pattern running through it.

"Perilynn, finally we found you! Louis and Cyndi were amazing. I don't think anyone could have better friends than them. Perilynn, can you help us get home now? I must go home; my family really needs me." Devon crossed the room to stand behind Perilynn and place his hand on Perilynn's shoulder. His Alonis began to glow, highlighting his face, which was vibrant with excitement. He was about to go save his mother and sister.

Perilynn loved Louis and Cyndi. If he had to end one of them, he'd do it, but it would be painful. He'd fought for this child Devon, but he didn't know him. And here he stood, asking to be sent home. Devon didn't know what that really meant, but Perilynn would oblige.

"Yes, Devon. I'll send you home. You'll be with your family before you know it, my friend," Perilynn said, still staring out the window.

Devon smiled. Perilynn turned and swiftly plunged a sword into Devon's heart. Devon grabbed the blade, damaging his hands. His sliced fingers were fading away. Multiple thoughts flashed through his head. He knew his time here would soon end. The most important thought stuck out like a golden flame.

"Perilynn, my mom . . . I think . . . I figured it out. I know what you all are . . . energy cannot be created or destroyed. It's eternal. We all contain energy," Devon said.

"What are you saying? What are we? What am I?" Perilynn

had struck too soon. He grabbed the child in his arms. Could he undo what he'd just done?

"Perilynn . . . you . . . are . . . ," Devon said. Then his Alonis went dark. Its chain split, and it rocketed away, breaking through the wall of the palace in search of DiVarion's laboratory.

Louis rushed through the door just as Devon's life slipped away. "Perilynn! What did you do? No. Not you! Not you!" Louis yelled.

"Louis, I had to do it. To become a Favorite, I had to destroy a Favorite. I didn't know Devon, but I know you. You're my friend. I have no reason to kill you. It was a choice that had to be made. As a Favorite, I'll find a way to make this right. This wasn't what I wanted. Had I crossed the Gate with you, Devon would be alive now." Perilynn thought his words would console Louis.

Cyndi felt it. Eynd tried to stop her, but Cyndi forced her out of the way. Racing into Perilynn's room, she halted abruptly at the sight before her.

"Cyndi, I had no choice. I had to destroy a Favorite to become a Favorite. You understand, don't you?" Perilynn said as Olivion's Gate appeared right beside him.

Louis couldn't believe it. Olivion's Gate *had* appeared for him, for killing Louis's friend. For killing *her* Favorite? What game was Olivion playing at? Did he, Cyndi, and Devon mean anything to her? Were they interchangeable? Were they disposable?

"Cyndi, we have to leave here! We have to go," Louis pleaded.

It hit Cyndi like the street after a thousand-story fall. The decision was upon her. She saw the two distinct paths that she'd seen in the Entity's dark city. One led to Perilynn and one led to Louis. She loved Louis. He was her friend. But the path with him and her on it ended in darkness. She didn't know who Perilynn was anymore. But his path held a future. It contained good and bad, pain and joy. It was something. What's more, it contained sacred knowledge. She couldn't let that slip away again. Louis couldn't come with her on this path. She had to break away from him, because all would be lost, including Louis and herself, if someone didn't gain that knowledge. Her heart told her this even though her mind didn't yet understand it.

Do I have to give up Louis for our own good? Cyndi wondered.

So be it.

"Louis, I don't understand everything that's going on here. But I will. What I do know is that I'm not safe with you or the iLone. My place is here with the eNoli. Go! Just leave." Cyndi's words cut into her as well as Louis.

"No! Come on!" Louis grabbed Cyndi's arm, but she only pulled away.

"Louis, I can't go with you. I have to stay with the eNoli. Leave. You don't belong here! Get away from here! Get away from me!" Louis had never heard that acerbic tone come out of the mouth of a friend.

Cyndi's Alonis began to glow furiously. It was finally working. She'd found her path. Louis may have thought he was an eNoli, but he acted like an iLone; he'd always been on his path. Cyndi felt her Alonis's power and knew her decision was the right one.

Bathed in the stunning light of Cyndi's Alonis, Louis frantically wondered where all of this came from—not just the light but
everything. He fell to his knees, helpless, confused, and angry.
Deep inside he could feel a pull, and he heard Olivion speak.

"This is why you're both so important.
One to aid those who want to leave.
One to force those who would never leave to do so.
They'll come to any place at any time.
You only have to call."

Olivion's voice angered him, but he called his kind.

Kiyonrae and Vivionya found themselves traveling without
their doing. They were drawn to Louis by a stream of wispy
glowing light created by his Alonis. And then, surprised, they
stood on either side of Louis. Kiyonrae recognized Cyndi, drew
glowing blades, and charged at her while Vivionya remained by
Louis.

Kiyonrae came to a screeching stop, caught off guard by the
appearance of Olivion's Gate about six feet in front of Cyndi. It
slowly opened. There was a silence as Perilynn exited, reborn as a
Favorite, victorious. His Alonis hung proudly from his neck.

Kiyonrae stood down, not out of fear but because Perilynn
had escaped the Abyss and also was now a Favorite. He may have
been on an opposite side, but he deserved respect.

Kiyonrae would have to face him before he could get to
Cyndi.

"The end of Devon's hope has brought my new beginning. Let us remember him." Perilynn bowed his head. His Alonis began to glow and wind began to stir his clothing. Two swords formed in his hands.

"Cyndi, you must stay behind me," Perilynn said as the Gate disappeared and he took his stance.

"Are you going to stick around this time and not flee after the children?" Kiyonrae asked.

"I didn't flee last time! I fought as long as I could, and I knew when to make my exit. Kiyonrae. Vivionya. You won't harm this child. Let us begin," Perilynn said.

The CEs' Alonises began to glow like hot liquid metal, as if even the Alonises were ready to battle one another. Perilynn charged at Kiyonrae.

Their swords locked and so did their eyes. Favorite vs. Favorite. Kiyonrae flipped backward. Before he landed, he propelled himself at Perilynn, but an energy shield appeared, blocking his way. It sparked red projectiles before fading.

"Cyndi, stay back!" Perilynn shouted. She'd stepped forward. She'd seen the fear and disappointment in Louis's face as Vivionya kept him back. She wanted to run to him but couldn't. Not only was that the wrong path but she'd be killed.

Perilynn and Kiyonrae burned powerfully with beaming Celestial Energy and started to ascend to fight within the high ceiling of the room. They took airborne stances. But Myth and a crowd of eNoli entered the room. Kiyonrae was taken aback at the sight of Myth. Not only had he returned but he was a Favorite.

The iLone would be foolish to fight so many while trying to protect Louis.

"Kiyonrae! We must take the child from here!" Vivionya shouted. She snatched up Louis, and with the help of their Alonises, all three disappeared.

Devon had met his Midlandian end.
Louis had been taken by the iLone.
Cyndi remained with the eNoli.

There was now a balance on both sides.
Things were as they were supposed to be.

Marvelous World

A.K.A.

The Marvelous World of the Supposedly Soon to Be Phenomenal Young Mr. Louis Proof

Book 1.5: Olivion's Favorites

Level IV

Chapter Forty-one

Have you ever felt so sick that you hugged the toilet bowl 'cause you felt it was your only friend? You only had the quickest thought about whether it was clean. Did you ever experience that right before you vomited out all of your innards—your intestines, kidneys, spleen, liver, everything? It all could go, as long as you felt better.

Louis would have been right at that toilet, but this is Midlandia. So there was no toilet, not to mention that here he didn't have any organs—they were back home, rapidly changing. But he was still down on his knees and palms, feeling horrible. He wasn't vomiting, but with every heave and convulsion, his form expanded with energy. This was dangerous. He could become so powerful that his human body couldn't sustain its link. He could explode throughout Midlandia.

No one on Midlandia could console him. Hey, they couldn't even get near him. Vivionya and Kiyonrae stood back, Alonises activated to form armor and barriers to shield them from each wave of energy, but even they were feeling the effects.

"He has to be stopped. I don't know what will happen, but this is dangerous," Kiyonrae shouted.

"We can't do anything to help him. He'll have to find his own way back. If he can't, then he's not up for what's ahead," Vivionya yelled over the pulsing noise from Louis's energy waves.

Louis heard none of this. He was just in pain. He wished to be back home.

That is what you want? By all means . . . wish granted.

Home. Louis stood at his front door. It was a welcome sight, but the agony of losing two friends ran deep, and anger still pumped through his heart.

Devon killed!

Cyndi a traitor!

Instead of opening the door of his house, Louis punched it and banged his head against it at the same time. He rested his face there for a moment before entering.

There was an even more welcome sight! Mom and Dad were sitting on the couch. "Mom! Dad! I'm back! I'm home!" Louis said, tearing up.

No response. They couldn't hear him. Wait . . . his parents felt a comforting warmth and looked at each other.

"I'm back, but I'm not back," Louis said to himself. The sight of his parents did much to calm Louis's fury, but it didn't wipe it away.

Louis heard eerie giggles. Who was that? All was quiet again, and then Louis saw something tear into this reality behind his unsuspecting mother and father. *No way!* Louis thought. Instinctively he released a burst of energy from his body. It caught whatever was trying to enter off guard, forced it back, and closed the portal.

The portal may have been closed, but something or someone was still there. Louis could see it bending and displacing reality as if it were pushing against a sheet drying on a line. It moved behind the walls, under the floor, above the ceiling, creating waves in the surface of each. Moving. Moving. Moving.

For now his parents seemed to be safe. But Louis was still angry, so he chased it out of his house, around the corner, and into Dodd Street, where kids were running amuck on a hot summer day. They'd just opened a fire hydrant for relief from the 101-degree weather. Louis was still steaming, but there was a glimmer of the old him left. *Wouldn't it be cool if it spewed cookies-and-cream ice cream?* Louis thought. Done.

News crews would soon report the miracle of Dodd Street.

Chase again! Turn right on Prospect Avenue. There's that homeless Mr. Brinkley from Eighth Street using that old hook and line to fish in the middle of the road. Nothing unusual but . . . *Does everything have to be so messed up for this guy? What if this time he caught a few?* Louis thought. Done.

Brandon would soon witness the miracle of Prospect Avenue.

Why the heck is Willy Beans walking down the street backward, wearing pajamas? Does he think he's in one of those anime films? What if . . . , Louis thought. Done. Willy Beans began to walk forward, speaking Japanese.

The miracle of Springdale Avenue.

Run. Run. Run. Whatever he was chasing was still displacing the pavement, buildings, and streets. Surprisingly, Louis found himself coming up on the JunkYard JunkLot.

They led me here? Louis thought as memories rushed him: the race, the weird event that had made him lose, and Glitch (or Stacia, which he'd learned was her real name). He'd call her Glitch. The thought of her pushed more of his anger away.

Louis expected to enter by way of the obstacles and elevator, but when he reached the pile of cars, he found a bluish beam of light about six feet tall and two feet in diameter.

I wonder, he thought, fearlessly stepping into the light. Immediately, he was in the heart of the JunkYard JunkLot. What he saw was criminal. Kids were fleeing, some hurt and crying. A voice boomed through the sound system:

Shut down sequence has begun.
Please evacuate through your corresponding elevator.
Have a safe return. We'll be back in full glory. Just you wait and see . . .

The elevators were packed, transporting everyone back to their cities.

Is Glitch here? Is she safe? Louis looked all about. There she was! He felt woozy for a second. Even in his panic that quick glimpse of her stirred strong emotion. Whoa!

"Glitch! I've got something to tell you. I know who's giving you the info. It's DiVarion and Lynda Alonis . . . ," Louis yelled to her, but she ran past him to the lab entrance, where her brother shut the door behind them. Before long, all of the kids had safely evacuated and everything in the JunkYard JunkLot went sadly silent and dark.

Louis stood alone in that which he never expected to find here: loss, shadow, dread. It reminded him of Devon. He wanted to fight but didn't know whom to lash out at. He'd lost his target.

Strange feelings began to invade his body. It started as a tingle. Then a shudder. Then depression. Then a bit of pain. The growing power of a hidden, dark domain that had been seeping into this dimension for some time sparked these feelings. Louis could see the domain staking its claim on the JunkYard JunkLot. A thin band of light now ran across the ceiling, down the walls, and over the floor of the JunkYard JunkLot, creating a ring around it.

It was like watching a burning cigarette. You know how that orange-red light slowly moves down the cigarette, leaving ash in its wake? That's what this looked like, but instead of ash, the glowing band of light revealed another dimension as it advanced toward Louis. Louis didn't realize it, but this was the thought dimension where Galonious and Trife were trapped.

It was breathtaking in its malevolent glory. A dark gray and white sky hung over a city of technology whose buildings were built close, tight, and tall. The city stretched as far as Louis could see. At its center a finely chiseled staircase climbed into the sky. From the high-tech throne of metal and light atop that staircase, a king could view this entire domain.

Who sits there? Louis wondered as he gazed at the city's

centerpiece. This place reminded Louis of Midlandian cities, but it was different. It didn't feel right. Its aura was twisted and warped.

This is what caused the JunkYard JunkLot to be shut down, Louis thought before . . .

Laughs.

Giggles.

It had returned but this time it wasn't alone.

They came up behind Louis, bending and stretching everything. When they ran past the burning light, they could be seen. It was a pack of Crims. Of course!

Where are you leading me now? Louis followed them into the new world. He turned to look back at the JunkYard JunkLot, but it was gone.

More and more Crims ran into the city until they were everywhere, scampering about. They didn't seem to know he was there, so he could freely walk through the city. But he was dead set on following the ones who had led him here.

They wound up in a place filled with unbridled desire, passion, and sovereignty. Galonious was touching and shaping this whimsical matter. "My masterful artistry is . . . masterfully artistic. A little desire, a little rage, a tiny pinch of relentlessness. That is the recipe for a great Crim," Galonious said as he took bits of people's most passionate thoughts to mold the Crims. They were not lifeless when they first claimed their shape, but they were not aware. They were simply molded desires and emotions. Galonious would inspect a Crim, then whisper a few words before breathing into the Crim's ear. That's when the Crim would become aware; it would immediately look intent and purposeful, then dart away.

The process continued.

Louis gasped. The matter being crafted into this Crim was familiar to Louis . . .

An unrelenting passion to help.

An unrelenting passion to win.

An unrelenting passion to fight for the cause at hand.

An unrelenting passion to have fun.

An unrelenting passion to break you in half if you threatened what he held dear.

His own desires were being molded into a unique Crim. It was *his* Crim. Galonious spoke into its ear and it became aware— so aware that it thought of a name.

"Quinlan. My name is Quinlan," it said, nodding to Galonious.

Curious, Galonious thought. He'd have special uses for this one.

Galonious went back to work while Quinlan stood around to observe.

"I think it's time for a bit more," Galonious said. He began to use much more matter than he'd been using before to shape seven full-size beings. They were more humanlike than the Crims, and Galonious gave them each a sampling of his own

CE energy. Its electric charge woke them. They were obviously far more powerful and capable than the Crims. Looking into their eyes, Louis saw deviant thoughtfulness and intention.

"Welcome, my generals. You will go to every continent, spreading my influence as my emissaries to the world," Galonious said. Quinlan left his side and walked toward Louis. Louis would've sworn Quinlan could see him as he paused two feet away, looking into his eyes. Quinlan could *not* see him, but he could feel him.

Not knowing what to do, Louis left Quinlan and Galonious to wander this place. He didn't have to walk far before he saw something interesting. *What the heck? Why are they here?* The parents of kids he knew were walking about. He yelled to them just as he had to Glitch, but they couldn't hear him.

Some were frightened by Crims that were taunting them. One father, though, was having a blast driving an expensive car, chasing after the pesky Crims. Farther on, Louis saw a house being built right in front of a mother, and a pile of money fell from the sky for another parent. It was all so strange.

They were going to bring my mom and dad here. What is this place? Louis thought. *Everything is messed up here, on Midlandia—everywhere!* He was angry again. He wouldn't even have peace and a normal life at home.

What's this about? What's going to happen? Louis thought.

Now, Louis may not have actually left Midlandia, but a tiny part of him did make it back home and had traveled to the thought dimension. Louis stood there with an angry heart and a growing power, and the combination of both provoked the dimension to answer his questions the best way it saw fit.

The sky turned red, streaked with obsidian. The terrain reconfigured itself into a street where cars were overturned, the pavement was cracked, street lamps had fallen, and lifeless bodies were everywhere. Death was not the worst thing here. Vacant holes were eating away at everything. No one was alive except for a lone figure about fifty yards ahead of Louis.

Nearing the figure, Louis recognized him from the images that had poured from the FyneStory device. "Arminion. You did this?"

"Did this? Some. I brought what really did it with me," he said before looking up to see who was speaking to him. "Louis Proof. I defeated you and destroyed that Alonis. Hmmm. You're not here, are you? You're just a memory, aren't you? Maybe I'm not here? Even I am going insane among this."

"I'm here. I think . . . ," Louis said.

"No. I killed you. It was such fun, but not even *I* knew what that would mean—" He stopped as he began to flash and flicker. Then everything started to vibrate and tremble.

"It's too late. Olivion was wrong about you!" Arminion said before he exploded from the inside out amid a chaos that was swallowing everything up.

Too late? Olivion wrong? Louis thought as the blast that came from Arminion sent him back to Midlandia. He awoke trying to piece everything together.

Weak? A failure? All of this will end because I will fail? Is Olivion wrong? He'd given up because Devon had been killed. Maybe it was true. Maybe Olivion was wrong.

No! Louis thought. *I'll make it back home. I'll save my mom and dad. I'll save everyone. I won't lose.*

Will you, Louis?

Am I wrong?

If so, this will not turn out for the better . . .

Chapter **Forty-two**

Young Miss Cyndi Victoria Chase is in quite a precarious situation, to say the least. The iLone had tried to kill her once again. She had forced Louis away. She had sided with the person who had killed her friend.

    Was she heartless?
    Was she foolish?
    Was she a traitor?
    Most important, was she in danger?

    Surprisingly, the answer to all of the above is: NO.

    Cyndi was just as important as Louis, and for anyone to have an inkling of a chance, they *had* to stand on opposite sides. But the bond created between them during their time here on Midlandia was so strong that nothing could break it.

    As soon as Perilynn had returned from beyond Olivion's Gate he had to defend Cyndi. That was so engrossing that only after Louis, Kiyonrae, and Vivionya escaped did he have a chance to let the entire situation sink in.

    The room had grown dark, as it was lit only by the Midlandian day, which had quickly turned to night. However, both Cyndi's and Perilynn's Alonis Medallions were shining and they provided enough light. Their glows sparked and colors played with one another, dancing on the walls of the dark room and on the faces of Cyndi and Perilynn.

"I have done it," Perilynn said, smiling as he took the Alonis from around his neck. He held it, he admired it, but he was still driven. Now he had to protect Cyndi and make sure she got home. If he failed, all would come to an end. There were many other things that he'd learned, but none of them would matter if Cyndi met her demise here.

Cyndi looked at her hands. They were shaking and her face was red, yet she felt no danger. Her glowing Alonis began to gentle her disturbed thoughts. Gazing at Perilynn, she saw that he had changed, but he was still the person who'd risked everything to ensure her safety—the same safety that he'd robbed from Devon, no matter what his reasons were. Through his responsibility and her own purpose he was bound to her in a way she could not explain but only feel. He was crucial for her safety and for the future of all. She had finally chosen a side. Now she needed to understand it.

"Why did you do that? How could you kill Devon and still defend me?" Cyndi said.

"I did it so that I could become a Favorite. I did it for myself. I also served Devon because he asked me to go home. But it was for a larger reason too. It was so everything could be set into motion. We must get you home and you must free us from this place," Perilynn said, and Cyndi could sense no dishonesty in his words. Her bond with her Alonis, coupled with her heightened Celestial Infection Rate, had given her the ability to tell lies from truths. Such was her responsibility—one that would come with a huge burden.

"I saw that if I went with Louis, there'd be no future. Farther down his path, I couldn't even see Louis. I only saw him, my family, friends, and all of the answers I'm after if I sided with you and set out on my own path," Cyndi said.

"Olivion allowed me to see my purpose. I am to protect you. It is our only future. So we must get you home. Galonious and Trife are oblivious to all of this. He and Trife are trapped in a powerful place—nearly as powerful as this one—and they're trying to escape. Something very dangerous is coming. When you return, Galonious and Trife will help you until you're able to call us all to Earth. I didn't want to leave Midlandia, but I must to remain a Favorite. We must fulfill our duties in order to continue as Favorites. After all I've been through, all I want to do is hold on to this," Perilynn said, once again placing the Alonis around his neck.

"Perilynn, without you I know I'd be dead. But you killed my friend," Cyndi said.

"Killed your friend? Was he really your friend or were you just traveling with him? You say I killed him. I did nothing of the sort. I killed his ability to fully become a Favorite. He's back home, exactly where he belongs. He's alive. He won't have to take part in this war, and he's free to do whatever it was that he wanted to return home for. I did that child a favor!"

Did you really, Perilynn?

Are you sure all you did to him was return him home?

Will he be able to help his family?

"Don't forget that the iLone were just here trying to kill you. What I did to him is no different from what they'd have done to you. You're smart. You know what side you sway to, and you know I have and always will protect you. You have no other option!" said Perilynn.

Cyndi understood but wondered if Perilynn actually cared about anything but maintaining his status as a Favorite. It didn't matter, though, because that would make him fight for her just as he had before.

"So what now?" Cyndi said.

"What now? Countless eNoli would like to meet you. You are a princess—no, a queen—and we are your court. Please, let's not keep them waiting," Perilynn said as he took her hand, leading her through the large, ornate doors of the room.

"Wait. I have to do something first. We have a debt to pay to some friends," Perilynn said.

"Okay," Cyndi said, glancing down at her glowing Alonis.

Now that her Alonis was finally working, she wished she still had that FyneStory device.

Yeah, if only . . .

Chapter **Forty-three**

Louis had never been unconscious. He had never been unaware even when he traveled home.

He knew he had to go on and he had the strength to do so, but everything was crazy and utterly confusing. He laid it all out for himself.

He now hated Perilynn, who once was a friend.

Perilynn had killed Devon.

Olivion made Perilynn a Favorite for doing so.

The iLone sought to kill Cyndi.

Cyndi had betrayed him and left him with the iLone.

The iLone, whom he despised, were now his protectors.

Did any of this make sense?

Not really . . .

He just wanted to go home for real and forget all of this.

He heard voices. He opened his eyes to see children looking at him, hesitantly smiling and whispering to one another.

"Okay, all of you, I hope you've had a good look. The way you were fussing over him . . . it's time for you to leave us alone," said a familiar female voice, drawing closer to Louis. The little guys ran out of the room, and Louis caught sight of Paris. He hadn't expected to see her here.

"Louis Proof. You had us worried for so long. We were afraid you were going to literally explode. Vivionya and Kiyonrae figured that since we've already met on quiet and friendly terms, I should talk to you. I'm happy to do so. So how are you feeling?" said Paris.

"I feel fine. I don't hurt anywhere," Louis answered.

"Louis, no one hit you, so I didn't expect you to. I mean about what happened . . . to Devon. Do you know that he's not dead? When Perilynn struck him, Devon was simply sent back to his body in your world. Your friend won't have the powers that you will have when you return, but he's okay," Paris said.

"Really?" Louis took a deep breath as he pondered this. "You know, I could've gone home. Olivion was practically rushing us all out the door, but I had to try to help Perilynn. And then he . . . and Cyndi . . . she decided to stay with Perilynn after what he did . . . how could she betray me like that?" Louis said.

"You have a right to be angry, but can you really be upset with Cyndi? Would you have her stay with you and be attacked by the iLone? Or better yet, would you stay with her and be attacked by the eNoli? Louis, it may not seem that way, but you two are on opposite sides of a war; you couldn't have stayed together. Not much of this is going to get easier. Horrible things may happen so

that better things can come about. After all you've been through,
you don't need me to tell you that it's going to be an uphill climb
on a rope laced with razor blades."

"Sides?! I don't believe in sides. From what I know, I don't
think it's that easy! But you know what? I don't care! Everyone I
care about is home, and that's where I'm going."

"Glad to hear it!"

"And we can't wait to get you back there," a new voice said as
Vivionya and then Kiyonrae entered the room.

"Kiyonrae! You tried to attack Cyndi. eNoli? iLone? Friends?
Enemies? I don't know how to call it anymore. Nothing makes
sense." Louis's tone wasn't angry but confused, which now seemed
to be the norm.

"I promise it will. You had me scared there. You pack a massive punch with that power of yours. If you hadn't calmed down, I
don't know what would have happened," Kiyonrae said.

"Louis, we're here to help you get ready to return home, so
that you'll be able to master who you are," Vivionya said.

"I remember you, you were in the city when we came to get
Devon," Louis said.

"Yes, my name is Vivionya, and you know Kiyonrae. Thank
you for calling us so we could save you. You belong with us. Do
you know that?" Vivionya asked.

Louis searched himself. His Alonis began to glow, and with
it came a feeling of belonging. He felt as if he were with his
family even though Paris and iLone were the only ones here.
Why do I feel this way? I hate the iLone, right? For the first time he

took in his surroundings. It all put him at ease and the feelings did not change.

The others led Louis out of the room, and to his surprise, when he exited he was alone again. At least it was beautiful here.

Midlandia is such a wacky place.

Chapter **Forty-four**

Perilynn had done much, but he owed something to a few. He was indeed going to lead Cyndi to meet the eNoli; first, though, he took her into the room that contained the Four.

They looked up at Perilynn; however in their state they had nothing to say. Although they'd forced themselves to speak to Louis, they had no desire to speak again.

"You fought hard so that I could become a Favorite. Actually, you fought hard so that you could destroy. Regardless of anything, when I needed you, you were there." Perilynn nodded at the silent Four. "You guys are really screwed up—an enigma of sorts. A part of you is gone, leaving you useless, yet you can't make the ascension to come back as something else. I can't let that be." Perilynn's Alonis began to glow. He raised his hands and opened his palms, and a pulse of energy began to gather there. The Four could see the outline of their brother in that energy. He was there but not completely intact and unaware of his own presence.

"This is the energy of your severed self. Think wisely. I may restore him, or you may each have your own independence. Understand me. You will each be whole to think and act entirely on your own," Perilynn said.

They gazed at the brother they loved and needed so much. He could come back; all they had to do was desire it. They could even feel one another's thoughts running through their minds. They were close to being one again. But that wasn't what they wanted.

Feast! They tore their brother's energy apart and devoured it until it was gone. They would now serve themselves. They would chase their own eNoli desires.

As they stood, they grew in size and age. No longer were they children. Rather, they seemed to be teens, each a different vibrant color. They weren't exaggerated Day-Glo colors but rich and deep. They were of four unique minds, two boys and two girls. For this they would forever be loyal to Perilynn. Perilynn's goal was to send Cyndi back home and they knew that would mean more destruction and fighting. So of course they were on board.

Now it was time to for Cyndi to meet all of the eNoli . . .

Chapter Forty-five

Perilynn, the Four, and Cyndi arrived at Lefton Rack, and it was a homecoming—an occasion for true celebration.

An iLone child had been killed.

The eNoli child was here, ready to be sent home to grant them freedom.

A rumor was spreading that Myth had returned.

Three million brilliant cheers for the eNoli future ahead!

The eNoli parted as Perilynn led Cyndi to the center of Lefton Rack. Then they hushed themselves so that every word that either of them spoke could be heard.

"We all know who this child is and why she's so important to us. Welcome Cyndi Victoria Chase!" Perilynn said.

They were silent as with great reverence and joy they saluted her. Then, simultaneously, they all bowed, Perilynn included. They appreciated and recognized her as their savior. Cyndi felt a lump in her throat and her eyes got watery.

"Freedom!"

"Freedom!"

"Freedom!"

The eNoli began to shout until one called for silence. "I speak for us all. We deeply apologize for our, you know, for trying to destroy you. We didn't know you were eNoli. Now we will lose our forms to ensure that you make it home. I and all eNoli are in your service and soon we will be in your debt," Holliston said, bowing again.

They are all in my debt? I'm responsible for their happiness? There are so many. They are all looking to me, Cyndi thought. She felt as if she'd been caught by a tsunami but there was no drowning, just the shock of being swept away in the massive wave. *I won't mess this up.*

Such was the way of Cyndi Victoria Chase.

Even at this moment, she missed Louis. Pushing him away had stung. But obviously it had been necessary. How could it not be when she was now revered as a queen? All this attention was bound to fill the hole he'd left behind.

She could sense the eNoli's passion, ambition, greed, and desire. Not just those qualities. They were complicated. They also burned with the same fuel that allowed David to defeat Goliath and made Martin Luther King Jr. stand up to a nation. They were fighters. They built countries. They were those who would never give up.

Cyndi felt as if she could do anything. She was eNoli. They weren't bad, just passionate and driven beyond belief. She would free them. She would vow to do so.

"Thank you. I appreciate your willingness to help me get home. Really, I want to totally go home. I've seen how it can be crazy here and I've seen how you've been trapped in those wicked capsules. I've been told that I have the ability to call you from this place. I will master that and free you all. Everyone deserves to be free!" Cyndi shouted, even further endearing herself to the eNoli. Needless to say, they cheered wildly.

"Cyndi, we'll get you home, but what of Myth? Is it true that he's returned?" one eNoli asked.

"Myth. I've seen and traveled with Myth. He's the one who brought me and my . . ." Cyndi paused. But, yes, they were her friends even as she stood on this side. ". . . friends to Perilynn so that I could be here right now. Myth is back. I don't know where he is now but he's back," Cyndi said.

"So, Perilynn, what does that mean to you? Will he reclaim his former position among us? He is the most powerful," an eNoli said.

"It's also said that he's a Favorite now. Is that true too?" another eNoli asked.

"Yes, it's all true. I saw him and his Alonis. He is a Favorite!" Reign shouted.

"So who will lead us, Perilynn? You or him?" Holliston said.

"What makes you think I want to lead you all again? What did my leadership gain you?" a loud voice said from the entrance of Lefton Rack. It was Myth. The rumors were indeed true, and the eNoli were in awe. "Young Perilynn. I've seen much. Maybe more or less than you as a Favorite. I don't want to retrace my old life. This is a new beginning, yes it is, with that marvelous child, Cyndi Victoria Chase.

"I'll tell you this. I've come back much more powerful than when I left—too powerful to be held to leading you all. The screaming of Midlandia, the appearance of the children, my return: Something beyond dangerous is coming and I don't think it will give a damn about either iLone or eNoli. So get Cyndi home, because I believe she has a much bigger role to play in this than just granting us freedom." Myth turned to leave.

"Well, there you have it! But, Myth, where are you going? What will you do?" Perilynn said.

"You have to ask? I'm going to find my beloved eLynori. It seems she and the Lost put you all to shame. Are you really afraid of them? Are they really that vicious? What a delight! Finding her is all I care about for now. I have a plan for her . . . ," Myth said.

Perilynn spoke quietly to Cyndi while all eyes watched Myth's majestic exit. "Cyndi, now we'll organize a massive convoy and seek out the Midland Isle. We *will* find it, because Olivion has no intention of keeping you here."

"What about the riddle? I haven't solved the riddle. You've visited Olivion and you're a Favorite. Maybe you know. She said, 'I am everything. All things come from me. But there is only one thing I cannot be. That is the key to everything,'" Cyndi said.

"I have seen Olivion. Olivion is everything. I can answer that riddle with nothing. Sorry," Perilynn said.

Cyndi shook her head with disappointment. She'd come this far and it was time to go home and she still didn't have the answer.

"The child looks sad," an onlooking eNoli said.

"Well then, let's show her how we party!" another said.

"Yes, it's a celebration!" many called in unison.

With those words, the best music ever heard flowed into Lefton Rack. It was music of elation and passion. Fun! Fun! Fun! Fun! Cyndi saw the eNoli's playful side and joined in the festivities.

But not everyone partied. Perilynn and others left to prepare an armada to face the iLone, who undoubtedly would challenge their plan to get Cyndi home.

Chapter **Forty-six**

Louis was alone in the middle of a smoothly paved street. It was wide and surrounded by nothing but green acres. He looked up at an inviting blue sky. The grass was shockingly even; blowing in the wind, it looked like a lush green ocean. He heard the hum of an engine—no, it was three engines . . . no, it was the sound of a cycle and cars. *Could they be racing?* Louis wondered.

In the distance Louis could see three magnificent vehicles, and they were indeed one cycle and two cars. The figure riding the cycle signaled to the others, and when they were not more than thirty yards from Louis, the vehicles began to disassemble. The cars broke apart; the pieces circled around until they turned into little rectangles that trailed the drivers. When only the seats were left, each hurled its driver into the air toward Louis. At the same time the cycle split apart, its driver running at the same speed as the bike had been going, and its pieces turned into glowing squares that flew into her back. In an instant they all stood in front of Louis.

"Louis Proof," one of the car drivers said, grinning.

"Yes," Louis said.

"See, I told you," the driver said.

"You told me? I mean, who else could he be? Who else is here that's not from here?" the other car driver said.

"Guys, how do you do that? The car and bike thing. The way you can just disassemble them. Can you show me? Maybe if you show me, I can do it too," Louis said.

"Sure. I'll be happy to," said the car driver who'd spoken first. "It's simple for a Favorite." He stepped into the middle of the road and began to run.

"Louis, it's all about one turn around the neck. Only one not two," the other said.

Louis watched the running one fling his Alonis Medallion around his neck. As soon as it completed one revolution, a blue rectangular light appeared at his back, and glowing rectangles came out of it. They spun around his body as he continued to race forward. A rectangle morphed into a seat that scooped him up, and others morphed into car parts. The car that Louis had seen just a few moments ago built itself again.

"See. Easy," the other said.

"That's so cool," Louis said as the car turned around to race back toward them. It disassembled and the driver stopped near Louis.

"How was that?" the driver said.

"That was great! I can do that? Wow! I'm going to try," Louis said. He hadn't thought about the possibility of his doing it as he'd watched Vivionya and Kiyonrae travel and fight. He hadn't realized how important paying attention was. He sure was paying attention now.

"Wait a . . . ," said one of them, but Louis wasn't listening. He ran off as fast as he could. With earnest determination he grabbed the Alonis Medallion and swung it around his neck. This is a tricky move. Wouldn't you know it, he hit himself in the head with the medallion and knocked himself over.

The three iLone laughed riotously before running to Louis to help him up.

"What happened?" Louis said as they were lifting him from the ground.

"You just ran off and almost knocked yourself out. You have to be careful," they said between chuckles.

"Why would you just take off like that? We showed you; we didn't tell you," the girl said.

"I just figured it would work for me." Louis still felt a bit dazed.

"Louis, I'm Lorlani, this is Dryft, and this is Oberlyn." Lorlani had been driving the cycle.

"It's great to meet you," Louis said.

"Likewise. Hey, we have to get back. Would you like to come with us? We can teach you plenty about your Alonis. And so many people would like to meet you."

"Hey, we insist. It'll be great," Dryft said.

"How will we get there?" Louis said.

"How will we get there?" Lorlani repeated with a laugh.

She stepped to the side and spun the Alonis once around her neck. The entire process of the light, the morphing squares, and everything else happened before Louis's eyes once again.

Soon there stood the best-looking cycle he'd ever seen.

"Get on," she said.

"Really? Wait. No, I want to try again. I'd like to ride my own," Louis said.

"Great! I hoped it would take more than getting knocked in the head to discourage you. This time don't rush. Swing the Alonis safely around your neck. As you do, you can think of the vehicle you want, but it would be even better to think about what the vehicle needs to be. It has to be fast. It has to be agile. It has to be strong. It has to travel on land. And of course make it really cool. You got it? Just ask the Alonis for what you need and it'll communicate with you in a special way. Trust me. You'll see," Lorlani said.

"Yeah, go for it, Louis," Oberlyn said.

"Stand back," Dryft said to his friends, only half joking.

"You can stand still or run," Lorlani said as they all stepped back to give Louis room.

Louis grabbed the Alonis Medallion, respecting both its power and wonder for the first time.

Only one turn.
Ask for what you need.
Go!

Louis took off down the street. Suddenly, it was as if he and his Alonis were two distinct entities but of one connected mind. Louis couldn't tell if he was saying the words or if they were being said to him:

How fast should I be?

So fast I can only be seen as Midlandian streaks.

How strong should I be?

So strong that I could crash from a million miles above and walk it off.

How agile should I be?

So agile I can maneuver with the precision of our wildest thoughts.

How cool should be I be?

So cool all who see me will take burning notice.

As the Alonis Medallion completed its rotation around Louis's neck, a panel of light about the same height and width of Louis's back grew three inches above his back. Glowing rectangles flew from the light and circled Louis's body. They morphed into car parts, connecting to build the car of Louis's dreams right around him. He immediately raced off in it at breakneck speed.

The other three began to run and swung their Alonis Medallions. Quickly, they were chasing after Louis in their vehicles and soon sped past him to lead the way.

This was beyond any RC car race Louis had ever participated in, even on the grand track of the JunkYard JunkLot. They drove through caves. When they got to a canyon they didn't stop. Each Alonis resifted itself to become a flying vehicle. There were wide, smooth, twisting, and looping paths that led over seemingly bottomless chasms that spread for miles.

Then there was a wall of water as high and wide as he could see. It was like a vertical ocean. It was like the wall he and his friends had had to overcome when they were seeking Olivion's Gate. The others sped into the water without hesitation.

I'll need something different if I'm going to travel through that. In an instant Louis's Alonis vehicle changed into an aquatic car. He drove into the water and was able to easily maneuver in it. Here he saw gigantic underwater cities crafted of brilliant multicolored transparent materials. Many of the surfaces were on a slant and they all looked utterly artful, more beautiful even than the city he'd rearranged not long ago.

The iLone waved to Louis and the others as they sped by. Louis happily waved back. In one of the nearby buildings Louis was surprised to see the Painters at work on the glasslike walls, creating another image of Midlandian lore. They nodded at Louis, then went right back to work.

Lorlani sped upward and broke the surface of the water. Each vehicle changed into a miraculous flying machine. With a thought Louis did the same for his. As they traveled, day turned into night, and on the horizon Louis could see a radiant city coming into view. It seemed beyond massive. The lights of the city created a white aura with a delicate blue tint, buildings cut the sky, and large and small airships flew overhead. This was the city Louis had seen when he'd first arrived in Midlandia. Far in the distance was the mountain he'd crashed into.

They entered the city under a huge archway. It seemed to be made of ivory and luminous words were etched on its front, welcoming all iLone to enter.

The streets were solid and perfect: no cracks, no debris of any kind. The buildings were so tall and beautiful they were almost beyond words. Each seemed to shed a thin, almost invisible, glowing mist.

Louis and the others dipped aggressively through the streets as iLone watched and waved at Louis. He drove with one hand and waved with the other. It felt like a homecoming.

They drove until they reached what probably was the center of the city. There was a small bit of sadness here, along with a tree of vibrant fruit and light. It seemed tough and unwavering in its power but Louis could see that some of the leaves had fallen.

Now, of course, it was a tree, and leaves always fall from trees. That's just the way things are, but not on Midlandia. This was the tree of eternity and it was supposed to be forever radiant and its leaves were never supposed to fall.

Louis got out of his car, walked over to one of the fallen leaves, and picked it up. Its light spoke sorrowfully to him. Without words, the leaf told him he had to be strong and fight so that all could be safe and glorious. As soon as it delivered its message, it faded away.

"Louis, just like Midlandia is crying, the tree is shedding its leaves; neither of those things is supposed to happen," a voice said from behind him. Louis turned to see Kiyonrae.

"We don't know what's causing this, but things are dying.

Things are never supposed to die here. That leaf was connected to something somewhere in the universe and it's now gone. We thought that impossible," Vivionya said.

"You have to find out what's happening and stop it," Dryft said.

"Why just me? Why is all of this my responsibility? How come you can't help?" Louis asked.

"We have no business on your world. We stay here so you can live your lives as your own. Galonious and Trife are there now. They're trapped, but if they get free, you'll all lose yourselves. Their presence will unlock everything buried deep within you, and everyone will act without conscience or restraint. You will all lose what makes you human," Vivionya said.

"Yes, the eNoli are self-serving demons. You've seen this for yourself. Perilynn sacrificed everything to deliver you safely to Olivion and then turned around and destroyed Devon," Kiyonrae said.

"But you were trying to kill Cyndi. You still want to kill her! She *was* my friend. What's the difference?" Louis said.

"I won't lie. Both iLone and eNoli fight for our goals. We iLone don't receive any pleasure from the duty of killing; we do it for your benefit, not our own. I sought to end Cyndi's existence here so that the eNoli won't have the chance to fester among your kind. You've had close company with the Five. They destroy for fun and sport. How did you feel when you walked through the City of Chance and saw the effects of their carnage? They relished what they did," Kiyonrae said.

Louis remembered the iLone woman who'd had just her upper torso left when she'd called to him. Other images flickered in his

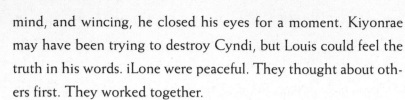

mind, and wincing, he closed his eyes for a moment. Kiyonrae may have been trying to destroy Cyndi, but Louis could feel the truth in his words. iLone were peaceful. They thought about others first. They worked together.

The only thing that made the iLone similar to the eNoli was war. There are always those who would have you ended so they may be supreme. If the iLone weren't warriors, they'd be wiped out.

The iLone must fight.

The eNoli must fight.

"Louis, Cyndi is here because we broke the treaty. But how could we have you face everything on your own with no help at all? However, this will prove to have been a critical mistake if we let Cyndi return safely. Perhaps we shouldn't have gotten involved. When you get home, you'll meet Timioosiyan. Your cousin Lacey has already met him. He'll assist you. It'll be up to you, though, to save your people by extinguishing Galonious and Trife. It's your destiny," Vivionya said.

"What's to stop all eNoli from going to Earth and messing everything up?" Louis asked.

"The Midland Isle is a place that only a few can find," Oberlyn said.

"Until recently. Many were there when the three eNoli escaped," Vivionya said.

"Throughout time, a rare iLone or eNoli stumbled upon the path to the Midland Isle and some came to your world. Whenever this happened, Earth experienced its most promising and horrific periods. The CE were in the shadows and their influence was felt. They caused monumental events to happen," Kiyonrae stated.

"A war was fought to find the Gate. Myth quested for it," Vivionya said.

"I know about that. He didn't enter the Gate, but Arminion did," Louis said.

"Yes, that changed everything. The treaty was established, which is the reason you're here. Before that there were no safe-guards against either iLone or eNoli leaving Midlandia to set foot on physical ground," Kiyonrae explained.

"But there's a dark side to that. If you and Cyndi return safely, unlike Devon, you'll have the ability to call countless iLone to your location, and Cyndi will have the ability to call countless eNoli. They want to send her home so that she may call each and every one of them to Earth. That'll end everything as you know it," Vivionya said.

"No matter what happens, you are *not* to call us to Earth. You can do what needs to be done. You have power. Your abilities are limited only by your imagination, so you are limited only by yourself," Vivionya said, thinking about the last conversation she'd had with Devon.

"But you must be careful. You are something like us but not quite. You still have a physical body that you're bound to. You'll have to rejoin it. While you've been here, it's been changing and

adapting to welcome you back. Take care not to go too far—"
Kiyonrae said.

A shout interrupted them as an iLone ran into the center of
the city. "The eNoli are beginning to search for the Midland Isle!
They are ready for war!"

"But he's not ready. You should have seen him. He hit his head
with the Alonis. We're doomed," said Lorlani with a laugh.

"We have no choice. We have to get him home," Vivionya
said.

H. O. M. E.

Such a welcome combination of four simple letters! thought Louis.

HOME!

FINALLY!

Chapter **Forty-seven**

The festivities were long over and Cyndi was outside looking up into the sky. Wondrous airships streaked overhead. Until now she hadn't realized the size of this operation. There had to be more than a thousand elegant battle cruisers above and on the ground. All of them were to protect her during their quest to return her home.

"So, Cyndi, you've come into who you are?" DiVarion said from behind.

"Hey, where did you come from? I didn't expect to see you here. Are you disappointed because I took the ship? Did it return to you?" Cyndi asked.

"Please don't worry about that ship. I think you know I guided you to it. Besides, I have plenty," DiVarion said.

"Thanks, DiVarion. What about everything else? Do you know what happened . . . to Devon?"

"Yes, Cyndi, I know all about that. It's a shame because he was your friend. But it seems he had a role to play and he fulfilled it. I guess he wasn't supposed to be like you and Louis—"

"It was so that Perilynn could become a Favorite and I would have to choose my side. I am eNoli . . . I *am* eNoli. I had no choice. Am I bad?" Cyndi said.

"Are you bad? What we may consider good and bad here is gray. The question is: Are you disappointed?" DiVarion said.

"You know, it sounds terrible, but I know that I'm supposed to be with the eNoli and free them from this place. I don't think they're good and I don't think they're bad. Who is really either? I've seen a bit of them in everyone I know. I can't explain it. Do you know what I mean?" Cyndi said.

"I understand. I really do, but do you have any idea what will happen if they're called from this place?" DiVarion asked.

"Honestly, I know it won't be all good, and I also know I have to do it. If I don't, it will be horribly wrong. I know this like I know I have to breathe and like I know I have to go home and see my dad, brother, and even that mother of mine. Louis won't understand, and he's going to try to stop me. He thinks I betrayed him with my decision, but I can't let him stop me."

"Well, my dear, I guess you know what you have to do. If you didn't have a specific duty, you wouldn't be a Favorite. Favorites always seem to find their way, and it seems you're well along your path. I've given you your Alonis. I can do no more than that. I will tell you this, though: I know you're on your proper path because look at how your Alonis glows and welcomes you. It won't lie to you." DiVarion gazed proudly at Cyndi.

His look gave her comfort. She knew that this was good-bye, so she gave him a hug of farewell and thanks. Hugging was out of character for her, and her desire to do this startled her. However, he *had* given her an Alonis, a safe place to stay, and guidance. She was deeply grateful.

"DiVarion, there's something else. I've been looking for something, but I don't know what it is. This drives me crazy. I keep
thinking that one day I'll open a book and find that special bit of
information that'll make me say, 'That's it!' I think this is all part of
me finding whatever it is that I'm looking for," Cyndi said, realizing this truth for the first time.

"I understand. Maybe what you've been looking for was
something that you couldn't handle before becoming a Favorite.
Maybe now you'll find it. Regardless of anything, I think both
you and Louis will be okay. Perilynn is waiting for you," DiVarion
said as he pointed toward a fleet of airships. Perilynn stood in
front of one. Cyndi caught Perilynn's eye and he signaled for her
to come aboard.

"Wait!" Cyndi shouted. "DiVarion, Louis and Devon left their
FyneStory books in your city. Can you make sure they get them?
Maybe it's too late for Devon, but Louis will definitely need his."

"Sure. I'll see if I can arrange for them to find the books when
they return home. That's very considerate of you," DiVarion said,
walking away. Soon he was gone.

Hoping that she'd see him again, Cyndi strode toward
Perilynn. Lines of eNoli were now boarding the ships. She wondered if there'd even been a war fought on Earth with as many
soldiers. It seemed unthinkable. No doubt she'd soon be with her
family.

"Perilynn, is all of this really necessary?"

"Necessary? Oh yes. The iLone aren't going to want you to
go home. We're about to go to war. There are far more iLone

Favorites and they pose a huge threat. Not to mention, if they trained Louis, he'd be a foe like none we've seen. But I'm not worried. I guided you to the Gate safely; I'll do the same now. Besides, there's only one of you this time. That should be easy, right? Oh, how I wish that was true!" Perilynn was firm but joking at the same time.

"There's only one of you this time," Cyndi repeated to herself. Why would Perilynn bring that up? She had no time to be thinskinned, so she boarded the ship.

"How will we find the Midland Isle? It was at Olivion's Gate. Besides, Olivion told me that neither Louis nor I would be able to return home until we answered her riddle. I don't have the answer," Cyndi said.

"Well, I don't know what that's about. It's my duty to guide you, and you *will* find the Midland Isle. I guarantee that," Perilynn said.

Cyndi felt terrible about Devon, but something made her feel as if it was okay; as if he'd found what he wanted. He'd wanted to go home and he got what he asked for. It wasn't like he was dead for real. He was just home.

Well protected among the eNoli ranks, Cyndi began her own journey home.

Chapter **Forty-eight**

The final leg of Louis's Midlandian adventure was about to begin. While it seemed that the eNoli were seriously prepared for a war, it looked as if the iLone were not. They had no visible cruisers or reinforcements. However, there's more than one way to wage a war.

"We're going to travel inside Midlandia," Kiyonrae said as he began to lead Louis from the tree through a crowd of countless iLone onlookers.

Louis remembered his journey with Perilynn in inner Midlandia. It was nice and safe there.

"He'll have to face Galonious and Trife when he returns, and you'll have him hide from battle?" Lorlani asked.

"We've lost one child, or have you forgotten? Louis will find his way to the Midland Isle within Midlandia, where it's much safer. Yet, I have a feeling Midlandia and Olivion won't allow him to return without the skills he needs," Kiyonrae said.

"But still, a Favorite evading battle? Will you accompany him?" Lorlani asked.

"Funny that you ask. In fact I won't; you three will," Kiyonrae said.

"Of course we will. We never planned to leave his side anyway," Dryft said.

"Wait. We have to go inside Midlandia? I think I can help," Louis said. To reach inner Midlandia, he wouldn't have to force through as Perilynn had. With the right technique, Midlandia would bend and shape itself to his will. If it were in the mood to do so, it would. All he had to do was ask politely. Louis stood within the glowing Midlandian city, and a silence gathered around him as streaks of blue-tinted energy began to circle his body.

Alonis Glow—Midlandian Blue.
Hands Glow—Midlandian Blue.

Midlandia began to cry, but Louis would bring it calm. He fell to his knees, pressing both of his hands to the ground to soothe and comfort it. Passionately and quietly he asked,

Will you open for me? I want to go home.
Yes, Louis. Just make sure you save me.

Midlandia opened up right then, revealing its inner wonder. Lights. Twisting and winding pathways. Louis was now kneeling at the landing of a large stairway that led deep into Midlandia. There was more. A graceful flying eLebrion came out of the opening and greeted the iLone before it took off into the sky, trailing sparking light behind it.

"Hey! He may be new at it, but he's a Favorite," Dryft said.

"Great, Louis!" Lorlani said.

"So that settles it," Oberlyn said.

"Yeah, we're off in search of the Midland Isle, I guess. Kiyonrae, Vivionya, all of you: Good-bye, I'm going home. When I get there . . ." Louis paused, thinking of what everyone had hinted lay on the path ahead of him. It seemed impossible for him to handle this on his own. He saw so many brilliant iLone faces looking eagerly at him. They were all relying on him. Even Midlandia had just asked him to save it.

What *would* he do when he got home?

What *could* he do when he got home?

"When I get there, I promise I won't give up," he said as he and his trusty chaperones entered inner Midlandia. While many other iLone would face the eNoli in a war, four would try to evade it by using the back door.

Louis was once again traveling through the hidden passageways and opposite spaces of Midlandia. The paths ran in spirals and concave to one another. This time Louis seemed to understand it all, and although he was following, he felt he could lead.

Surprisingly, someone else was here. He could see this figure yards away speeding along a spiraled path, having what seemed to be a great time. It was almost as if this person was surfing as he did wild acrobatic tricks on the path. But there was no surfboard. Who could be cavorting at a time such as this? It was Orenci! Louis called to him, but Orenci didn't hear him, or knowing Orenci, he

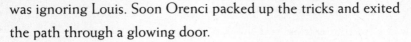

was ignoring Louis. Soon Orenci packed up the tricks and exited the path through a glowing door.

He'd told Louis and Cyndi, "You'll each know when you need to find me." Well, Louis and his new friends were trying to find a path to the Midland Isle, so if he didn't need Orenci now, he figured he never would. Without warning, he jumped from his path to the one that Orenci had been on and ran into a passageway, which quickly closed behind him.

"Kiyonrae is going to beat us senseless!" Dryft shouted.

Chapter **Forty-nine**

There are many doors throughout Midlandia, although they aren't always visible. Of course, if you enter a door, it's the one you're supposed to enter and it will lead you to the place you're supposed to be. *That is the way of Midlandia and of all other places, including your own.*

"So you've finally found the time to pay me a visit. Speaking of paying, have you been paying attention? Louis, have you?"

"Paying attention to what?" Louis asked.

"Are you thick? Louis Proof, have you been stricken with idiocy? Let me ask again. Have you been paying attention to everything?"

"Everything?" Louis asked. What was everything? That surely was a lot.

The eNoli?
Yes.

The iLone?
Yes.

The fighting?

Yes.

The Horribly Marvelous Wonder of Midlandia?

Oh yes! Definitely!

"Yes, Orenci, I've been paying attention. I really have. This place has many wonders, but it's not a good place. I lost a friend, and someone for whom I'd have laid my life down killed him. Matter of fact, I did lay my life down for him. Me and Cyndi both did. Orenci, I have to go home. My Alonis is powerful, but I don't think it'll be enough. I'm going to have to fight. Can you help me?" Louis said.

"Louis, so I ask again . . . have you been paying attention?" Orenci charged at Louis. Louis moved, but not fast enough to avoid being hit. He didn't fall, but he stumbled backward. The pain of the blow shuddered through him. The land became dark and it began to rain. Orenci charged again, this time connecting with one of his signature moves: a smack followed by a slap. Rain fell but Louis was vibrating, and oddly, none of the rain hit him. A shield of glowing energy around his body blocked the rain.

Instinctively, Louis rushed at Orenci.

"Louis, you won't meet kindness once you return home. I hate to tell you this, but your home is under attack. Parents are being stolen. Galonious is building an army made from people's most supreme desires. Do you know how dangerous that type of army is? You had to help your cousin Lacey fight them when you were in the Celestial Drifts. You'll have to deal with that, and *that* is only a distraction. There's something coming unlike anything you've seen. It's even making Midlandia cry for help. I don't know what it is, but it's coming. Louis, even I don't have time for my own enigmatic ways. I need you stronger! You must fight harder!"

"I've seen how messed up my home is! I've seen Galonious!" Louis tried to ready himself for whatever Orenci did next.

"You saw Perilynn fight much of Midlandia. The FyneStory device showed you Reign and Kyll fighting. Were you paying attention?" Orenci now charged at Louis with multiple acrobatic attacks.

Louis *had* been paying attention to the eNoli's moves. He battled back in the rain, but soon the sky cleared and the sun came out. Orenci shot beams of light at Louis, and the Alonis created shields to protect him. Louis figured out how to fire back by calling to Midlandia's energy and forcing it toward his attacker, but Orenci dodged Louis's glowing projectile.

"Very nice! So come on, chase me, if you can!" Orenci began to run at hyper cheetah speeds. Tearing up the Midlandian ground, Louis tailed him until Orenci flew into the sky.

"What's stopping you? I thought you had no limits," Orenci shouted.

No limits. No limits. Louis had never considered that he might be able to fly. He felt a pull inside of himself sort of like the one he'd felt when Perilynn had first rescued him by pulling him back from Reign. He thought of flying and easily took off into the sky after Orenci. Actually, he'd flown when he first got here, but he'd hit a mountain. This time he knew it wasn't a dream and he was in control.

Chasing Orenci, he rocketed faster and faster for hundreds of miles yet couldn't catch up. He flew for so long that the utterly unexpected happened. He felt tired and weak. Was that even possible? Quickly, he lost speed and altitude. Orenci slowed down as Louis plummeted to the ground, hitting it like a laundry bag full of scrap metal.

"That, Young Louis, is why you need an Alonis." Orenci landed right beside him. "You're powerful, but you're still tied to your finite human self. If you exhaust too much of your energy, you will fall weak. Your body is an anchor that keeps you bound to those you love and those you'll have to fight for. Only if you give up your ties to your humanity will you be strong enough to face what's coming. It's an enormous sacrifice. But on a lighter note, with the Alonis Medallion you don't have to use your own energy all the time. So use your Alonis to chase me! Let's go!" Orenci took off once again.

Slowly Louis gathered himself and stood. Feeling his strength coming back, he began to run and, with a thought, swung the Alonis around his neck. Soon he was in a small, high-tech jet that built itself the same way the car had. Now he could reach speeds that left Orenci in the dust—and he wasn't tired. Orenci smiled and began to leap alongside mountains that were building themselves around them.

Dismantling the Alonis vehicle, Louis chased Orenci on land. They soared from peak to peak. Louis whooped with joy.

Orenci stopped on one of the peaks, and Louis landed beside him. "Louis, you have great potential. I've taught you some things, but I can't teach you what you need to know. If I show you too much, you'll be limited by what you think you should do. You have to be open for everything. You must think without limits. That's the most important thing I can teach you. I'm sure you'll be able to do things that will amaze me. Yours is a hard path that you'll have to see to the end. Know that we're relying on you and you are very special. You are more powerful than you can imagine."

"Orenci, you seem to know almost everything. Cyndi was my friend and now we're on opposite sides. We both can't win. Is she is really eNoli now? Which one of us will win?" Louis said as Orenci threw a mountain peak—yes, a mountain peak—at Louis. Louis leaped to punch right through it. Its energy shattered, then quickly gathered itself to reattach to the mountain.

"Nice try! Answer my questions!" Louis shouted.

"I don't know everything, but I do have an idea of how this may turn out. So you or Cyndi—who will win? I say—" Orenci had stopped on another mountaintop, and as Louis landed next to him, Midlandia began to vibrate.

"You've got to love this place," Orenci said with a laugh, and the wind seemed to carry him away.

"Oh, come on! Who's going to win? Her or me? I know you know," Louis asked.

"Next time I see you, I promise I'll tell you who I think will win. That'll give you something to look forward to. Also, remember that there's sort of a science—and science has laws—behind being an iLone Favorite. It's not *my* job to teach you that. Nonetheless, don't you think it's time for you to get back, since you have a fighting chance now? Fight your way home! And fight some more when you get there," Orenci said, flying off.

Louis felt ready now. However, there was one thing he was going to do before he left. He was going to make sure he wasn't the only one to return home.

Without warning, his newfound confidence was shaken as Louis began to fall through the air. The mountains and everything were gone. Such is possible on Midlandia.

Chapter Fifty

Louis landed with a massive thud that jolted the Midlandian ground. No one was near, but behind him he could see eNoli coming in daring numbers. Massive aircrafts were with them as they searched for the Midland Isle. Louis could feel Cyndi. She was on one of the ships, well guarded, while he was exposed to all of his enemies.

Reign was already in pursuit. Louis ran as fast as he could, swinging the Alonis around his neck, and his Alonis car swiftly built itself. He had no choice but to flee against so many. Louis wasn't scared, but he needed a plan—which he didn't have.

"Louis. Death is creeping in on you. All we want to do is send you home. Home, Louis, home. My blade will do it easily," Reign shouted.

"Oh no! You can't get that," Louis shouted back as he spotted a lone figure in the distance. Louis had never seen him before, but he could feel that he wasn't a friend.

It was an eNoli only known to few: Laugh of the Lost. He wore a long red jacket that blew in the wind and was torn and worn. The scythe he clutched looked deadly sharp. He let it fall to the ground to clap his hands. The sound was deafening.

Unfazed, Louis raced toward him at least until the Midlandian ground disappeared under Louis.

Darn! Once again he began to fall, this time into a pitch-black abyss. Laugh picked up his scythe and flew over the abyss. *Had Laugh's clap created the abyss?* He did not even have to touch Midlandia to shape it. Louis stared hard at Laugh as he targeted Louis with beams of light that disrupted the energy of Louis's Alonis. The car disassembled—and that was only the first hit. Once again Laugh besieged Louis with solid, fierce beams of jagged light that struck their target. Louis screamed in pain.

Reign and his followers halted, reminded why eNoli like Laugh were not to be messed with even without being Favorites. Landing in front of them, Laugh just smiled with his head cocked to the left as if it would fall off, looking like a psychopathic twenty-something-year-old. Reign backed off, wanting nothing to do with him and the band of misfits that had appeared behind him.

Laugh clapped his hands again. As the thunderous sound died, the abyss filled with solid ground. Louis had surely met his end. Satisfied, Laugh began to walk back to wherever he'd come from.

"Sicko!" Reign said under his breath.

Laugh turned around to see who dared insult him.

Wait. Midlandia had begun to rumble and . . .

Louis was back! In a mini Alonis vehicle, he shot right out of Midlandia. And he was not alone. Countless iLone were with him, ready to fight.

The Young Armada landed in front of Reign. Reign knew that he and the eNoli with him were in trouble.

The Young Armanda stood in a perfect V formation with aMaya in the front. She looked into the sky and all around, calculating how many they'd have to face.

"Oberlyn, Lorlani, Dryft, take Louis away from here. We'll deal with this," aMaya said as the Young Armada's Alonises began to glow.

It seems as if both sides *are* evenly matched.

Chapter **Fifty-one**

Cyndi was unaware of the progress of the war or that Louis had just been attacked. Safe in a quiet room, she could've sworn she saw someone run past her open door. She'd know that person anywhere: Orenci. Quickly, she left the room, only to jump in surprise. He stood not two feet from the door.

Orenci laughed, and they were no longer on the ship—or at least they didn't appear to be. Dust and wind blew about this sandy, rocky place. It wasn't appealing but it wasn't bad either.

"So, Cyndi, what am I supposed to teach you? You can already fight, can't you? Your father gave you karate lessons so you'd be able to protect yourself. With your power and with what you've seen here, you'll be fine. But you're not after a chance to protect and save others. You're after truths. You have to be, because there are secrets solely for you to unlock. I'll start you off with one," Orenci said.

Extending his hands, Orenci moved violently backward and upward until he was about seven feet away and five feet off the ground. He was suspended in the air and a smile came across his face and it was as if Midlandia was holding him.

"Can you see it? Can you see it all?"

See what? Everything was blowing around and the dust was everywhere. Cyndi could hardly see anything.

"There'll always be something to distract you. But the truth is always there. Fight through the madness and confusion so that you may see it," Orenci said.

The madness. The confusion. What was it for her? High school? Boys? Grades? Getting into college? The confusion of life? Oh yeah, let's not forget this war. What was beyond all of that? What is there to see?

Cyndi could see it. There were infinite connections from here to all other places. There was energy everywhere—not just here—and she could also see it as it was back home. Nothing was alone and nothing was unaffected. She couldn't believe she and Louis hadn't seen this before.

"I see the connections! What do they mean? There's so much information, and I can't understand it!"

"Cyndi, to be able to see is the first step. To be able to understand is another."

"Thank you. I have more to do before I can understand, don't I?" Cyndi asked.

"Yes, you do. Remember, every journey is a twisted path and you never know where it'll lead you. You may have to do some things that don't seem to make sense, but trust in your feelings and not in what you see. Things are always changing and recreating themselves. Trust your feelings," Orenci said.

Cyndi suddenly found herself at the helm of the ship with Perilynn.

"Where did you come from?" Perilynn said.

"That doesn't matter. Are we any closer to the Midland Isle?"

"Who knows? I'm working on it, Cyndi. I'm working on it!"

They both looked at the massive battle that lay in front of them.

Chapter **Fifty-two**

Louis and the iLone met countless eNoli in battle. The eNoli were swarms of deadly Celestial bees ready to protect their young queen, as well they should. But Louis and his Alonis soared toward where he knew Cyndi had to be.

He felt he'd figured it out. They could only get to Olivion's Gate together. So he was sure that he and Cyndi would also have to get to the Midland Isle together. He was set on convincing Cyndi of this obvious possibility. All he had to do was get to her. She'd betrayed him, but this was bigger than that. He had to get home, and he wasn't going to let the iLone destroy her.

With lightning-quick moves, Dryft, Oberlyn, and Lorlani sliced through eNoli ranks using well-targeted blasts and maneuvers fueled by pure energy. They fought their way above one of the grand silver and purple eNoli airships. Louis's flying Alonis deactivated, dropping him on top of the ship. He removed the Alonis Medallion from his neck and held its chain. When the medallion touched the surface of the ship, the medallion spun, cutting through the ship's skin like a blade. As the ship began to crumble and fall apart, eNoli tried to escape.

Louis flipped off of the exploding ship and was once again

in his flying Alonis vehicle. He swept through eNoli attacks and blasts until he was able to drop on top of the next ship. Now, though, the eNoli, wise to his intentions, met him upon landing. And Dryft, Oberlyn, and Lorlani were right there to support Louis. Battle on the airship! Could the eNoli defeat four Favorites?

Louis bounded from ship to ship, breaking them apart with his Alonis. These ships were just in his way as he tried to get to the one he was sure Cyndi was on.

Speed up, Louis, and stop wasting time.
Your brethren will be upon her soon.

Vivionya and Kiyonrae were not with Louis or the other Favorites. They were iLone assassins set on destroying Cyndi Victoria Chase. While Louis was trying to reach her, they'd already infiltrated her airship and stealthily sought out her location. She was with Perilynn and the Five who were now Four. There was no better team to protect her, except for Myth, who'd left to find eLynori. As far as Vivionya and Kiyonrae were concerned, as Favorites they'd been in much worse situations. Anyway, they cared not for their own safety as long as they could destroy the child.

Louis, you cannot let that happen.

They fought and dismantled many eNoli on their way to their target. As soon as they broke through the doors to the ship's helm, their Alonises created a storm of light, as they knew there was nothing for them besides battle.

The Four met Kiyonrae and Vivionya with a wildly crafted and coordinated acrobatic display of martial artistry. Flips. Kicks. Punches. High. Low. From every which way. It was overwhelming, but the Favorites blocked all and threw their own attacks into the mix. Kiyonrae used his Alonis to continue to fend them off while Vivionya went for Cyndi and Perilynn.

Perilynn met Vivionya head-on. He wasn't about to let Cyndi fall. They fought until Vivionya managed to force Perilynn away. It was only for a second, but it gave Vivionya a chance.

Vivionya was about to end Cyndi and the havoc she would rain on Earth with her return. A blade appeared in her hand.

You would all be saved?

You would all be condemned?

Louis entered the room with Oberlyn, Dryft, and Lorlani chasing him. They had no idea that he was there to help Cyndi. He arrived just in time to see Vivionya get blasted back. Apparently Cyndi didn't need to be saved. She was quite capable of saving herself.

Cyndi became aware of Louis's presence. An unexpected calm came over the room as Cyndi's and Louis's Alonises created an impenetrable stream of solid light between them. Not even the other Favorites could breach this. Louis could see the CE shouting and trying to penetrate the light, but he couldn't hear them. Louis walked up to Cyndi, his eyes filled with disgust and disappointment.

If Perilynn reached Earth, Louis would deal with him there, but there was no time to think about that now.

"Cyndi, we're going home! We can only get home if we leave together—just as we could only find Olivion's Gate together. You should know that," Louis said.

"Louis, I want to go home, but you don't understand. We can't go together."

"That doesn't make sense! We can't get home without each other! Come on!"

"Louis, don't yell at me and stop looking at me like that. You're my friend, but I've seen it. You don't know!"

"Fine, when we get back, we can be on opposite sides. But right now you're coming with me so we can get home!" Louis screamed, holding out his hand to Cyndi.

She took it. With that their Alonises began to glow, and a sphere of light encased them, sweeping them from the airship to the center of the battle. iLone and eNoli were streaking through the sky, destroying one another. Battleships blasted one another. There were deafening explosions everywhere.

The children observed from their bubble of light. Were there no friends here? Was there no love here? When these two sides got together, would there be only war?

Cyndi, terribly shaken by what she saw, clenched her hands into fists. All of this destruction was because of not knowing!

Both sides have a version of the truth, which neither really understands. The iLone were wrong about why Perilynn wanted to cross the Gate. Maybe all this could have been avoided if they knew that Perilynn was only after answers that he deserved. The iLone were even wrong about why the eNoli wanted to leave.

Just as Orenci had allowed her to see, everything was connected. The energy that flowed here created problems everywhere, especially back home. She thought about high school: that hotbed of ignorance. More important, she thought about all the conflicts over religion. Everyone had his or her own perspective and everyone was ignorant. How could you understand something such as the Olivion? Let alone package up what you think you know but don't and then condemn those who have their own ideas. But who was right?

I will be right. There had to be one truth. That's what she was after: pure truth without any perspective to mess it up. But did that exist, and what would it take to gain it? Was that what was on the top floor of the library that she'd left behind to find Louis? Is that what the power in her Alonis, when combined with the FyneStory device, would unlock? Without that truth, Cyndi realized that . . .

Louis watched it all just as Cyndi did. A friend had died, a new and precious friendship had been destroyed, and now there was a full-blown war. It was not fun. It was not exciting. It was harrowing. What about love? What about understanding? He wanted to stop this. But what would it take? He'd been told he'd have to fight what was coming. What would carry him through that?

Was it love of home?

Was it love of family?

He wouldn't let this come to his home and destroy every-thing. He loved his home too much. Without that love fueling him to fight he realized that . . .

That was it . . .

At that moment, and as of if one mind, Louis and Cyndi came to the conclusion that if this continued

THERE WOULD BE *NOTHING* LEFT . . .

The answer had been staring them in the face since the begin-ning.

DiVarion, Emyli, Paris, Myth, the Librarian, and Perilynn had all said what Olivion could not be:

"Sorry, children. There's *nothing* I can think of, *nothing* at all," DiVarion said.

"The Olivion is everything; there's *nothing* the Olivion cannot be," Emyli said.

"That's quite a riddle. Too much for me. There's *nothing* that I can think of," Paris said.

"Olivion's Gate showed me *nothing*, but Olivion was every-thing," Myth said.

"I have seen Olivion. Olivion is everything. I can answer that riddle with *nothing* . . . ," Perilynn said.

If I am everything and all things come from me
There is only one thing I cannot be.

Olivion cannot be nothing!
Nothing is the key to everything.

"Where are we now?" Louis asked as they were walking along the chaos of another war.

"I know this . . . we saw this when we were with Emyli," Cyndi said.

"Yes, there's the Gate," Louis said.

"There's Arminion," Cyndi said.

They saw him cross the Gate, and this time the Gate stayed open. They followed Arminion through.

Arminion, unaware of them, was bent on destroying Olivion. Her Domain was different from when they'd seen it. It was a dim blackness. The only light came from the sparking path left by his dragging blades as they cut into Midlandia.

Louis and Cyndi followed Arminion to Olivion's Observatory. Where they'd once seen a glowing light that rejuvenated them, they now saw an image of a sleeping young woman who was the epitome of beauty. Although they didn't realize it, she looked different to each of them. Louis saw strength and bravery in her magnetic presence and modeled cheekbones. Cyndi saw cleverness in her arched eyebrows. And Arminion saw power in her command-ing aura, stunning body, and in the light that rose from her like a mist, electrifying the air around her.

Arminion dropped his blades to gaze upon her. He was so enamored that he actually forgot why he was there. He wanted to know who she was and everything about her. This was like nothing he'd ever felt before. It even greatly surpassed his desire to destroy the Olivion.

"You've come to destroy me? Why do you wait? Come on, so you may leave this place. I won't stop you," Olivion said to Arminion, appearing near him.

"Who is she? Where is she?" Arminion said.

"Never mind her. You didn't come here for her, did you? You've come to destroy me—so try," Olivion shouted. Her tone and insolence reminded Arminion of exactly why he'd sought her. Yes, he was here to destroy her, but not before he found out who this woman was.

"I will end you with these blades, but I may spare you if you tell me her name!" Arminion said, picking up his blades from the ground.

"I will not tell you," Olivion said.

"Yes, you'll tell me as you beg for your life," Arminion said.

He rushed at Olivion and plunged his blades into her. She stood there unharmed. Arminion kept stabbing her with no effect.

Eventually, he fell to his knees in defeat. There was no hope for escape as there was no hope of destroying the Olivion.

"Arminion, don't you see that you can't destroy me with what I am? That blade, you, all CE, the world you seek to escape Midlandia for are all parts of me. If I were to be destroyed, all would cease to exist. I am everything and all things come from me. I am not your enemy," Olivion said.

"I want to leave Midlandia. This place is a prison. There's an entire world that we aren't a part of. Please let us leave," Arminion said.

"You want to leave? Do you even remember that place? Is that why? That's a world of death and endings. There are no such things for you here," Olivion said.

"Yes. But there's something other than here, and I want a part of all things. That drives me insane. I can dream of that place, I know it's real, and you've just admitted it exists. However, now, above that, I want to find her," Arminion shouted.

"You want to find her?"

"Yes! Who is she? What is her name? Where is she? I must know!"

"Well, if that person is to have a name, it shall be Alorion. She's asleep, waiting for someone to wake her," Olivion said.

"Alorion? That name . . . it's a perfect name. Where does she sleep? Tell me where so I can wake her!" Arminion demanded.

Olivion had always known he was the one. He had a passion unmatched by all of her CE. He wouldn't fail her. She was sure of it.

"But you've tried to destroy me. Why should I let you leave to wake her? If I did, you'd have to be punished first. What would your punishment be?"

"Anything! I wasn't alone in my quest to find and destroy

you! You can ban all CE from leaving, but let me go. I have to meet that woman. She calls to me. She wants me to wake her!" Arminion shouted.

"Then that's it! It officially stands that you and all CE shall not be allowed to leave this place. If you do there will be strict consequences: Children will be created with the potential to harness powers that surpass your own. But you shall be one of my Favorites and you, my special child, will be able to leave, only when I say it's time. Then you may search for Alorion, and if others follow you . . ."

"Fine, so where is she? Is she far from here?" Arminion said.

"Yes, she is. Everywhere is close to here, but she is far far from you. Yet you can find her. You can reach her. If that's what you really want to do. That's how Myth was able to lead you to my Gate. So, I ask you: Are you sure that is what you really want to do?" Olivion said.

"Of course I do!" Arminion said, realizing for the first time what love was.

"You'll have to search long and hard to find her, and when you do you must awaken her."

"I'll do it. How can I awaken her when I find her?"

"You'll have to take her to the end of all that is known and unknown and throw her beyond that. Only then will she awaken to you. Can you do that? Will you do that?"

"Yes, I will," Arminion said.

"But look at you. You're a child! How can you do that as a child?" Olivion said.

"A child? I don't have to be a child." Arminion chose to grow into a young man about the same age as the woman he'd seen. He looked to be in his mid-twenties and was strikingly handsome.

"Very well. If I'm to let you leave, you'll have to do many things to clear your way. They involve the eNoli and their eventual exit from this place. I will have you leave. I will have all of you leave . . ." Olivion then detailed what she had in store for the CE. She divulged much of what had recently happened. When she finished, a door floated in front of Arminion. He grabbed the handle . . .

The Olivion is the epitome of is.

The Alorion is the epitome of not.

"Arminion, you're forgetting something."

He turned to Olivion, and before he could even think of what he had forgotten, she threw a silver medallion toward him. He caught it in one hand, amazed that he was now holding an Alonis.

"Does this mean . . ."

"Yes. You best not fail me."

Arminion nodded and put it around his neck. He then turned back to the door, opened it, and made his duty-laden exit.

Louis and Cyndi saw this scene and didn't understand why it was important. It seemed senseless.

"Did you see that, children? Do you understand?"

"No! He's in love with some girl he doesn't know? That's what this is all about?" Louis said.

"There's a great plan here. I know because it's of my own design. You see,

with Midlandia's screams, all that is gets smaller and smaller. It's closing in on itself," Olivion said.

"What's closing in?" Cyndi asked.

"All that is. Here and everywhere else. There was no beginning but there was a time when all you know didn't exist," Olivion said, and with that Louis and Cyndi saw it—better yet, they felt it.

It was a feeling worse than pain yet without pain. It was the most horrid thing conceivable. It was unbearable. There was no energy. No life. Total absence. Complete void.

That was worse than the most horrid war with the most heinous acts. Even in war there's always hope that it'll pass. In the face of this enemy there wasn't even hope. This was an enemy that could not be attacked. It had no form and could not be fought.

The infinite moment ended. *"Children, come here,"* Olivion said, motioning to them. She stretched out her arms and held them close. She kissed them both on the tops of their heads and then began to tell them a story.

"You see, what you felt and saw is the worst fate imaginable by you and me. That was all there was at one point long ago. Eons passed, and then there was something, just a glimmer, and that was me, Olivion. So all things and I could be, I forced that epitome of not from myself. I did it just like that." Olivion snapped her fingers and they saw an explosion and the universe expanding from it. They watched all things being created.

"You see, that explosion was the first something, and from there all things were created by my energy. It spread as naught rushed outward from me. Everything came into being. With this energy there would be life.

"So that you could have lives of your own, I hid myself behind my Gate

and in my Domain, in this grand place known as Midlandia. I put a portion of the most important part of myself into the Midland Isle, which connects to every place and every time and is the only way to travel here. But there was a problem. Although I forced that nonentity from myself, it would eventually want to return. If that were to happen, everything it came in contact with would cease to exist. Not be destroyed. Literally cease to exist in the sense that it never was there. There'd be no memory of it and all of its effects on the world would be erased. That would create holes in space and time. Can you imagine such a thing?

"The ripple effects will be so complicated. What's worse is that you cannot fight something without shape or form. What would you fight? If it touched you, you'd be gone.

"I had to give a form to that which is totally without form so that it may be defeated.

"Do you now understand what the threat is, children? If it returns, I don't know if I'll be able to force it from myself again," Olivion said.

"What? What? What?" Cyndi said.

"Yeah, are you serious?" Louis said.

"We're supposed to deal with that? By ourselves?" Cyndi said.

"If you don't have a chance, we don't have a chance," Louis said.

"Oh yes, you do! Arminion is both your hope and ultimate doom. The total void will seep into the body of Alorion and with that it will have thoughts, desires, wishes, and most important, form. It will be the most powerful being imaginable, but at least you will have a chance to face it. Within that is hope," Olivion said.

"So you set Arminion up. He has no clue what he's doing?" Cyndi said.

"Yes, and you know I thought it might take a little more convincing, but

341

the eNoli always want to do what pleases them. He just wanted to find her and awaken her, no matter what the consequences." Olivion laughed.

"So what's he going to do?" Louis asked.

"He's going to bring her to Earth of course. That's where the eNoli most want to be. And you'll have to fight! Fight! Fight! Fight!" Olivion sounded lighthearted, as if this was all a joke, but they knew she was deadly serious.

Cyndi and Louis were stunned. They wanted to forget that this was happening. Cyndi thought that maybe she didn't really want to know everything.

"Well, what are we supposed to do?" Louis asked.

"I've told you much. You each have a side you are on and you'd best stick to them and do what needs to be done. I can't tell you everything. Some things will be revealed along your journey," Olivion said.

"You are one twisted person!" Cyndi said, thinking about her conversation with the Standing Man.

Olivion laughed. *"Did you forget that all things come from me?"*

"No. All things come from you. You are as good as you are evil. As insane as you are sane. You don't have a side. You are all sides," Cyndi said.

"But all of those sides are in danger. That's why all of this is happening!" Louis said.

"Yes, so I think you'd better get going." Olivion whisked herself away. This time two doors opened on opposite sides of the Observatory. Cyndi knew that she couldn't leave with Louis. Louis knew it too.

Words were inadequate. So they nodded to each other and then set out separately for the Midland Isle and home.

Epilogue

Arminion traveled as far as he could with Alorion's lifeless yet beautiful body. He passed VY Canis Majoris. Not even its enormous size could intimidate him. Farther than any telescope could see. He traveled until he actually met the edge of all things known and unknown.

As a CE he was eternal, even if he changed form to come back as something new, but beyond the edge of all things known and unknown he saw his end. It caused him a pain he'd never experienced before. He could feel it just as Cyndi and Louis had. Whatever it was, it was getting closer, swallowing up all existence. Arminion had to move back to avoid meeting his destruction.

What was it? It continued to hurt his senses as he tried to comprehend what the minus, the absence, and the without was. He couldn't imagine that he was supposed to throw his love into that.

Do not cower now.

You crossed my Gate and chose your own destiny.

Throw Alorion in and she will be yours.

Arminion heard Olivion's words. He'd come this far and he wouldn't fail. He caressed Alorion's face, then forced himself to lovingly toss her into the void.

The very edge of the *not* shook and vibrated and brilliant lights flashed. It was the ultimate storm, then all things went calm. Within the *not* Arminion could see Alorion. She began to move and the *not* was drawn into her body. All that was not was replaced with all that was. It began to grow and stretch outward at the speed of light until the *not* could no longer be seen or felt.

The *not* claimed Alorion as herself.

The Ultimate Danger had been reborn.

Arminion flew within inches of Alorion and hovered by her body. He was ignorant of the threat she posed, but if he'd known, it would have excited him to no end. He waited for her to speak:

"Who are you?"

"I am Arminion."

"Who am I?"

"You are Alorion."

"Am I really?"

"Yes. I've done so much to be able to meet you. Please, come with me."

"You've done so much to meet me? Curious. I will come with you."

Arminion took her hand. It would take them some time to get there, but they were headed for a place that was:

Louis's home
Cyndi's home
Devon's home
Your home

Get Ready!